THE BOOK OF LIES

THE LAST ORACLE BOOK FOUR

MELISSA MCSHANE

Night Harbor Publishing

For DawnRay and Jenna and all the hardworking people who make conventions possible

The front room of Abernathy's felt close and warm and comforting thanks to the overcast, which dimmed the evening light to almost nothing. Winter in Portland was usually a cold, rainy time, but this year, an unexpected amount of snow had fallen, and dirty piles of slush filled the gutters. It made for a depressing sight, especially in daylight, when I couldn't ignore it. So I'd decided to fight back.

The fir tree I'd bought at the specialty lot was the smallest one I'd ever seen that wasn't a bush. It stood about two feet tall, though what it lost in height it made up for in perfection of shape, conical and even on all sides. Its needles were a deep blue-green and gave off a rich scent that brought the forest indoors. Judy steadied it in its pot and adjusted a few of the branches. "I think it's too small."

"There's not a lot of room on that side of the counter, and I think it's exactly the right size if we put it on that box." I carefully lifted the little tree off the counter and set it on the box I'd covered with a spare white sheet from my apartment. "Go outside and make sure it's centered."

"This was your idea. You go outside. It's freezing out there."

I shrugged and ran outside, not bothering with a coat even

though it was as cold as Judy had said, cold and windy with the scent of more snow in the air. I backed away from Abernathy's plate glass window with the name of the store painted across the top and accidentally stepped off the curb into slushy, frigid snowmelt. It slopped over the top of my shoe and instantly soaked my foot. I cursed and shook the slush off my shoe, then took a few more careful steps until I was standing between two cars parked at the curb.

Christmas lights burned blue and gold and green all around the window, framing the tiny tree like something off a Christmas card, though with petite Judy standing behind it, arms folded across her chest, it would be a card from a disgruntled elf. I could imagine her tapping her toe impatiently.

"To the left," I said, though she couldn't hear me, and gestured to convey my meaning more clearly. Judy rolled her eyes and hitched the box in the indicated direction. "Perfect."

"Oh, that is so adorable," Viv said, startling me. She had a large cardboard box in her arms and the tip of her nose matched the pink of her hair.

"If that box is full of ornaments, we're never going to fit them all on the tree."

"Mostly it's full of menorahs I picked up at a vintage store. I think we should put some up, show our holiday spirit."

"Well, Abernathy's is religion-neutral, so it's a good idea."

Behind the window, Judy turned and walked away. "I think she's impatient," I said.

"Let's get this finished," Viv said, hitching the box higher.

The warm air of Abernathy's, scented with pine and cinnamon, wrapped me in its embrace when I opened the door. As far as I knew, Abernathy's was indifferent to human customs and holidays, but it had made the store smell like hot rolls at Thanksgiving, so I wondered if I was right.

I stopped for a moment just inside the door and looked around. Bookcases, dozens of them, stood at all angles to each other, extending deep into the store. At times like this, I could imagine them huddled together, some close enough for only one person to pass abreast, sharing secrets and laughing over the books they contained. It was whimsy, but Abernathy's was unique —no mere bookstore, but the greatest oracle the world had ever seen.

"Come on, Helena, let's set these out," Viv said. "Judy, you know you want to."

"I'm not a big fan of Christmas," Judy said, but she held a string of tiny LED lights in one hand and a mug in the other. "I made cider. Well, I heated it up."

"Thanks." I accepted the mug from her and took a long drink. It set a little fire burning in my belly that sent out trickles of warmth throughout my body. "What do you think, white or multicolored lights? Or all one color?"

"White," Judy said, "so it doesn't clash with the window. I don't know about this. Nathaniel never decorated for the holidays. You didn't decorate last year."

Viv set a menorah made of art glass, colorful and beautiful, in the window sill to one side of the tree. "It's not just for the holidays, it's for the big convention, or whatever you called it."

"Conference of Neutralities," I said. "Lucia said a lot of people would be coming to visit Abernathy's. I'm nervous about that."

"Why? You outrank most of them," Judy said.

"There's no ranking among Neutralities—"

"Not officially. But everyone knows who's more important, and they all behave accordingly. No one's in a position to judge you except Claude Gauthier from the Athenaeum and maybe whoever comes from the Sanctuary, and Claude's not that kind of man."

"At least it only happens every three years, right?" I set down my mug on the counter. "They're all so much more experienced than me, and I'm sure there are traditions I don't know about."

"Don't worry so much," Viv said. "It gives you wrinkles."

"I don't think I'm at an age where I have to worry about wrinkles forming, thanks."

The door flew open, letting in a blast of cold air. "Good after-noon," Jeremiah Washburn said with his characteristic smile that always drew one out of me, it was that charming. "I see you've been infected by holiday cheer."

"You make it sound like a disease," Viv said.

"A good one, maybe. Don't you tend to say 'Merry Christmas' when someone says it to you?"

"I say 'Happy Halloween.' It throws people off their game, and sometimes I get candy."

"Not everyone is as creative as you." Jeremiah swept her a little bow. Viv smiled at him and went back to digging in the box, but I was pretty sure I saw her blush.

Jeremiah's smile broadened, if that was possible. He unzipped his coat, revealing a T-shirt with a picture of a turtle with four elephants standing on its back, bearing up a disc with waterfalls pouring over the edges. I'd known him for five months and I couldn't remember ever seeing the same shirt twice, though he'd given up his Birkenstocks for tennis shoes in deference to the weather.

"Can I help you with something? Or is this a friendly visit?" I couldn't help glancing at Viv, who had her back to us and was fussing with the second menorah, a bright silver sculpture with golden candles.

"Safe deposit box, please."

I led the way through the store, past the bookcases and into the back hallway that led to the basement stairs. In addition to the oracle that gave auguries to customers, Abernathy's had safe deposit boxes in the basement, protected by powerful magic. I took the keys off the wall and waited for Jeremiah to extract his key from his jeans pocket. "How have things been? The hunt goes well?"

"As well as you'd expect. Things are finally returning to normal after that serial killer business last July. Fewer invaders, and they're easier to destroy." Jeremiah was a wood magus, and unlike other magi I knew who hunted the monsters trying to destroy humanity, he worked alone. Not totally alone—he also had a familiar, a tamed—or was that subdued?—invader he used to fight and destroy its kin.

"You don't capture them, then? I thought that was what Nicolliens did."

"I leave that to the hunting teams. Familiars are essential to the fight, but I don't want any part in creating them. I'm satisfied with what I do."

I nodded, and turned away to give him some privacy, but he stopped me in my tracks with "Helena. Do you think..."

"What?"

"Nothing. Never mind. I'll be done here in a minute."

I ascended the steps and shut the basement door behind me. I almost thought...but no, if Jeremiah were going to ask Viv out, he would have done it by now. Viv, for her part, seemed uncharacteristically shy around him, but I'd never known her to be coy in her interest in men. And Jeremiah wasn't her type—short and skinny and a true product of geek culture. She'd certainly never said anything that indicated she was interested in him. Yet she'd been single for nearly three months now, which in Viv's world was more like three years. I shook my head and proceeded back through the store. I could just ask her, but the fact that I needed to ask was so unlike my best friend I felt funny about doing it.

Viv and Judy were having an amiable argument about the tree topper when I arrived. "This isn't going to be one of those *A Charlie Brown Christmas* incidents you read about, is it?" I said. "Hanging one giant ornament that makes the tree bend in half?"

"I say angel. Judy says star," Viv said, holding out a simpering cherub with a hollowed-out bottom.

"Stars are traditional. The star on our tree has been through three generations of Rasmussens," Judy said.

"Do I get the tie-breaking vote?"

"Choose me and I'll bake you cookies," Viv said.

Judy rolled her eyes. "Bribery. How juvenile. *I'd* bake a cake."

"Now you've made it impossible for me to choose."

Viv flew the angel around my head. "Pick me, Hel," she sang in a falsetto voice, "and I'll put in a good word for you with Santa."

"Wrong part of the Christmas story," Judy said.

My phone rang. The display read *Rick Blaine.*

My heart gave its usual thump. "Sorry, I have to take this," I said.

"Let Jeremiah choose. He's Jewish, he's got no preferences." *Though if I'm right about his preferences, that angel will be swaying atop the tree when I come back.* Jewish. And Viv had brought menorahs. Maybe I was wrong about her feelings.

I hustled into the office and shut the door. "Hello?"

"Sorry to call so early," Malcolm said.

"I don't care when you call so long as you do. How are you?"

"Better now. I miss you."

"I miss you, too." I sat in my office chair and put my feet up on the desk. "We're putting up a little Christmas tree. I wish you could see it. It looks like something a Munchkin would have."

Malcolm chuckled. "Where I am, they don't celebrate Christmas, and it's incredibly early in the morning. I destroyed two invaders a few hours ago and now I can't sleep."

"No more details. If I don't know where you are, I can't tell anyone."

"I know. Has anyone asked?"

"No. Lucia gives me skeptical looks sometimes when your name comes up, but she does that to me all the time anyway. And they'd have to be fans of *Casablanca* to recognize what I named your number in my phone."

"Still no luck with the Accords, then."

"Unfortunately, no." I'd started studying the Accords, the rules by which Neutralities like Abernathy's were governed, almost the moment Malcolm had gone into hiding. But five months of study hadn't found me a loophole that would allow me, custodian of a Neutrality, to have a relationship with an Ambrosite, one of the two factions magery was divided into. I was expected to be impartial in my treatment of both, and I was, but the rules didn't think that was good enough. They were very clear: no custodian was allowed romantic attachments to members of either faction.

"Keep trying," Malcolm said. "I don't want to get your hopes up with specifics, but I think I'll be able to return home soon. In the next month or so."

"Too late. My heart is already light. You think the storm has passed?" Malcolm had killed a high-ranking Nicollien in self-defense, a woman who'd turned out to be a murderer, but that didn't stop most of the Nicolliens from wanting him dead in retribution.

"I'm sure there will still be a few who want to duel, but from what I hear, the initial outrage has faded, and word of Ms. Guittard's actions has spread widely. Anyone who wants to kill me will have no official support."

"Do you really think Mr. Rasmussen would have defended someone who tried to kill you?"

"As head of the local Nicolliens, he might have believed it his duty to do so, despite the Nicollien Archmagus's instructions."

I twined the curly cord of the office phone around my fingers and shifted my grip on my cell phone. "The Nicollien Archmagus wanted you punished. I think his instructions were half-hearted."

"So do I, but that will be irrelevant shortly. Will you be happy to see me?"

That made me smile. "Malcolm, 'happy' is a weak word for what I feel when I think about seeing you again. I love you."

"And I love you." I heard him yawn. "I think I might be able to sleep now. Just speaking to you relaxes me. Though not as much as having you in my arms would."

"I can think of much better things to do if I were in your arms than relax."

Malcolm laughed. "Soon enough, love. I'll talk with you again tomorrow."

"Sleep well. I love you."

I disconnected and stretched, tilting farther back in my chair. It was unfair that Malcolm and I had only had a few hours together before he'd gone on the run. Five months of phone conversations, getting to know each other better over long distances, was better than nothing, but it was nothing compared to how wonderful it was to have him near.

I leaned over awkwardly and opened the bottom drawer of the desk, pulling out a thick sheaf of pages bound only by three silver rings. Slips of colored Post-Its stuck out on every side, giving it a cheerful look that was completely inappropriate. The Accords were *huge*, covering every conceivable aspect of magery and life as a magus. They'd been written seventy-two years ago, after magery had split into the Ambrosite and Nicollien factions, and delineated clearly the responsibilities and rights of each, as well as the rules governing Neutralities. I slapped the Accords on the desk and retrieved a slimmer notebook from the drawer. My notes, for all the good they'd done me so far.

I'd spent the first couple of months reading the sections specifically about Neutralities, cross-referencing, checking definitions, taking copious notes, and obliquely asking Lucia questions to confirm my understanding, and now I'd moved on to the Accords in general. Lucia already believed Malcolm and I were together, but I didn't think I should confirm that supposition. Though it did make me wonder why she never lectured me about him. Maybe I ought to take a chance on asking her about Malcolm. She might know something I didn't. Or maybe her silence was a warning, some kind of 'don't ask, don't tell' policy the Neutralities operated by.

I flipped the pages of the Accords idly, then pushed it away and stood. I was having fun with friends today, not beating my head against the iron wall that stood between me and the man I loved.

The angel stood proudly atop the tree when I returned. The star nestled into the branches just below. "I see you figured it out," I said.

"Jeremiah is a traitor," Judy said irritably.

"Just because he didn't pick his leader's daughter," Viv said, not even bothering not to sound smug.

"Would you two stop bickering? Let's have more cider. Only an hour left before closing, and the weekend," I said, picking up my mug. The cider was cold, but I swigged it down anyway.

"How's the famous Mr. Blaine?" Viv asked.

"As well as ever. I don't know where he is."

"Just talking to him is a violation of the Accords," Judy said, but without making it an accusation.

"I know that, Judy, you don't have to keep pointing it out."

"You're going to end up in trouble, and I don't want that." Judy scowled and collected her mug. "There's more cider in the break room."

Telling Judy the truth about me and Malcolm had been the biggest risk I'd ever taken. Her father, William Rasmussen, disliked me and hated Malcolm, and if he knew what we were doing he'd have brought us both before a tribunal. I'd dithered about it for a week, torn between fear that she'd feel it her duty to tell him and the sense that a real friend didn't keep those kinds of secrets. But when I'd told her the truth, she'd sat there staring at me for several seconds, then said, "You didn't have to tell me."

"I couldn't help thinking how you'd feel if you found out some other way," I'd said.

Judy had nodded and said, "Thanks for trusting me," and that had been it, except for her frequent reminders that I needed to find a better solution than not telling people and renaming my boyfriend's contact number in my phone. I knew it was just Judy's way of showing affection, but sometimes it got on my nerves.

Viv danced past me, holding her mug close to her heart. "I love cider, it's so Christmassy," she sang.

I followed her more slowly, but came up short when the bells above the door rang. "I'm here for an augury," said the tall, willowy woman who entered. Between her paleness, and her white floor-length skirt and white fur-trimmed parka, she looked like an ice-touched elf queen. I remembered her, though I didn't recall her name; she'd been one of my former employer's blackmail victims. Did she think I knew her secret? She certainly behaved as unselfconsciously as if she didn't.

"Certainly," I said, taking the augury slip from her white-gloved hand. "Just a moment." I took three steps away, between the bookcases, and entered the timeless silence of the oracle.

The air within was cooler than the rest of the store and smelled, not of pine and cinnamon, but of ripe apples. Abernathy's enjoyed experimenting with fragrances. Here, the blue glow of twilight was tinged with gold, and motes of dust floated past, gleaming within the last rays of the sun as if the overcast had cleared.

I paused with my hand on a nearby shelf and breathed it all in. I never felt so at peace as when I was within the oracle, being its hands as it chose the books to answer customers' questions. I'd never had an augury for myself—that, too, was against the Accords—but I knew what it was like to give someone the answer to an important question, and it filled me with joy.

This time, it took me a few minutes to find the woman's augury, which turned out to be a book called *Fascinating Womanhood*. Interesting title. I brought it back to the front counter and found the woman waiting for me, standing perfectly still in the center of the space between the counter and the shelves as if she'd been drawn there by a magnet. She turned her pale face toward me, unsmiling, as I approached. "$1000," I said.

She reached into a fur-trimmed white purse and withdrew a white checkbook and a black pen. "A check is acceptable?"

"Yes, unless it bounces, and then Abernathy's won't accept any more from you."

"It won't bounce." She filled it out, tore it off and handed it to me. Georgina Eisen. I vaguely remembered the name.

"I'll write you a receipt." I scribbled her name quickly in the ledger under the antique cash register, then pulled out the receipt book. "Looks like it's started snowing," I said, feeling an obscure need to keep the conversation going.

"It has," Eisen said. "Hunting will be poor tonight."

"You're a hunter?"

"My husband. Though with these new attacks, hunting isn't the most dangerous game in town anymore, no matter the weather."

"What new attacks?"

The pale face made the faintest look of surprise. "Familiars attacking their masters, of course."

"Oh, that. That rumor goes around every couple of months. It's not true. Familiars can't break containment."

Eisen raised her eyebrow, again the faintest of expressions, as if her face really was made of ice. "You're not a Nicollien," she said.

"No, but I know history. It's been almost seventy-five years since the first familiars were harnessed, and not one has ever escaped or attacked a human."

"Believe that if you like, but the news out of Philadelphia says otherwise." She tilted her head as if listening to distant music. I handed her the receipt. "Thank you."

"You're welcome. Merry Christmas."

"Is it?" She peered at me nearsightedly. Uncomfortable, I flapped my hand in the direction of the Munchkin tree. "Oh. Yes. Merry Christmas."

I watched her through the glass as she got into a small white car parked in the spot magically reserved for Abernathy's customers and drove away. I wasn't sure if I admired her commitment to her signature color or just thought it was weird. Shrugging, I walked back to the break room, where Judy and Viv were drinking from steaming mugs and talking rapidly about some designer I'd never heard of. "Half an hour to go," I said. "I'm impatient for the day to be over."

"What should we do?" Viv said. "Three young, beautiful women, free and unattached—well, two of us are—with plenty of time and money—well, one of us does—isn't it funny that the one of us who's loaded is also the one with a hot boyfriend?"

"I'm not loaded," I said, "I'm comfortably well-off."

"You earn commissions on your auguries," Judy pointed out.

"It's not a commission, and it's only one percent. Hardly the stuff fortunes are made of."

"Well, you can afford to buy dinner, and then we can see a movie," Viv said.

The door bells jingled. This time of year, it was hard not to hear it as a Christmas sound. This time of *day*, it was hard not to hear it as a funeral dirge. I sighed. "Last one of the day, if I'm lucky."

The man waiting by the door was, to my surprise, a Nicollien. The Nicollien and Ambrosite leaders, William Rasmussen and Ryan Parish, had lessened tensions between their people by decreeing that Nicolliens would only use Abernathy's in the morning and Ambrosites in the afternoon. I'd told everyone I wasn't enforcing the rule, but magi in general cared more about their leaders' dictates than the opinion of a custodian, even if it was my Neutrality they were making rules about. Jeremiah was an exception. "Freddy. I'm surprised to see you here at this time."

"I hope you were serious about not enforcing the time constraints. I need this augury and I don't want to wait until Monday." Freddy Whittaker was someone I considered a friend, even if his enormous familiar made me nervous. I glanced beyond him through the window to where the thing waited; no familiars were allowed inside Abernathy's. The monster was a horrible creature with a massive black and violet carapace that gleamed with a black-light radiance, hundreds of shark-like serrated black teeth, and a dozen tiny eyes glittering with malice. Everyone else would see a huge, snarling Rottweiler or Doberman, but I, as Abernathy's custodian, could see through the illusion. Lucky me.

The familiar saw me watching and made a leap at the window, but was brought up short by the leash tethering it to the lamp post. I shied away involuntarily.

"It's all right, Helena, Vicious can't hurt you," Freddy said, holding out an augury slip for me to take. "Though I admit I've never seen it so eager to reach someone. You must look good to it."

"That's not comforting." The familiar made another lunge, and howled in frustration, a terrible sound that made me long for some kind of weapon to defend myself. "Why'd you bring it, anyway?"

"I'm going out of town for a few days and I don't like to leave it alone in my house. It's torn up furniture before."

"That makes sense. I'll hurry and get this for you." But I took one last look at Vicious, whose black tongue lolled out of its mouth, dripping lilac-colored goo, and thought of what Georgina Eisen had said. It wasn't at all hard to understand how rumors like that one got started.

2

$\mathcal{I}$ stood by my living room window, looking down on the snow-covered cars lining the street. We didn't usually get this much snow in December, and it made me grateful I lived above my work—no slipping around on the narrow Portland streets, no inching along the freeway at rush hour. The Christmas lights I'd put up around my window lit my hands, holding a mug of what was left of the cider. Sunday nights were one of my favorite times, when the weekend was winding down and I started looking forward to Monday morning. It was so peaceful even without the hush of a billion falling snowflakes.

I let the curtains fall and reclined on my maroon velvet couch, leaning back against the armrest and putting my feet up on the cushions. Malcolm might call soon, which would make this evening even better. I could watch a movie, or read a book. Anything to avoid thinking about the Conference of Neutralities, which started tomorrow afternoon and bode well to ruin my calm if I got to worrying about it again.

My phone rang, and I snatched it up. Judy. I suppressed a twinge of disappointment. "Hello, Judy."

"Have you heard the news?"

"What news?"

"The worst kind. Father just confirmed these rumors coming out of the East Coast are true. A familiar escaped containment and attacked its master."

"No. That's impossible."

"Apparently not. Do you realize what this means?"

"Disaster. Do they know what caused it?"

"Not yet. They think it was the binding in the harness—it makes the most sense. Helena, this is disastrous."

I took a drink of cider, trying to calm myself. "It's just one familiar, though, right?"

Judy let out a low *hah*. "One is more than enough for the Ambrosites to be up in arms about how they were right all along."

"But you're not a Nicollien."

"You think that matters? If it *isn't* a lone occurrence, and it happens here, we're both going to be in the middle of the conflict. And I have to live with Father, who's about two seconds away from packing up and flying to Philadelphia to consult with the Nicollien East Coast leader. I keep telling him he needs to stay close to home in case the worst happens."

"You're right. If familiars start breaking containment here, the Nicolliens will need his leadership." Familiars getting free to attack people, savage them with tooth and claw and drain the magic from their bodies, was one of my nightmares. "Did the familiar kill its master?"

"Yes. Horribly, so we hear." Judy paused, and in the background I heard William Rasmussen shouting about something. "Helena, what if it happens here?"

"I don't know. What would they do? The Nicolliens?"

"They might have to start destroying familiars proactively."

"That's not so horrible, is it? If the alternative is human death?"

"It would weaken the Nicollien hunting teams significantly." Judy drew a deep breath. "This is ridiculous. I'm panicking over nothing. Really, what are the odds that a harness failure would happen more than once? And if it *is* harness failure, we make our own, so whatever happened in Philadelphia couldn't affect us."

"That's a better way to look at it." I took my empty mug to the sink and rinsed it out. "You remember the store hours are reduced this week?"

"Yes, and for me it's like a nice Christmas holiday. I'm not so sure you benefit."

"Working ten to two, then going to the conference from three to eight, and then there's the after-hours mingling...it does sound like work. Lucia said most of the networking happens after eight. I have no idea what kind of networking custodians do."

"Bitch about the Board of Neutralities, probably. Look, I have to go, Father's calling me. I'll see you in the morning."

I sat on my couch after she hung up and cradled my phone in my hands. I'd never been so grateful not to be a magus as I was right then. The Ambrosite and Nicollien split had been over the use of familiars, with the Nicolliens insisting they were a powerful weapon and the Ambrosites saying they were too dangerous to be used. I was certain Judy was right, and this one incident was more than enough for the Ambrosites to renew their charge that the Nicolliens should give up all the familiars and fight invaders only with magic and weapons as they did. I'd seen familiars fight invaders, and they were effective, reducing the risk to their human handlers, but familiars also terrified me, and I couldn't fully support either side in their argument. As was appropriate for a custodian of a Neutrality.

My phone rang again, and once again I felt a pang of disappointment. "Hi, Viv."

"What are you doing? Not watching one of those old black and white movies you're nuts about, are you?"

"No, just waiting for...just waiting."

"Malcolm hasn't called, has he?"

"I'm just as happy to talk to you."

"That's a nice white lie. I'll take it. Hel, you don't think I'm frivolous, do you?"

"What? Of course not!"

"But I am a little. I like to party, and I have a hard time being serious about things—"

I sighed. "Viv, did you talk to your mother again? You know that always makes you question your life choices, when really you're a wonderful person who makes life fun for everyone around you."

"It's not about Mom. It's...you're going to think this is stupid."

"I promise I won't."

"No, you really will. *I* think it's stupid."

"Viv, just tell me."

There was a long pause. "What do you think of Jeremiah?"

Hah. I was right. "I like him a lot. You're interested in him, aren't you?"

"I don't know. It's probably just his smile—but I never have trouble telling a man I'm interested, and now I don't know what to say!"

"Just ask him out, Viv. I bet he'd say yes."

"But he probably thinks I'm crazy. I know I talk like I'm crazy when he's around. And he's a magus, and he kills monsters...those are serious things, and I'm not like that. I have pink hair!" Viv's voice, higher pitched than mine, nearly became a shriek.

"This is sounding like you're thinking of more than your usual fling."

"I don't know if I am."

She sounded so forlorn, so unlike herself, that my heart went out to her. "Viv, Jeremiah wore a T-shirt last week with a flamingo on it that said 'Majestically Awkward.' He's not that serious. And these days he comes into the store later than he used to, I think because he's looking for you."

"Really?"

"It's not like I've asked him or anything, but I really do think you have a chance."

Viv sighed, a long, drawn-out exhalation. "I haven't felt this awkward in years. I don't know why."

"Maybe because you've finally met someone you could see yourself with indefinitely? You've never had that before."

"Maybe. You don't think it's bad that I've—"

"Viv. You see the best in a lot of different men, and you're comfortable with your emotions. This is not a bad thing. Are you *sure* you haven't been talking to your mom?"

Viv laughed. "I don't suppose you have his number? If I call him now, I'll stop freaking out about it."

"It's in his record downstairs. But it's a violation of his privacy if I give it to you, even if I suspect he wouldn't mind."

"I'll just have to wait until I see him again. If I survive that long."

"Patience, grasshopper."

"I am a master of patience. And I can tell you want me off the line so *your* monster hunter can call you. It must be driving you nuts that you can't see him."

"A little. But I'm a master of patience too."

Viv laughed again and said good night. I went back to lying on the couch. Viv and Jeremiah. Wasn't she taller than he was? And normally she went for the burly type. But attraction was what it was, and I wanted Viv to be happy, whether that meant a string of boyfriends or a single steady one.

The phone rang again. *Finally.* "Hi."

"I can't talk long, but I wanted to hear your voice," Malcolm said. I heard a distant humming in the background, low and throbbing. "It may be a while before I can call you again."

"A while? That sounds bad. I wish I could think of something romantic and memorable to say."

"Tell me you love me."

He sounded unusually tense, which propelled me upright. "I love you. Are you all right?"

"Under a lot of stress. I'm about to board a plane that looks like it was built during the Eisenhower administration, heading off for —never mind, I can't tell you. But for some place not very pleasant."

"I'm sorry. I take it this is for work?"

"Yes. Things have gotten complicated. You heard about Philadelphia?"

"Judy told me." The thought of loose familiars made me even more uneasy than Malcolm's too-serious tone.

"It's not just Philadelphia. I've heard of at least two more incidents and I'm going to check one of them out. Stupid Nicolliens and their insistence on keeping dangerous creatures in their own homes...it's just ridiculous." I'd never heard him sound so frustrated.

"What exactly is happening? Judy said the bindings failed."

"I don't know much more than that. The magic that prevents a familiar from draining a human is created by a bone magus, and it's complicated enough that I don't understand it. But it alters an invader to make it more like a human, and the harness they put on it works like an aegis in reverse—prevents them using magic instead of permitting it the way a human's aegis does. My understanding is the alteration magic is failing, so the binding is intact but no longer has anything to attach to."

"I think I understand. Malcolm, how serious is this?"

He was quiet for a long time. "I'd like to tell you it's under control," he finally said, "but I don't want to lie to you. If the problem persists, or worse, accelerates, it could be very serious. You need to stay in warded places. Don't walk anywhere if you can help it."

"You don't think it could happen here?"

"There's no reason to believe otherwise. And we already know invaders are attracted to you. Just promise me you'll behave as if the worst has already happened."

"I promise. Trust me, I don't want to encounter any familiar, even one on a leash. They scare me."

"That's because you're sensible. I wish I could be home with you."

"You're doing what you were made to do. But I wish you were here, too."

The humming sound in the background grew suddenly louder and higher-pitched. "That's the plane," Malcolm said. "I have to go. I love you."

"I love you," I said, and the line went dead. I checked the time. Plenty of time to watch a movie until the ache in my heart lessened.

I decided on *The Maltese Falcon* and went to the kitchen to pop

THE BOOK OF LIES

some popcorn. My phone rang as the paper sack rotated in the microwave.

"Are you ready for tomorrow?" Lucia said.

I leaned against the counter and watched the paper sack inflate. "I...guess so? I have directions to the hotel and I printed out the schedule. What more is there?"

"Have you ever been to *any* kind of business conference before?"

"No."

"Then you won't be ready. It's a small conference by most standards, no more than a hundred and fifty attendees, but it's not a big hotel and you'll get to know people just by using the elevator. You won't have any idea of the politics, but if you just nod politely and never agree to anything, you'll be just fine."

I jerked upright. "Politics? You didn't say anything about politics. I thought these were all Neutralities."

"Neutral only counts as far as the factions go. The Neutralities have their own interests and aren't shy about promoting them. And stay away from Rebecca Greenough. That woman is pure poison."

"Who is she?"

Lucia made a dismissive, irritated noise that was part snort and part raspberry. "Custodian of the Bailey Node in London. She and I have a long, long history of antagonism, mostly her fault, but she may let that spill over onto you because you and I work so closely together. Just a heads-up."

That didn't sound encouraging, but maybe I could stay out of Greenough's way. "Okay. Anything else I should know?"

"The after-parties are important. A few of them are traditional, and you'll want to go to those. The rest...just be careful who you accept invitations from, if you don't want to send the wrong message."

Once again panic tried to set in. "But I don't know anyone! What if I accidentally send the wrong message?"

"You can always ask me if you're not sure. Don't worry too much about it. The custodian of Abernathy's has a lot of pull among the Neutralities, and you won't find many who will judge you on your behavior."

The microwave beeped. "Judy said there was an unofficial ranking. Is that true?"

"Yes, but you're at the top and not likely to lose that position, so don't worry about that either. It's the rest of us node custodians who have to fight for a place in the pecking order." I had a feeling Lucia didn't worry too much about her ranking, either. "Just be at the Grandison after three and you'll be fine." She hung up abruptly.

I poured my popcorn into a bowl and sat on my couch, drawing up my feet beneath me and cuddling into the corner. Lucia had succeeded in making me more nervous than before, but she'd also given me something to think about that wasn't missing Malcolm or roving, uncontained familiars, so that was an improvement.

I ate popcorn and watched Humphrey Bogart solve the mystery of the Maltese Falcon. Sometimes I wished life could be as uncomplicated as a movie. Not that *The Maltese Falcon* was uncomplicated, far from it, but Bogie never had to worry about a hundred and fifty men and women all watching to see if he was going to do something stupid. No, he had hundreds of thousands of fans watching and judging his every move. Maybe I didn't want to trade places with him, after all.

3

The Grandison Hotel was on the waterfront by the Willamette, just a few blocks from the red brick building where tribunals were held. It was a tall, narrow structure built of gray stone, with a green awning over the door near which stood the valet parking stand. I hoped parking wasn't too expensive; some of these hotels charged as much as forty dollars for the service. But there was nowhere to park on the street, so I handed my keys to the nice young man and received a ticket in return. I settled my purse over my shoulder, straightened my coat, and walked toward the door as if I stayed in hotels as expensive as this one all the time.

I gratefully left the December afternoon chill behind, but I wished the interior were a little brighter. It was a clear, cloudless day, and my eyes took a moment to adjust to the lobby, which was dimly lit by comparison. The light from the giant crystal chandelier hanging at the center of the room, blazing like a glittering sun, didn't reach the farthest edges of the space. I walked forward, hoping for some hint as to where to go. I wasn't checking in, though my conference registration packet had said there was a room for me. Traveling to and from the store every morning seemed like more of a hassle than sleeping in my own bed every night.

The rose and gold figured carpet was soft underfoot, but faded from the passage of thousands of feet. Polished ruddy wood pillars held up the balcony of the mezzanine, and I saw men and women strolling around it, some stopping to look down at where I stood. I didn't think they were looking at me, since I wasn't very remarkable, just another blonde young woman in a tailored skirt and blouse under a gray wool coat and sensible low-heeled pumps. Christmas trees decorated all in white—ornaments, lights, everything—stood at the four corners of the room, making the lobby smell of distant pine forests and, faintly, a hint of snow.

As I approached the reception desk, I saw what I was looking for —a sandwich board sign reading WELCOME TO THE CONFER-ENCE OF NEUTRALITIES and, in smaller letters, *Registration on the mezzanine.* What did ordinary people think when they read that name? The Board of Neutralities had bought out all the rooms for this conference, so there wouldn't be any non-Warden guests, but the hotel employees couldn't possibly be in on the secret.

I looked around for stairs and found them to the left, carpeted in the same rose and gold and next to an elevator. I figured I didn't need the elevator and ascended the stairs, passing a couple of people wearing name badges on lanyards. It gave me an unexpected thrill I felt embarrassed about. This was no big deal. Just my first meeting with other people like me, who shared the same responsi-bilities and interests. Nothing worth getting excited about. I walked a little faster.

The mezzanine circled the lobby on three sides and had several doors leading off it, all named for mountains—Denali, Kilimanjaro, Rainier. Between two doors on the side nearest the stairs stood a long folding table with three people seated behind it. All wore navy blue suits with pale blue shirts and maroon ties, even the woman. There were a couple of short queues in front of the table, mostly people dressed as I was, but some of them wearing jeans, making me wish I'd known that was an option. Well, the custodian of Abernathy's was probably held to a higher standard.

I lined up behind a sign with the letters A-G, smiling politely at the woman next to me, then stepped forward to face the middle-aged man in the navy suit. "Name?" he said.

"Helena Davies."

"Davies..." The woman beside me gasped, but the man didn't notice. "Davies...here. Oh." He stopped, lanyard and badge in hand, and gaped at me. "Custodian of Abernathy's."

"Yes." I held out my hand for the badge, trying not to feel awkward and conspicuous.

"You're younger than I expected," he said with a lopsided smile. "You can't be more than twenty."

"I'm twenty-two, actually." That had sounded defensive. I didn't need to explain myself to this guy.

"Sorry." Finally he handed me my badge, then reached down into a box beside him and brought out a bulging cloth bag, the kind you get at upscale grocery stores. "Welcome to the conference, Ms. Davies. It's a pleasure to have you."

Feeling certain I was going to trip and fall in my embarrassment, I nodded at him and walked away in a random direction. If that was going to be everyone's reaction, and not just the way the employees of the Board of Neutralities were going to behave, this would be a very long conference. I'd come prepared to be stared at, but not with quite so much...awe.

I found a bench and sat with the bag on my lap. Most of the bulk turned out to be a very nice metal water bottle, the refillable kind, heavy enough to use as a weapon. I didn't know why that comparison occurred to me, unless I was still nervous about the possibility of familiars breaking free and roving around the city looking for prey. There was a leather-bound notebook and an expensive pen that looked like something you'd use to sign billion-dollar deals. I opened another bound notebook to find a printed copy of the conference schedule, more complete than the one I'd printed off the Board's secure website at home. It also had little bios of important presenters and a big picture of Claude Gauthier, Curator of the Athenaeum, who was giving the keynote address on Wednesday.

There were also some brochures and a glossy booklet listing

exciting things to see and do in Portland, and some loose sheets with coupons and discounts for several of those things. And way down deep at the bottom of the bag I found a fob with an inch-wide lens fixed in it. The lens was attached to a retractable string and looked like an old-fashioned monocle. I held it up to my eye, but it just made things blurry. Something to ask Lucia about when I saw her.

I packed everything away except the keychain, which I hooked onto my lanyard the way it looked like it was supposed to go, and the water bottle, which was empty. Unfortunate, because just looking at it made me thirsty. I guessed someone had wanted to cut down on plastic bottle waste, but at the moment I'd have preferred a nice, full, non-recyclable bottle. Well, searching for water would give me something to do until pre-dinner drinks began at 5:30.

Almost immediately I found a drinking fountain that was set up with a spigot to refill bottles. Fascinating. I drank until my stomach was too full to be nervous, then filled the bottle and capped it tightly. I could just picture the water spilling all over that nice notebook. I checked the time on my phone—4:57. I could probably go to the bar now.

I slung the lanyard around my neck and went back to the stairs. The voices of the people at the registration table had taken on an echoing quality, some weird effect of the mezzanine, probably. I carefully didn't meet the eyes of the man who'd welcomed me and trotted quickly down the stairs.

I glanced at the sign as I passed it, and had to stop for a moment, dizzied by the play of sparkling light from the chandelier over its surface. All the letters were highlighted in rainbow colors and shimmered like heat haze. I took another drink, and the dizziness subsided but didn't go away. I looked toward the front door, which shone with natural sunlight—no dizziness. Maybe I'd run down the steps too quickly. I hoped it didn't mean I was coming down with a cold.

The bar was through a door to the right of the hotel entrance. It was warmly lit by sconces on all the walls and the pillars bearing up the roof. Leather armchairs that looked butter-soft sat facing the two fireplaces, and tables of the same warm red wood as the foyer stood here and there throughout the room. The bar took up most of one wall, and the bar stools were upholstered in the same leather as the chairs. It looked like someone's idea of a Victorian smoking room, minus the Victorian. The blocky, blobby pictures over the fireplaces reminded me of that artist whose name I could never remember, but in maroon and ruddy brown instead of primary colors. It smelled faintly of varnish, like it had been recently remodeled.

The couple I'd passed on the stairs were seated at the bar, a couple of bottled beers in front of them. Other than them, the place was empty. It was a little early for me, but I didn't want to sit around in the comfortable chairs without a drink. "Beer," I told the bartender, a very attractive man with a shaved head and skin as dark as my friend Derrick's. "Something local, please."

The bartender presented me with a bottle and opened it for me with a practiced twist and a smile. Too bad I was already spoken for, because he was *extremely* handsome and that smile was killer. I thanked him and took my beer to one of the fireplaces, where I sat in one of the leather armchairs and promptly flailed my way upright. Those cushions were deep. I took a drink and closed my eyes, enjoying the heat of the fire on my face.

"Hello there," said a man to my left. I looked up and saw the couple from the stairs, standing over me. "Do you mind if we join you?" He spoke with a strong Hispanic accent.

"Please do."

They sat in a couple of leather armchairs opposite me. Both were in their mid-forties, the man with graying black hair, the woman red-headed, and both were dressed far more expensively than I was. "I thought I knew all the custodians, but you're not familiar," the woman said. She too had an accent, but I couldn't place it beyond somewhere eastern European.

"I'm Helena Davies from Abernathy's. This is my first conference."

The two exchanged surprised glances. "Then it's *very* good to meet you," the man said. "I'm Carlos Ramirez y Mendoza of the Vargas Node, and this is Elisabeta Vaduva of the Ionescu Node."

"I apologize for our surprise, it is just that we did not expect the custodian of Abernathy's to be drinking beer alone in the hotel bar," Vaduva said. "Rubbing elbows with the rest of the named Neutralities, perhaps."

"Are they here already?"

"Of course. They all have suites. Don't you?"

"I have to work still. It was easier to sleep at home." Under their curious gazes, I reconsidered my decision.

"Of course, closing Abernathy's entirely would be unthinkable," Ramirez said. "This must be a busy week for you, and the week before Christmas at that."

"What the Board was thinking to set it at such a time, I don't know," Vaduva said. "It usually falls much earlier in the year."

"They choose to show that they are not so Anglocentric as it appears, with five of the nine current Board members hailing from English-speaking countries, and the need to hold the conference in the United States, where the oracle is," Ramirez said. "Though I think they have gone somewhat overboard in trying to prove this."

"I'm sorry, but I don't know where your nodes are," I said.

"The Vargas Node is outside Madrid some twenty kilometers," Ramirez said.

"And the Ionescu Node is in Romania, on the shores of the Black Sea," Vaduva said. She reached out and took Ramirez's hand. "Far enough apart that Carlos and I see one another only at this time, every three years."

"That's...you must miss each other terribly. I didn't realize you were so tied to your nodes. You can't travel?"

Ramirez and Vaduva exchanged glances again, this time amused. "Our respective spouses would not be so understanding," Vaduva said.

I blushed. "Um..."

"What is your saying? What happens in Portland, stays in Portland?" Ramirez laughed. "We spend this week together, and our spouses look the other way, and all is well in Romania and España."

I still had no idea what to say. I pretended I was open-minded. "I understand."

"We have begun our relationship with the new custodian in awkwardness," Ramirez said, laughing again. "Let us speak of something else. I host a party on the next to last night of the conference; you will come, yes?"

"I...think so." Lucia's warnings rang in my ears like a Chinese gong. "I don't know my schedule yet."

"It is the only party that night. Everyone comes. You will be very welcome. Now, I am Carlos and this is Elisabeta, yes? And we will call you Helena and we will all be very friendly."

"I'd like that." Their unusual romantic arrangement aside, the two were funny and interesting and I felt comfortable around them. This might not be so bad.

Carlos fixed on something past my shoulder. "Ah, I think this is your...is it insulting to refer to her as your chaperone?"

I turned to see Lucia speaking to the gorgeous bartender. "No, that might be accurate. I know I depend on Lucia to keep me from screwing up too badly."

"No one will judge you," Elisabeta said, raising her bottle to me in a toast. "You have too much influence."

I was prevented from asking what kind of influence that was by Lucia saying, "Davies. Good. You sure you don't want to take a suite here?"

"I...actually, yeah, I think I will." I still wasn't sure about sleeping here, but having a place to retreat to seemed like a good idea. And I was less likely to miss out on the after-hours gatherings, if Carlos's statement about his being the only party Thursday night meant there were normally many more than that.

"Smart choice. They're nice. Ramirez, Vaduva, good to see you still together."

"We are nothing if not consistent, Lucia," Elisabeta said with a smile.

"I'm going to steal Davies for a while. You don't mind, do you?"

"Not at all," Carlos said. "Helena, it was good to meet you, and I hope we will see you again."

"I hope so, too," I said, and let Lucia take me by the elbow and steer me away toward the far corner of the room. "They're all right, aren't they?"

"Who? Oh, yes. Look, don't be too worried about what I said. Just be yourself. You're not stupid and you aren't easily fooled. Ramirez hosts a big bash on Thursday you'll want to go to. It's fun, and people stop politicking long enough to relax for real."

"He already invited me."

"Good. Now, did you look at the revised schedule?"

"No."

"Too bad. You're on it."

"I'm *what?*"

"Last minute addition. There's a panel addressing the issues Abernathy's has with dividing its time between the factions. Apparently some other Neutralities have latched on to the idea, and now the Board is toying with adding it to the Accords."

"Making it permanent? What a terrible idea!"

"Which is what you'll get to say on the panel. It's Thursday— you'll see it listed with the other breakout sessions."

I yanked the conference book out of my bag and flipped to the correct page. Sure enough, there was my name with a bunch of other people I didn't know. "I've never been on a panel before. What do I say?"

"There'll be a moderator who directs the discussion. Just speak your mind and it will be fine."

"I don't like the idea of being responsible for something that goes into the Accords. That's a lot of, well, responsibility."

"You don't want the division of time to become permanent, do you?"

"Of course not."

"Then you've already got responsibility. Stop whingeing and be the woman I know you are."

That made me blush. "Lucia—"

"I'll deny I ever said that. Now, go mingle, and I'll see you later."

"Can we sit together at dinner?"

"The named Neutralities have their own table. Good chance for you to meet your counterparts. I'm sure Gauthier is looking forward to meeting you in person. He said as much upstairs."

"You're staying here?"

"This is the only vacation I ever get, Davies. You think I can afford a hotel this swanky on what the Board pays me?"

"Yes, actually. I know what the Board pays you."

"Well, if I get the chance to stay at a four-star hotel on someone else's dime, I'll take it. Sorry you have to work. It's probably not much of a vacation for you."

"Not really, but it's kind of fun, getting to know all these people. Though I don't know how they manage to keep it a secret from the hotel employees."

"There are two dozen paper magi doing nothing but maintaining full-on magnifica illusions so nobody who works here has any idea we're anything but a conference of heating and cooling system salesmen and -women." She tapped the monocle attached to my lanyard. "The magic for seeing through the illusion is bound to that."

"But it just makes things look blurry."

"You're not supposed to use it, you're just supposed to hang it around your neck like you did. Though you probably don't need one, seeing through illusions like you do."

"I'll hang onto it anyway. It's kind of pretty."

Lucia shrugged. "Suit yourself." She drained her glass of wine. "I'm going back for seconds. That bartender is easy on the eyes."

She left me standing alone with half a beer, toying with the monocle. Would it make me extra-able to see through illusions? Or just have no effect? I'd find out eventually, but until then, I intended to enjoy myself. More people had entered the bar, all of them wearing badges on lanyards. I didn't know any of them. I hesitated, unwilling to walk up to strangers and introduce myself, even if they were strangers who had everything in common with me.

"Ms. Davies!" A big, broad man with the thickest mustache I'd ever seen approached me, his arms spread wide. "Good to finally meet you! I'm Herman Goetz, custodian of the Wernher Node, and I feel I know you already, you have been of so much help to me."

"Mr. Goetz, how nice to meet you." I did remember Goetz, who was a frequent customer via mail-in orders. "It feels odd, speaking to you in person. You're much...taller than I imagined."

Goetz laughed, a booming noise that drew attention from everyone around us. He wrapped me in an enormous hug, and I was overwhelmed by the scent of peppermint schnapps. "Good girl! Sit, talk with me, I wish to know what happens when you receive my letters."

I didn't exactly want to talk shop, but I didn't know how to turn him down, so I sat at one of the tables across from him and let him buy me another beer. I told him the routine, which was to my mind fairly boring, but Goetz sat with his beefy elbows on the table, drinking it in. About the time I realized we had an audience, Goetz boomed out, "I will come to Abernathy's in the morning and you will for me do an augury in person, and you are all invited to watch!"

"Oh, um, Mr. Goetz, actually the oracle prefers to—"

"Nonsense! Everyone should know of the great work you do!" He banged his fist on the table, rattling my bottle. I made a quick grab to keep it from falling over.

Red-faced and extremely conscious of the people surrounding our table, I said, "I'd love for anyone who's interested to visit the store. We're open from ten until two."

"Excellent!" Goetz banged the table again. "You should speak to these people as well. I do not wish to dominate your time." He shoved back from the table, forcing a couple of people to hop out of the way, and bowed. I smiled weakly and gave a little wave of the fingers, and stood as well.

The bar was full now of lanyard-wearing men and women, all dressed in some variation on business attire. I saw no more blue jeans. And all of them wanted to talk to me. After another fifteen minutes I felt dizzy and over-warm, since I was still wearing my coat, and the beer was telling me it had been a bad idea on a mostly empty stomach. I smiled, and answered questions, and rarely got a chance to pose questions of my own, not even important ones like "where is the bathroom?"

Finally, my bladder protesting that it had had enough, I excused myself and almost ran back to the lobby, where I found a short hallway leading to the restrooms. Even those were upscale and beautiful, with marble counters and stalls with doors that went from floor to ceiling. I was grateful there wasn't a bathroom attendant, though I did wish there were some way to tell whether a stall was occupied other than by knocking on the door.

Eventually, relieved in body and spirit, I washed my hands and crept from the restroom, hoping not to run into anyone else who might want to talk to me. I'd never thought being Abernathy's custodian would be so overwhelming.

4

I decided to take the opportunity to check in. The woman at the desk had my name on a list and shortly handed me an envelope with two key cards. She looked dismayed when I said I had no luggage, but politely directed me to the elevators. "Welcome to the Grandison, Ms. Davies," she said, just as if I were some visiting dignitary. Hers was the only voice that hadn't echoed since I registered, and I thanked her and strolled across the lobby, avoiding the eyes of the uniformed men who looked as if they resented me for not having luggage for them to carry.

In the elevator, I shed my coat and draped it over my arm and immediately felt better. I watched the display as the numbers climbed higher...and higher...what floor was this suite on, anyway? The top one, apparently. The elevator chimed, and the doors slid open on a hallway carpeted in plush navy blue. It was so silent I could hear the hum of the elevator, or maybe it was the blood rushing through my ears. In either case, it was eerie.

I walked slowly down the hall, looking for my room number. The doors were spaced very far apart, with light sconces on the walls between and, at every third sconce, a flower arrangement set in a fan-shaped brass holder mounted beneath the light. Dark purple and white flowers with five petals stood out against the creamy wallpaper. I didn't know enough about flowers to recognize what these were, but they looked real and smelled sweet enough to make my head ache a little.

I walked more rapidly, turned a corner, and kept going. I hadn't thought the hotel was all that big from the outside, but maybe that was an illusion, the non-magical kind, generated by expensive architects. To my relief—I'd begun to wonder if I would just circle this floor endlessly—my room was about halfway down the new hall, white with a brass peephole and a key card reader next to a lever door handle. With only a couple of tries, I managed to work the key and let myself in.

The sun had set, and the room was unlit. I groped for the light switch and then stood just inside the door, gaping. This wasn't a hotel bedroom; it was a sitting room, with blue and gold overstuffed chairs grouped near one side of the window that took up the entire wall. At the other end of the window was a dinette table, glossy in the soft track lighting, surrounded by chairs that looked as if they were waiting for dinner to be served. A cabinet next to the dinette turned out to contain a small refrigerator and mini-bar, fully stocked, with an expensive coffee maker atop the cabinet. The room was bigger than my living room and kitchen combined.

I opened the door nearest me and found a bathroom, complete with shower and vanity table. Brown and gold wallpaper made it look cozy, and the marble countertop made it look expensive. I fingered the plush white towels and the thick terrycloth bathrobe. They probably added a bundle to your bill if you kept it. I would bet my next month's salary that Lucia took hers home every time.

The next door led to the bedroom, and again I gaped at the king-sized bed with royal blue bedspread and four enormous white pillows, the blue and gold striped chairs with square ottoman off to one side of the room, the flat-screen TV bigger than my own. I could picture myself cuddled up in the bed, watching movies while rain beat against the big picture window nearby. There was *another* bathroom, done in rose marble and shades of pink and gold, and a safe in the wall, and I made the sudden decision that I *was* sleeping here tonight, thank you very much. As long as I had to travel back and forth for work, I might as well enjoy a little comfort. Well. A *lot* of comfort.

I hung my coat in the closet and put my conference bag beneath it, then freshened up a bit in the rose-colored bathroom. Why the suite needed two bathrooms, I had no idea, but I guessed rich people could make demands the rest of us couldn't. I dithered about carrying my purse downstairs and finally decided I needed somewhere to keep my key cards—and, again, why I needed two key cards was a mystery I didn't care to unravel.

No one had missed me. The crowd in the bar was noisy the way any crowd gets when its members are sufficiently lubricated with alcohol. I decided against any more beer and settled in to a seat in one corner, watching my peers and wondering what they were like. Which one was Rebecca Greenough, Lucia's archenemy? Who would be my fellow panel members? I caught the bartender looking at me and smiled politely. He was cute enough, but I missed Malcolm, even though he wouldn't have been here if he was home. Too bad, because that enormous bed had all sorts of possibilities.

A clear tone rang out, like a church bell, and someone said, "If you'll all make your way to the ballroom, dinner is served."

I let the tide of people sweep me along, out of the bar and across the lobby to the stairs. I felt even more dizzy caught up in the crush, and over-warm even though I'd left my coat in my suite. If I was getting sick, this was going to be a miserable week.

The ballroom, Kilimanjaro, was to the left of the stairs, filled with round tables covered with white tablecloths and sparkling with crystal and silverware. I searched the room for the table Lucia had referred to and saw Claude Gauthier holding a chair for an unknown woman. I hurried in that direction, giving the tables a wide berth and politely smiling at everyone I passed. The noise of over a hundred people chattering echoed in my ears, adding to my dizziness, and I reached the table and sat with a feeling of profound relief.

"Helena!" Claude stood again and came around the table to

embrace me. "How good to see you in the flesh. You look warm. Here, let me assist you." That strange echoing effect was back.

I tucked my purse under my chair. "Thank you, I do feel a little warm," I said, and sipped the ice water in the glass he handed me.

"You must allow me to make introductions," Claude said, "as the rest of us are well-known to one another." He gestured toward the elderly man on my left. "May I present Iakkhos Kalivas, custodian of the Labyrinth."

Kalivas' face was a mass of wrinkles, and he wore his white hair long in back, possibly to balance how it was receding in front. The overall effect was as if his hair was sliding off his head. He also wore a headset strapped to his forehead, covering one ear and with a slim microphone bud extending from the earpiece to lie along his cheek next to his mouth. Both earpiece and microphone were made of clear glass that glimmered like an oil slick with shaky rainbows. "I'm pleased to meet you," he said with a perfect Midwestern accent. "I wish now that I'd made use of Abernathy's so we'd have something to talk about."

His lips weren't synchronized with his words. A translator, and a piece of glass magery, if I wasn't mistaken. "I know so little of the other named Neutralities, I'm sure I'll pester you with questions about yours," I said, making him laugh.

"See? Friends already," Claude said. "Next, we have Diane Lakin, custodian of the Fountain of Youth."

Diane Lakin looked no older than me, which I guessed made sense—except weren't custodians not allowed to use their Neutralities on their own behalf? Something of what I was thinking must have been visible in my expression, because Lakin chuckled and said, "I really am only twenty-five."

"Oh! I...was wondering about that. It's nice to meet you, Ms. Lakin."

"Call me Diane. I don't think I can keep a straight face with someone my age calling me Ms. Lakin."

"All right. In fact, I hope you'll all call me Helena. I'll feel less awkward."

"But of course," Claude said, as if that was an obvious conclusion. "On my other side is Parvesh Chhitri, and the lovely lady next to you is Nimisha Rai. Both are disciples of the Sanctuary."

"Samudra Magar is the custodian of the Sanctuary, and he cannot leave it," Nimisha said. With her smooth dark skin, she could have been any age from twenty to forty. "We represent him at this conference."

"The Sanctuary is in Nepal, isn't it? In the mountains?"

"That is correct."

"Then you've come a very long way."

Nimisha smiled, but it was a tired expression that told me I'd said something inane. I opened my mouth to apologize, but she overrode me with "Not quite so long as some, but it is a long journey, yes."

"I'm sorry, I'm—" Even my own words were ringing. "I think I must be unwell. Everything's echoing." I sipped water, and closed my eyes, but the echoing continued.

"Perhaps you need to lie down?" Nimisha said.

"I don't want to make a fuss." I felt over-warm again and reached up to unbutton the next button on my blouse, not caring if it was immodest. My hand brushed the monocle on the lanyard and I yelped—it burned like a match across my skin.

"Are you hurt?" Claude said.

"This thing burned me," I said, pointing at it. Nothing could induce me to touch it again.

"May I?" Iakkhos said. His fingers, which trembled slightly, removed the monocle from the lanyard. "I don't feel any heat."

Instantly the echoes ceased, and when I opened my eyes, the rainbow effect had disappeared from Iakkhos's translation device. "What did you do?"

"Just removed your illusion-piercing magic. Do you feel better?"

"I do. I wonder—I think it interferes with my own ability to see through illusions."

Claude began laughing. "I should have thought of that! Interference indeed, my dear. The two magics would be at war with each other. Give it to me, and I'll return it to the conference managers and have them make a note for next time."

"So the echoing—"

"The magnifica alter the perceptions of the hotel staff so they hear nothing but inane chatter no matter what we say, and see nothing extraordinary when magic is done. There is not much of that, given that we are Neutralities and non-magi, but Iakkhos's translation headset looks like an ordinary Bluetooth receiver to them."

I sighed. "I'm glad it was so simple. I was afraid I was coming down with something."

"Which would make this conference really unpleasant," Diane said.

A server approached our table carrying a laden tray in one hand and a folded stand in the other. She unfolded the stand and set the tray on it, picked up a wooden bowl, and cracked a couple of eggs one-handed into it. "What's that—are they serving raw eggs?" Diane said, craning her head to see more closely.

"Caesar salad dressing," I said. "I've heard really fancy restaurants and hotels make it right at the table, to show how fresh it is." I smelled mashed garlic and anchovies, and it took me back to my mother's kitchen.

"Fascinating," Iakkhos said. "It smells incredible even at this stage."

"You know about food, then," Claude said. "I did not realize you were a gourmand."

"I'm not, really, but my mother is a fabulous cook and she always makes her own Caesar salad dressing." There was the scent of fresh Parmesan, underlying the stronger odors. The server worked rapidly, whisking ingredients together without spilling a drop. I suspected the anchovy paste was fresh, too. I had never really appreciated how good my mother was until now, considering how much a meal like this one would cost if it weren't underwritten by the Board.

The server tilted the bowl and showed its contents to us, creamy and sharp-smelling and perfect. She then poured it over a bowl of romaine and tossed the lettuce thoroughly. Out came the block of

Parmesan and a grater—she wasn't stinting on the cheese, thankfully, it was my favorite part of a Caesar salad. We all watched in fascination as she tossed the salad again, then rapidly but respectfully served each of us. A sprinkling of croutons, some ground black pepper, and she whisked her tray away, leaving us watching her in silence. It was like being part of some ancient ritual, sacrificing heads of lettuce rather than people.

Claude cleared his throat. "Let us begin," he said. I took a bite. Heavenly. The dressing was maybe a little too salty, but Mom always said that was a possibility with Caesar dressing—it was the anchovies that did it. Besides, it was a tiny quibble.

A basket of sourdough rounds appeared on the table next to me, and I helped myself, then passed it to Iakkhos. "So, can I ask what the Labyrinth is? Or should we not talk shop at the table?"

"It's perfectly acceptable to discuss our Neutralities at dinner," Iakkhos said with a smile. I had to look at his eyes rather than his mouth, because I found the asynchrony disturbing. "The Labyrinth is the oldest of the extant named Neutralities—"

"I think the Fountain is actually older," Diane said. "But it was discovered rather than created, and we count from the time of its discovery."

"That's more accurate. At any rate, it was built in A.D. 1400 near Knossos in Crete—not on the site of the original labyrinth, fortunately, or we would have lost it to excavations in the 19th century. Magi use it to center themselves, to regain full use of their aegis when time and battle have worn them down. You walk the Labyrinth to see what its wisdom has to show you."

"So it doesn't have anything to do with the myth of the Minotaur?"

"Not really. The builders drew their inspiration from Daedalus's mythical creation, but there's no creature at the center of our maze." Iakkhos laughed. "Unless you bring it with you, in your heart."

I didn't understand what he meant, but felt awkward about asking when no one else looked confused. "I've wondered how much influence the oracle at Delphi had over Elizabeth Abernathy, when she created our oracle."

"*A History of Magic* says she intended it to work the same, with the prophetic power attached to a man or woman," Claude said, "but the power overwhelmed everyone who tried to take it on. A few people died."

"I'm just as happy not to be the embodiment of the oracle," I said, remembering the one time I had become its body to fight off a giant invader trying to destroy the store. That had nearly killed me.

"So what is it you do, if it isn't being the oracle yourself?" Diane said.

"I receive a question, and the oracle shows me what book will answer that question. It's pretty straightforward."

"Helena is being modest," Claude said. "She has faced many challenges to Abernathy's safety and defeated them all."

"I heard about that," Diane said. "The oracle was giving false prophecies?"

"It was under the influence of a powerful illusion," I said, feeling slightly defensive even though Diane's question hadn't sounded accusatory. "I helped find and destroy it."

"Claude's right, that doesn't sound straightforward at all," Diane said. "Would you pass the salt, Nimisha?"

I glanced at the woman next to me, who had remained silent ever since the salad had come out. "I'd never heard of the Sanctuary until this conference," I said, feeling a little uncomfortable at being the center of attention. "What is it?"

"It is a place for reflection and meditation," Nimisha said. "Some Wardens come to receive a vision of their future—not ambiguous like those provided by Abernathy's, but a clear revelation. Only one such vision is granted to a person in his or her lifetime."

I whistled. "Wow. I bet that's expensive."

"I know little of such matters. I focus on guiding Wardens through the meditation process."

She made it sound as if I'd suggested she do something indecent, and I reddened slightly. "The oracle doesn't care about money either."

"And yet Abernathy's makes a great deal of money for the Board of Neutralities. As we see from this rather vulgar display."

I glanced nervously at the server, who had just set down a new tray filled with plates that smelled delicious. Beef Wellington, with wilted greens and fingerling potatoes, and a lovely dark red merlot. My stomach rumbled just thinking about it. "I thought all the Neutralities brought in plenty of money."

"They do," Diane said, and I thought she gave Nimisha a warning look. "You may not care about money, but I'm sure Samudra pays careful attention to how much the Wardens pay for his service."

"We prefer not to think of it as a service," Parvesh said. "And we do not eat beef."

An uncomfortable silence descended over the table. I glanced at the server again. Her face was perfectly composed, and the plate she set down in front of Nimisha held not the delicious flaky pastry of beef Wellington, but an orange-glazed chicken that didn't look nearly so nice as what I was about to eat. Nimisha had been about to say something that by the look of her face would have been passive-aggressive, but she closed her mouth and picked up her knife and fork.

I took a bite of my beef. Heavenly. Mom made it rarely, so it was a real treat. Conversation stopped in favor of eating and also, I thought, to let the tension pass. Nimisha sure acted like she had a stick up her butt, and Parvesh wasn't much better. I'd been so eager to meet my counterparts I hadn't thought they might not all be eager to meet me. When had I started thinking of Abernathy's in terms of the money it made? Maybe the two from the Sanctuary had the right idea. And maybe I needed to stop obsessing about what they thought of me. I sipped my wine, which was dry and delicious. I didn't know enough about wine to recognize it, but it certainly went perfectly with the beef.

"I hope the Fountain is still running when I get back," Diane said, smiling wryly. "My assistant knows to turn people away, but she's not the most thorough when it comes to cleaning."

"I read in school that the Fountain of Youth was supposed to be in Florida," I said, gratefully grasping the end of this conversational rope. "Is that true?"

"Georgia, actually, but close enough. It's like your store—hidden in the open, disguised as something else. In this case, it's in a trailer park. You haven't seen vulgar until you've seen a square of grass outside a double-wide covered with pink flamingos. The plastic kind." Diane smiled sweetly at Nimisha, who ignored her. "But I imagine we don't get as many visitors as Abernathy's does."

"Does the water really make you young?"

"It has restorative properties, yes, but it can't keep you young indefinitely. It's more effective at making your insides young than your outsides. But it works."

"I've used the Fountain twice now, before your time, Diane," Iakkhos said. "I'm a hundred and two and I don't look a day over eighty-five."

His droll tone of voice surprised a laugh out of me, which made him smile. "Then you remember a time before magery was divided," I said.

"I do. A time before the nodes became Neutralities. Before there were all these regulations on custodians. I realize it's idealistic, but I hope to see it again in my lifetime."

"Not this again," Claude said, but in a friendly way. "Iakkhos, have you any evidence that Nicolliens and Ambrosites are close to making common cause? If anything, things have become worse."

"And what's this nonsense about restricting the times the factions can use a Neutrality?" Diane said. "Helena, tell us about it. I know that's happened at Abernathy's."

"The local faction heads arranged it. I'm not enforcing it, but they all do it anyway." I mopped up the last of my sauce with a piece of crust and popped it into my mouth. "I've heard the Board is thinking about making it official."

"Ridiculous," Nimisha said. "Ambrosites and Nicolliens live together in harmony at the Sanctuary. I wonder that you allow it."

Irritated, I shot back, "I just said I don't allow it. I have no control over what the faction members decide to do. And it turns out most of them choose to obey their leaders. I've had one Ambrosite and one Nicollien who ignore the whole thing, and I'd hoped they would set an example for the others, but not so far."

"I see," said Nimisha, somewhat mollified. "Then you will speak against it."

"I'm on a panel Thursday about it, so yes."

"I meant unofficially. You will give your opinion without fear or favor?"

"Of course."

"That is good."

Her approval warmed me, which then made me annoyed—there was no reason I should care what this woman thought. "I have to stand up for my principles. Maybe if I can get the Board behind me, I can force Mr. Parish and Mr. Rasmussen to repeal their dictates."

"Good luck with that," Iakkhos said. "The Board is notoriously slow to change its collective mind. Alterations to the Accords almost never happen. To be more specific, alterations not proposed by Board members almost never happen."

His certainty struck me to the heart, as if he'd laid my secret desires bare. "But if the change is sensible—"

"The Board members are conscious of their role as gatekeepers of history," Claude said, making a face. "They dislike ceding power to anyone, even a ranking custodian of a powerful Neutrality. But I don't imagine you have any changes in mind, Helena!"

I smiled, but inside I felt angry and miserable all at once. If the Board members were all so intractable, maybe my chance at changing the Accords was impossible. Especially since my change was ultimately selfish. I doubted many other custodians wanted the freedom to date faction members.

The server brought us a choice of coffee or tea, then set down a beautiful frozen key lime pie I just had to make room for. They were going to have to roll me out of here on a dolly. I took a bite, then, daringly, asked Nimisha, "Have you been to Portland before? As representatives of the Sanctuary, I mean."

"This is our first time out of Nepal," Nimisha said. "Though we make a thorough study of the world. It is why we speak your language well."

"It's said English is the language of business now," Diane said. "Convenient for us, but it also makes us less likely to learn other languages. That's unfortunate, I think."

"I can still understand Spanish, mostly, from my high school classes," I said, "but I wouldn't say I speak it at all."

Parvesh said something liquid-sounding in a language I didn't recognize. "That is Nepali," he said, "and I speak Maithali as well."

"It sounds beautiful," I said.

"I've never learned to speak anything but Greek," Iakkhos said. "I just don't have the head for it." He tapped his translator and added, "This is a real boon. Sixty years ago I had to have someone follow me around and translate for me."

"French is my native tongue, but I have learned German and Russian in addition to English," Claude said. "But Diane is correct that English is our *lingua franca*. You will be at no disadvantage," he told me.

I opened my mouth to respond, but a woman stood up from a nearby table, larger than ours, and ascended the steps of the dais some three feet away. It extended most of the length of the room and had a couple of potted plants looking alone and embarrassed about it. At the center stood a podium with a microphone and the hotel's logo on the front.

"Greetings, and welcome to the Conference of Neutralities," she said in a voice that would have carried to the corners of the room even without the microphone. She had skin the color of burnished copper and wore her hair shaved close to her scalp, and I was pretty sure her business suit cost as much as my annual salary. "We hope you feel welcome here. If you have any needs, please contact a member of the hotel staff, who will assist you in whatever way necessary.

"You have all received a copy of the program. We will post any corrections or changes each morning outside the registration table. For needs specific to your responsibilities or this conference, speak with one of our associates at that table."

The woman swept the room with her gaze. "We wish to remind you again of the seriousness of your duties. Enjoy yourselves, but never forget your purpose in being here. Thank you, and we will see you at the opening session tomorrow afternoon."

Sporadic clapping spread throughout the room as the woman returned to her seat. "Laverne Stirlaugson was born stuffy," Claude said under his breath. "Being chairwoman of the Board has not helped her disposition."

I concealed a smile behind my hand. Beside me, Nimisha said, "She is due respect because of her position."

"I respect her position. I merely wish she would allow herself some fun." Claude patted his lips with his napkin and laid it atop his empty plate. "I will retire now. I am tired from my journey. Ward-stepping is no easy thing."

"Didn't you fly?" I said.

"That takes far too long and is even more exhausting," Claude said. "Faster to skim between wards, if you have two people capable of carrying you. Wouldn't you agree, Iakkhos?"

"I wouldn't travel any other way." Iakkhos stood. "And I feel tired as well. I'll see you all in the morning."

I finished my dessert and rose from the table. If I was spending the night, I needed to run home and pack a few things. "Tomorrow, then," I said.

In the elevator, I checked my phone for messages I might have missed—nothing. I tried not to feel too disappointed. Malcolm had said it would be a while. I'd just become so used to talking to him practically every day, and I wanted to tell him about the other custodians. I liked them—well, I didn't really like Nimisha and Parvesh, but maybe they were just cranky from their trip. I still had several days to really get to know them.

In my suite, I collected my coat, gave the beautiful room one last loving look, and ran back to the elevator. Again, all I could hear was the hum of the motor and the *ding* of the door opening to admit a couple of lanyard-wearing people having an intense conversation in some Scandinavian language. They ignored me, which was nice.

Dimly I became aware of music playing. My phone. I dug it out of my purse and saw Judy's number on the screen. "What's up?"

"It's happened," Judy said. "Do you know Mark Woolston?"

"The really tall guy with the buck teeth? Comes in every Wednesday at eleven sharp?"

"Not anymore," Judy said. "He was killed by his familiar twenty minutes ago."

5

The sun shone brightly Tuesday morning, but inside Abernathy's it might as well have been a winter storm. Nicolliens huddled in groups of three or four, talking in quiet voices. Normally there were at least three familiars leashed outside the front door during Nicollien time, snarling and growling whenever they caught sight of me. Today there were none.

I did dozens of auguries that morning. Half were of the "how do we combat this new evil?" variety. The rest read, "Will my familiar turn on me?" The second kind were so inexpensive I wondered why Abernathy's didn't just give them for free the way it did auguries that might save a life. I looked into those men and women's faces and saw fear and despair, and handed over their books more gently than I normally might have.

Judy said very little, and that only to communicate about the store. "I saw his body," she'd told me when she came in that morning, and that was all she would say about it. I didn't press. Either she needed to talk about it, in which case she eventually would, or she needed to forget about it, and I shouldn't pry. I'd done my crying for Mark late last night and now I felt exhausted by my fears for my Nicollien friends and for Malcolm's safety.

Around eleven, the door flew open with a crash like it hadn't done for over a year. "I am here for an augury," Herman Goetz boomed.

"Oh, Mr. Goetz, I...certainly, but could you speak more quietly?"

"I am loud when I am happy," Goetz said, "but I will do as you ask." His voice became marginally quieter. "Why is this place silent? You Wardens all look as though you have lost a friend."

"Mr. Goetz, they *have* lost a friend," I said, taking his arm and drawing him closer to the counter and away from the grieving Nicolliens. "A Nicollien magus was killed last night, and they all knew him."

"Oh, the familiar. I have heard this. My apologies." Goetz took off his overcoat and wiped his vast forehead with its sleeve. "Here is my augury question."

I unfolded the much-creased piece of paper. *How do I expand my sphere of influence?* I thought Goetz already had plenty of influence, as custodian of the third-largest Neutrality in Europe, but I smiled and entered the oracle.

When I returned with Goetz's book, I found Nimisha Rai and Parvesh Chhitri waiting by the counter. "Oh!" I said. "Just a minute— here, Mr. Goetz, that will be two thousand dollars."

"Very well, thank you," Goetz said, handing me three vials of *sanguinis sapiens*. "Better than changing money, yes? But this store should become more modern, and receive bank transfers with automatic currency conversion. I tell you this as a friend."

"I agree, Mr. Goetz, and it's something we're working on," I said, ignoring how Judy rolled her eyes behind the man's back. Bringing Abernathy's into the 21st century was an ongoing struggle, one that Judy bore the brunt of, but I didn't feel like discussing it with him.

"Excellent, excellent. *Vielen Dank,* thank you so much," Goetz said, and let me usher him out the door.

"Welcome to Abernathy's," I said to the Sanctuary representatives. "This is Judy Rasmussen, my co-worker. Did you want an augury, or just to look around?"

"We were curious," Nimisha said. "We have heard much about this store. It seems so ordinary."

"That keeps it safe," Judy said.

Nimisha smiled, an unexpectedly friendly expression. "I meant no insult. It is simply a surprise to know what emerges from it and how that contrasts with how it looks."

Parvesh was looking at the nearest bookcase. "Do you have books in Nepali?"

"I don't know. It would damage the oracle if I knew what it contained. That's how it operates, by indeterminacy. Anything could be inside, therefore everything is."

"You could use it to locate missing books," Parvesh said, running his hand across a row of spines.

"I don't know what you mean."

"Books that no longer exist. Books lost to humanity. The missing plays of Kalidasa, for example. Or lost folios of Shakespeare. If anything could be inside, why not such works?"

"I...that might not be how it works, but it's an interesting idea," I said. Beside me, Judy's phone buzzed with an incoming text, and she turned away to read it. "I can't test it myself—I'm not allowed to use the oracle for myself, you know."

"And we have no money except what we need to return home," Nimisha said. "But it is, as you say, an interesting idea."

Judy gasped. "Another killing," she said. The Nicolliens in the room turned their attention on her. "Patty Henriksen."

A woman sobbed and was comforted by her companions. "Did you know her?" I asked Judy.

"No. But Father would have. Helena, this is getting serious."

"What killings do you mean?" Parvesh said.

"Familiars turning on their masters."

"I thought that was impossible."

Judy's lips thinned in a scowl. "So did we."

Parvesh and Nimisha exchanged glances. "What is done with the familiars?"

Judy stuffed her phone in her pocket. "They're destroyed. If they're caught. Patty's familiar escaped and it's loose in the city now."

I drew in a horrified breath. "It has to be caught."

"Brittany's team is on it. They'll find it before it hurts anyone." Judy didn't sound sure. It wasn't that Brittany Spinelli wasn't a skilled steel magus, almost as good a hunter as Malcolm; it was that Portland wasn't a small city, and a familiar could go anywhere with its dog-form illusion. I hoped Brittany had the equivalent of the illusion-piercing monocle.

"I hope this store is well warded," Nimisha said. "Invaders are drawn to custodians."

"I know. And it is." Maybe I needed to get a stone magus down to the store to check its wards. Just in case.

"We would like to see the rest of the store, if it is not too much trouble," Nimisha said.

"Of course not." They'd been so polite and not at all passive-aggressive. Last night had just been jet-lag, or whatever you got from traveling between wards. I waved them toward the back of the store, trying not to picture the familiar that was now roaming free in the streets of the city. I would feel a lot more comfortable if Malcolm were here to hunt it.

I SAT near the edge of the ballroom, which today was full of chairs rather than round tables, and covered my mouth to hide a yawn. The same woman who'd addressed us the night before, the chairwoman Laverne Stirlaugson, was talking about the marvelous opportunities for custodians here at the conference. She'd already invited us to check out the vendor room, which I fully intended to do, curious about what kinds of goods and services might appeal to custodians of magical Neutralities. Now she was talking about some last-minute changes to that afternoon's programming.

"...and there will be a buffet supper in this room starting at six," she said. "As always, if you have any questions, feel free to ask." Her expression said she didn't intend for us to ask *her*. A scattering of applause throughout the room signaled the end of the session. I stood and collected my bag and purse, flipping through my program book. There were a few breakout sessions I was interested in, particularly one about how Neutralities policed their people for signs of partiality. I hoped that might give me some ideas for fixing my own problem.

"Ms. Davies."

I looked up and saw a slender, olive-skinned middle-aged woman with frosted hair and cat's-eye spectacles extending her hand to me. I juggled what I was holding and clasped it. "Yes?"

"Rebecca Greenough," the woman said. Her voice was pure BBC announcer and her smile didn't make it all the way to her eyes. "How nice to finally meet you."

"Um...it's nice to meet you, too." I didn't know what else to say. If she was poison as Lucia said, I needed to stay far away from her. But I had no idea how to do that, short of fleeing rudely out of the ballroom.

"We have a connection, you know. I was an Abernathy before my marriage. My grandfather was Rowan Abernathy's younger brother."

Warning bells went off inside my head. Rowan was Silas's father, and if Silas had an uncle and cousins, one of them should have inherited the store when he abdicated—or maybe I was wrong about how the custodianship used to be transferred. "I didn't know Rowan had family other than Silas. You should come to the store...there's a picture of Silas—"

"I'll be sure to visit, thanks. It's just odd to think I might have been custodian of Abernathy's had things gone differently. Don't you agree?"

"You mean, if Silas hadn't abdicated? Yes, I agree that's an odd thought."

I'd just reflected her words back at her, but she frowned as if it had been an insult instead. "You don't know what happened, do you?"

"I don't. I just know they had to do auguries for three weeks to determine the next custodian."

"Mark—my grandfather—didn't want to move to Portland. I can hardly blame him. Such a small city."

Her dismissive tone of voice irritated me. I was pretty sure there was more to it than that. "I'm sure a lot of places are small compared to London."

"Indeed. Abernathy's thrived in Charing Cross Road."

"It's thriving here."

"I would hardly call it thriving." Greenough glanced around the ballroom as if assessing its qualities and coming up short. "No, hardly that. But it won't matter soon."

"I'm sorry?"

Her eyes widened in what I was sure was pretend surprise. "You haven't heard? I'm petitioning the Board of Neutralities to move the oracle back to London where it belongs."

"That's impossible. Abernathy's can't be moved."

"It was moved once. I'm sure it can be done again."

"You don't understand. That move was an act of desperation, to protect the store against the Blitz. It was extremely dangerous and shouldn't be repeated."

Greenough made a dismissive wave. "Times have changed. It no longer takes weeks to cross the ocean. I can assure the Board of the oracle's safety during the whole process. I've even purchased the store Abernathy's used to be housed in. I just need their authorization."

"They won't give it. They don't like change. And I'll persuade them otherwise."

"You? The girl under whose supervision the store has nearly been destroyed twice? You think they'll care anything at all about your opinion?"

Her casually dismissive tone infuriated me. "I've *saved* the store twice."

"I'm sure they'll see it otherwise." She smiled, a smug expression that made me itch to slap her.

"You mean you'll tell the story your way. You weren't even there, Ms. Greenough." I put enough disdain into my words to make them a weapon. Greenough didn't even flinch.

"I have influence with the Board. I think you should start getting your passport in order—if that's even necessary."

Now I felt cold. "What's that supposed to mean?"

The smug smile broadened. "The Board may decide the custodianship of Abernathy's should go to a London native. Someone familiar with the ways of the city."

"You mean, you?"

Greenough's eyes widened again. "I already have a custodianship, Ms. Davies. But I'm sure I wouldn't turn down Abernathy's if they offered it to me. I feel I have a right, after all."

My hand had closed into a fist. "You won't succeed."

"Keep telling yourself that, dear."

I made my fist relax and smiled pleasantly. "I have an idea," I said. "Why don't we ask the oracle what it thinks?"

That rattled her. "What?"

"Well, it's got more of an investment in your proposal than either of us. Let's ask it for an augury and see what it has to say."

Greenough's smile turned nasty. "Very well," she said. "Tomorrow morning. And don't even think about falsifying it."

"Ms. Greenough, I never falsify auguries. And the fact that the possibility occurred to you tells me you'd be a terrible custodian."

Greenough's lip curled derisively. She swept away out of the ballroom before I could slap her silly.

I drew in a deep, relaxing breath. This was ridiculous. If the Board hated change so much, it certainly wouldn't move Abernathy's for such a frivolous reason as one woman trying to recreate history. But I needed to make sure. I needed to talk to the Board. And hope Abernathy's would deliver an augury that would put the whole ridiculous notion to rest.

Laverne Stirlaugson was at the far side of the room, talking to a board member I knew named Ragsdale. I hurried across the room and stood politely to one side, waiting for her to finish telling Ragsdale something. Ragsdale saw me hovering and cleared his throat discreetly. Stirlaugson turned her head and assessed me with her eyes. I held myself upright and tried not to look like a puppy whining for a treat.

"See to it," she told Ragsdale, and turned to face me. "Yes, Ms. Davies?"

"Hi, um, Ms. Stirlaugson, I..." Now was not the time to stammer. Or to beat around the bush. "Is it true Ms. Greenough has petitioned to move Abernathy's back to London?"

"It is." Her face was closed-off, remote, and I suddenly felt I had no chance whatsoever. I persisted anyway.

"Does the Board know how dangerous it is to move the oracle? How difficult it was the first time?"

"The Board is aware, yes."

"Then why haven't you told Ms. Greenough no?"

Stirlaugson raised an eyebrow. "Ms. Davies, Ms. Greenough has some compelling arguments. London is far more central to our interests than Portland. Imagine how much more London has to offer this conference."

"The conference only happens once every three years. Abernathy's has to operate every day."

"If you have a statement to make, you'll be given the opportunity. We have not yet made our decision. Now, if there's nothing else...?"

I knew a dismissal when I heard one. "No, ma'am. Thank you. Nice to see you again, Mr. Ragsdale." I managed not to bow—Stirlaugson looked every inch a queen—and made my escape.

Outside in the hallway, I took a moment to gather myself. A statement, she'd said. I needed to marshal my best, most persuasive arguments, and I'd have the chance to present that to the Board. And at worst, well, I'd never lived abroad and it might be interesting. To live far away from my family. And how would Malcolm justify spending all his time in London? *Don't be stupid. The worst is that they take the custodianship away from you.* Which was about as awful a worst as I could imagine.

I breathed in deeply again. Fretting wouldn't solve the problem. I headed for the Everest room and my first presentation of the conference. I had plenty of time. And I wasn't going to let that bitch Greenough ruin my life.

But I had trouble paying attention to the presentations, which were mostly aimed at the node custodians. The panel on policing the Neutralities only made me discouraged, because it was just like the Accords—they looked for indications that you might someday be biased, not signs that you already were. Why couldn't they give us even a little credit?

After three breakout sessions, I was tired and hungry and disinclined to talk to people. The buffet was less intimidating than the formal dinner had been, though the food was still excellent, and I helped myself to roast chicken and new potatoes and found a table off to one side, hoping no one would try to talk to me.

"Helena! Why do you sit alone? Come, Elisabeta and I will sit with you." Carlos swung the seat next to me away from the table and dropped into it. "You look tired."

"I feel tired."

"Then you must join us for a drink after dinner, down in the bar," Elisabeta said. "The parties begin tonight. You will need your strength for that."

I smiled, half-heartedly. "I think I need a nap first."

"You have worked all morning, I forgot," said Carlos. "Yes, nap, but we will call for you at eight."

Their enthusiasm was infectious. "All right."

"Where do you go next?"

"I was going to look in the vendor room. I'm curious about what people sell to Neutralities."

"Many things. Specialized software that lets us track movement of *sanguinis sapiens*. Security systems. Items for law enforcement. Magical versions of common things. You may find it interesting."

I took a few more bites. The roast chicken was a little dry, but the potatoes made up for it. "I've only known about the magical world for a little over a year, so I'm still fascinated by the things you all come up with."

Carlos chuckled. "Very well. You will explore, and nap, and be ready for parties!"

"Drinks first," Elisabeta said. "You must talk to that divine bartender. I'm sure I saw him watching you yesterday."

"I already have a boyfriend," I said.

Elisabeta shrugged. "That doesn't mean you cannot flirt."

I was sure that wasn't true, so I smiled and took another bite so I'd have an excuse not to respond.

By the time I was finished eating, I felt more cheerful, not hard to explain when I had Carlos and Elisabeta laughing and teasing me. I walked away from the table feeling full and content. Being miserable wouldn't solve my problem. Drinks and, all right, some light flirtation with the bartender wouldn't solve it, either, but it would make my problem more distant.

The vendor room, Denali, was full of black curtains blocking off spaces where the vendors presented their wares. It reminded me of a dark, somber version of an Arabian souk, saved from joylessness only by the colorful awnings and cardboard cutouts thronging the room. Banners bearing the names of companies I'd never heard of hung from black backdrops. I'd barely taken two steps into the room before I was accosted by someone selling accounting software. "Guaranteed compliant with your current system," the man said, "just drop it atop whatever you're using and bingo! You're able to track magical deposits."

"I don't do the accounting," I said, and hurried on. Too bad Judy wasn't here. She'd know whether the man's product worked or not.

The next person gave me a pen I accepted gingerly, remembering my reaction to the monocle, but it just had the name of his company embossed on it. The one after that had a couple of gorgeous women handing out flyers. I stopped paying attention after that, because my eye had been caught by a display whose name I knew very well. I drifted toward it, pulled by an inexorable tide.

Campbell Security was one of the larger booths, staffed by eight people. One of those people reached up to straighten their banner, and my heart thudded painfully in my chest at how familiar he was. The next second revealed it wasn't Malcolm: the dark-haired man was tall, but his face was longer and his shoulders narrower. But the shape of the eyes, and the nose...those were the same, and I wished Malcolm were there so badly tears pricked my eyes. I blinked them away and continued to approach, pretending they were any other vendor.

"In the market for security for your node?" the lone woman said.

"You provide security for Abernathy's already," I said.

The tall, dark-haired man turned around and fixed me with an oh-so-familiar gaze. "Ms. Davies," he said. "Ewan Campbell. I understand you're friends with my brother."

"Mr. Campbell, it's nice to meet you." I wished I could say *Malcolm's mentioned you*, but Malcolm never talked about his family and I had no idea how he felt about them, except I thought he didn't get along with his mother very well.

"Call me Ewan. I don't suppose you'd like to give us a testimonial? Mal said you'd had an attempted break-in foiled by our alarm system."

It didn't sound as if Malcolm had mentioned I'd set off the alarm system to save myself from my attacker. "I don't mind. I feel safe in my home thanks to it."

"Perfect. Thanks. Terry, how about you give Ms. Davies one of those keychains?"

I shied away. "It doesn't have any illusion magic on it, does it?"

"No, just a jolter. It's a sample of our work." Ewan took the keychain, which had what looked like a laser pointer attached to it, and aimed it at the table. "Point it at an assailant, squeeze the middle, and it delivers a jolt of electromagical energy that will shake someone up long enough for you to get away. Plus, it's a flashlight if you press the button at the top." He squeezed the thing, and the table rattled, knocking over a basket of pens.

"Thanks. It's interesting."

"Anything for one of our best customers."

I took a risk. "I don't suppose...you've heard from Malcolm."

Ewan's face went cold. "Not a word, and I'm not sure I want to, given how he's treated our mother," he said.

"Oh."

"I'm sure he's fine, wherever he is. Throw the man in a dumpster and he'll come up covered in diamonds." Ewan smiled, but it looked forced. "Anything else we can help you with?"

"No, but thanks. Good luck."

Ewan was already turning away from me. I walked on, deep in thought. What had Malcolm done to his mother? All I knew was that Malcolm had had a girlfriend his mother liked more than he did, and I guessed Mrs. Campbell hadn't been happy when he dumped her, but I didn't know if that constituted poor treatment. It wasn't as if he'd dumped his mother, after all.

I visited a few more booths and collected some more tchotchkes, then headed upstairs around seven for a quick nap on the glorious bed. I could get used to luxury like this. As I drifted off, I wondered once again where Malcolm was. Probably not sleeping as luxuriously as I was.

A knock on the suite door woke me about half an hour later. Carlos and Elisabeta stood expectantly outside, dressed for clubbing rather than business. "No, that will not do," Elisabeta said when she saw me. "You must wear party clothes. Hurry, we will wait."

I invited them into the sitting room and retreated to my bedroom to change. I'd packed lightly, figuring I could always go home for anything I forgot, and now I dressed in an outfit Viv had picked for me, a fitted black dress with a short skirt and spaghetti straps under a rose-colored military-style twill jacket. I pulled on black ankle boots with a modest heel, brushed my hair free from its ponytail, and tucked my key card and phone into my jacket pocket. A little lip gloss, and I was ready to go.

Carlos and Elisabeta clapped when they saw me, and I blushed and turned in a half-circle to make the jacket flare out. "That bartender, he will not care you have a boyfriend when he sees you," Carlos said with a wink.

"I think my boyfriend would care, though." I wished Malcolm could see me, not just because his eyes would pop but because it would mean he was home.

"Oh, who says you can't flirt?" said Elisabeta. "It is just being friendly."

We bantered like that as we rode the elevator down to the ground floor and crossed the lobby to the bar. Sure enough, the gorgeous bartender was there, shaking up a martini for an older gentleman who sat at the bar. He saw us come in, and a slow smile spread across his face. Wow.

We sat at the bar some distance from the other gentleman and waited for the bartender to come our way. "What can I get you folks?" he finally said.

"Manhattan," Carlos said. "For both of us."

"Right up. And for you, miss?" He leaned forward and smiled at me again. In the face of that smile, I couldn't order a beer. I was tired of being boring. The trouble was I knew nothing about liquor.

"I don't know," I heard myself say. "What would you recommend?"

The smile broadened. "Dark rum," he said, "with ginger beer, served over ice with a lime garnish. Sweet and dark...just the way I think you like it." He winked, and I went red all over and very nearly blurted out that I had a boyfriend, thanks, and I didn't want to be flirted with. Carlos and Elisabeta roared with laughter. I nodded, inarticulate in my embarrassment. There was nothing wrong with letting him flirt with me, since I had no intention of letting it go farther than flirtation. I needed to relax and, as my sister Cynthia frequently told me, stop being so serious all the time.

"He likes you," Carlos said *sotto voce* as the bartender turned away to fix our drinks.

"I'm sure he flirts with all the young women," I said. "And I have a boyfriend."

"You make no promises," Elisabeta said. "Be friendly. Have fun."

I sat up straighter and smiled at the bartender when he returned with my drink. "Tell me what you think," he said.

I took a sip. It was rich, and a little spicy, and I liked it. "It's good."

He leaned on the bar, inclining his head and shoulders toward me. "I'm Kevin."

"Helena."

"Pleased to meet you, Helena. Hope you're not offended, but aren't you a little young for this crowd?"

Carlos and Elisabeta laughed again. "We are old, you see," Elisabeta said.

"I didn't mean—"

"They understood," I said. "I guess you're never too young to get into the...heating and cooling business."

"Glad to see you can party, too. Someone as beautiful as you, you shouldn't just wear those drab suits."

His expression was so admiring I blushed again and had to take another sip of my drink. "What's it called?"

"A Dark 'n' Stormy. Dark for the rum, stormy for the ginger beer, get it?"

"It's delicious. Thanks."

Kevin nodded and moved away down the bar to where someone else was signaling for his attention. "You sure you have a boyfriend?" Carlos teased.

"Very sure." The ache in my chest roused by seeing Ewan had mostly faded. Even so, as hot as Kevin was, my heart still belonged to Malcolm, and I missed him more every day.

Kevin returned to my side, polishing the counter with a white rag. "You know," he said in a low voice, "I get off at ten. Do you—"

I was saved from answering by a buzz from my phone signaling an incoming text. "Hang on," I said, and pulled it out. Judy.

KELLERS FAMILIAR ATTACKED THEM. HARRY CRITICALLY INJURED. COME NOW.

6

───────────

J sucked in a sharp, horrified breath. "I have to go," I said. "A
friend was attacked—I have to go *now*."

"Wait, Helena!" Carlos said. "Let us come with you."

"No, it's okay, stay here." I tossed those last words over my
shoulder as I ran from the bar and through the lobby. The valet stand
was busy, but I grabbed one of the uniformed men and said, "I need
my car, *please*. It's an emergency."

He remembered me, and the urgency in my voice propelled him
off into the darkness. I jigged in place, too late remembering I didn't
have my coat. The little jacket wasn't enough to keep me warm, but I
didn't dare waste time running back to my suite. I pulled out my
phone and texted Judy: COME WHERE?

Almost immediately came the reply: KELLERS HOME HURRY.

I choked back a sob. Did she mean Harry was dying? Was this to
give me a chance to say goodbye? So many questions thronged my
mind, driving my anxiety higher. Hot tears trickled down my cheeks
and were chilled by the wintry breeze that blew through the awning.
I wondered how long ago it had happened and hoped Harriet was all
right. Surely Judy would have said if Harriet had been injured too.

With a screech, my car pulled up to the curb, and the attendant hopped out. "Good luck, miss," he said so compassionately the tears started up again. I drove away as rapidly as I dared, heading for the freeway.

The night was dark, overcast with clouds that threatened freezing rain or possibly snow. I shook uncontrollably as the Civic's heating system struggled to fight back the cold. If Harry died...I hoped they'd destroyed Vitriol. It infuriated me that the monster had a name, like it was a pet or a friend. No pet could do something like this.

Everyone on the road tonight seemed intent on getting in my way, creeping along the freeway like they were afraid of excessive G-forces on their stupid cars and their stupid bodies. I swerved around a pickup truck and got honked at. *Fine. Honk. Just stay out of my way.* The roads were dry, the visibility was...well, it wasn't good, but it wasn't raining. There was no reason not to go a little faster than the speed limit, something I never did, but then I'd never had so much reason to before.

I took the curving streets and switchbacks of the Kellers' neighborhood at speed, my tires squealing sometimes, and skidded into their long driveway. William Rasmussen's BMW was parked there already, along with a few cars I didn't recognize. The house blazed with light at every window, as if they were hosting a Christmas party, but there was no music, no sound except the wind soughing through the branches of the fir trees surrounding the house. I parked and nearly fell getting out of my car, sprinted to the front door and flung it open without bothering to knock.

The pale gray living room I was so familiar with had been destroyed. The couches and chairs were tipped on their backs or sides and huge chunks had been torn out of them, turning them into splintered wood and shredded upholstery. The andirons and fireplace screen were bent and lay some distance from the fireplace, where the fire burned low and menacing. Several men and women I didn't know were picking up the furniture and holding its broken pieces together, and I smelled something sharp and bitter like burnt glue. They all looked up when I entered, then silently went back to what they were doing. I passed between them to enter the formal dining room, where the table's gleaming surface was covered in deep scratches and burn marks. Someone had fought a battle in this house, and if not for Judy's text, I would have believed the Kellers had lost.

Judy emerged from the hallway that led deeper into the house. "He's still alive," she said, her voice hoarse from crying. "Lucas is with him. Come talk to Harriet."

I followed Judy down the hall, which was covered with photos of the Kellers' children and grandchildren. I'd never been in this part of the house and it surprised me how normal it all looked. Harry and Harriet were glass magi and had fought in the Long War for years before going into semi-retirement, and part of me had trouble reconciling that with raising a family. "Did someone call their children?"

"Father arranged it all. He's in Harry's office making calls." Judy opened a door to a frilly pink bedroom that might have belonged to a pre-teen girl. Harriet sat in an overstuffed pink armchair, staring at nothing, while a magus I didn't know knelt at her feet, holding her hand. Harriet was covered in blood and the sleeve of her bright yellow sweater was torn and hung, blood-soaked, from her shoulder.

As we entered, she closed her eyes tight and hissed, her lips drawn back from her teeth in pain. I'd never seen a healing done before—at least, not on someone other than myself—and watched in astonishment as the angry wound beneath the torn sleeve glowed with amber light. I knew Harriet would be in agony from the healing, which could feel worse than the injury, and I closed my eyes in sympathy with her.

Then I heard Harriet breathing heavily, like someone who'd just run a grueling race, and I opened my eyes to see her put her free hand on the magus's head. "Thanks, Joanie," she said. She raised her head to look at us, and her lips quivered. "Oh, girls," she said, and Judy and I flung ourselves at her and held her tight. I cried again, not sure if it was for her pain, or for the danger Harry was still in, or for the terror so many others faced as well.

"I have to go to him," Harriet whispered. "Thank you both for coming. Judy, has Will called the children?"

"He's doing it now," Judy said. "Pete's on his way."

"I'm glad." Harriet disengaged from us and stood. "Come along, both of you. If…" She shook her head and was silent.

We followed her next door, which I would have called the master suite if it hadn't been so cozy. The rest of the Kellers' house looked like a spread from a home decorating magazine. Here, the furniture was mismatched and worn the way something well-loved would be, with a four-poster bed carved with fanciful images taking up most of the space.

Harry lay in the bed under the covers, looking unexpectedly small for a man over six feet tall. I couldn't see any injuries, none of the awful blood Harriet looked like she'd been drenched in, but he was barely breathing and he looked so pale I wondered if some of that blood hadn't been his. Lucas Yarnell, a Nicollien bone magus I knew from Abernathy's, stood beside the bed, looking down at Harry. Lucas looked as ashy-faced as Harry, and when he reached out to take Harry's hand I saw both of them tremble.

Harriet moved forward to sit next to Harry on the bed. "Well?" she said.

"He's over seventy years old," Lucas said.

"I know how old he is, damn you," Harriet said, startling me because I'd never heard Harriet use any stronger language than "darn." "Will he recover?"

"It will take time. He lost a lot of his magic and a lot of blood. I can't guarantee he'll ever work magic again."

"I don't care about that. I just want him to survive. Did you hear that, Harold Archibald Keller? You are *not allowed* to die." Tears were streaming down Harriet's face that she made no move to wipe away.

Harry's lips moved. Harriet leaned far over to lay her ear against his mouth. Then she laughed, a slightly hysterical sound. "He says my roast would bring a man back from the dead."

Judy and I laughed, and I felt some of the burden lift from my heart. "Is that a good sign? That he can talk?" I asked.

Lucas caught my eye and shook his head, the tiniest movement, and my heart chilled again. "Let's leave Harriet alone for a bit, okay?" he said, shooing us out of the room.

"What aren't you saying, Lucas?" Judy said.

Lucas carefully closed the door behind us and motioned us away from it. "His magic isn't regenerating the way it should," he said. "It happens as you age—the mechanism that causes your magic to replenish itself becomes less efficient, and recovering from the loss of magic is harder and sometimes impossible. He's going to need...not transfusions exactly, but some assistance for his natural processes to start working again. And it might not help."

"So...he could still..."

"I'm not giving up yet." He didn't look as certain as he sounded. "There are still things I can do. If Joan's finished, we can try to combine magic, see if that works. Right now I want Harriet to have as much time with him as possible, just in case..."

He went into the room we'd found Harriet in, and the muffled sound of conversation drifted from it. I focused on one of the pictures on the wall, of the Kellers' four sons. They were one of those families with a strong family resemblance, though in their case all the boys looked like Harriet. They were lined up in a football starting position, bent over and smiling at the camera, and I wondered which one was Pete. Whether they were all magi. Where they lived, and was it close enough for them to travel to be with their parents.

"It was so unexpected," Judy said quietly. "Harriet said they were just sitting in the living room after dinner, with Vitriol lying on the floor by the fireplace like it always does, and Harry stood up to get the paper and the monster launched itself at his chest. Harriet killed it with her cast iron skillet, but not before..." She took a shuddering breath. "They're analyzing its body and the harness, but it looks like the same as the others—the alteration magic is failing."

"What are the Nicolliens going to do? The problem's not going away!"

"I don't know. Father might order a mass extermination, if they can't figure out why some are failing and others aren't. It's terrifying." She looked me up and down. "Were you clubbing?"

She made it sound so horrifying I blushed and stammered, "Um, there are parties at the conference...I was going to one, and Carlos and Elisabeta said I should dress—"

"Never mind. Just so it wasn't anything important."

"No."

We fell silent. The conversation stopped, and Lucas and Joan emerged from the pink bedroom. "There's nothing else you can do here tonight," Lucas said. "No. Help Harriet move some of her clothes into this room. She can't stay in there with Harry, and she has to sleep sometime."

"All right."

Harriet was still sitting on the bed next to Harry, holding his hand. "Lucas wants you to move some things into Amelia's old room," Judy said. "We'll help you carry."

"I don't want to be away from him."

"You have to sleep eventually. And it will disturb him if you sleep in here."

Harriet raised her head. "If I'm gone when he—"

"Don't," said Judy. "Don't think like that. He'll be fine."

"And Lucas won't leave him alone," I said.

Harriet nodded and patted her husband's hand, then rose. "I should get out of these clothes and burn them. I just can't stop seeing Vitriol's smashed skull and wishing I'd been able to cut its damn head off."

We helped Harriet take some clothes and her toothbrush into the other room. The Kellers' one daughter, Amelia, had a frilly soul, and I wondered if Harriet would even be able to sleep in that pink nightmare. But eventually we got everything put away and left Harriet to change her clothes.

As we loitered in the hall, Judy's father emerged from a room at the far end of the hall and stumped toward us. William Rasmussen normally looked like a professor of some obscure science, but tonight he just looked weary, his eyes dark-circled and pouched, the corners of his mouth drawn down in a permanent frown. He glanced once at me and dismissed me—well, we weren't friends and probably never would be.

"I've reached all five of their children," he said to Judy. "Peter will be here in a few hours. The rest will come as they're able, and let's hope it's soon enough."

"What made the magic fail?" I asked.

It was a mistake. Rasmussen's lips compressed tight with anger. "This has nothing to do with you," he spat. "Stay out of it."

"One of my friends might be dying. It matters to me."

"So you can turn it into a weapon? Don't tell me you're not thrilled to see our weakness. You've always hated familiars, you—"

"Stop it!" Judy exclaimed. "Do you really think Helena's happy about this?"

Rasmussen and I glared at each other. I said, "I don't want anyone to get hurt. Yes, familiars scare me, but I've seen them in action and I think you're right that they help in the Long War. But if you don't know what's causing this to happen, I think I have a right, as a potential victim, to know what you plan to do about it."

Rasmussen was breathing heavily. "We won't let it go on," he said. "I'm waiting for word from the Archmagus. If we can't find a way to identify the familiars who are likely to break containment, we'll have to start destroying them."

"I'm sorry."

"So am I. Now get out. There's nothing more you can do here."

"Father—"

"It's all right, Judy. He's right. Call me if—if anything changes." I turned and walked away. The living room looked more like itself, though the fireplace screen was still bent; the couches were mostly whole, with the upholstery restored and the ash wood glossy and unblemished. The Nicolliens avoided my eyes the way someone who'd heard Rasmussen yell at me would. I let myself out the front door and trudged to my car, no longer feeling the cold.

I drove back to the hotel, barely seeing the road. It probably wasn't safe to drive like that, but I didn't care. I kept glancing at my phone where it lay on the passenger seat, willing it to stay silent. Harry would be all right. He had to be.

I left my car with the valet and slumped through the lobby, only just then realizing I'd left my purse in my room and had been driving without my license. Reckless driving, driving without a license...I was normally the most law-abiding person you could imagine, but none of that mattered now. I avoided the bar. It was after ten by now, so Kevin would be gone, but I didn't want to take any chances on meeting someone who'd want to talk. Talking felt like way too much work.

Inside my suite, I slung my jacket over one of the chairs and went into the bedroom to fall face-first onto the bed. I let it swallow me up, draining all the fear and sorrow and tension out of my body and sending it somewhere far away. I kicked off my boots and curled in on myself, listening to my breathing. I needed Malcolm so badly, and at that moment I didn't care if the entire Board of Neutralities and every custodian there was knew I'd violated the Accords. I just wanted him there.

Eventually I found myself drifting off and rolled off the bed, stretching. I stripped out of my party dress, leaving it puddled on the floor, and put on my pajamas. I plugged my phone in and set it on the nightstand, then stared at it for a few minutes, willing Malcolm to call. Nothing.

I turned off the lights and lay on my back with my arms flung wide. I was barely able to reach both sides when I lay like that. I rolled onto my side and curled into a ball again, and prayed, as I rarely did, for Harry and Harriet and all the other people affected by this nightmare. I slid into sleep and dreamed of being chased by monsters I fought with only a frying pan. It was a fitting weapon for Harriet. For me it was just futility.

7

*J*udy was at Abernathy's when I arrived, logy and exhausted from being jerked out of sleep so often by nightmares. "No change," she said before I could ask. "It's good news. It means he's holding steady."

"What will happen next?"

"Once his magic reserves reach a certain point, he'll do a sort of physical therapy, but for magic. His body needs to relearn how to generate magic naturally, not through the aegis. And when that's done, he can fully recover. But he may not be a magus anymore."

"I thought you were a magus as long as you had an aegis."

"If the aegis stops working, it's the same as not having one. With Harry's magic so depleted, it could fool his aegis into believing he's dead, which would render it inert."

"Isn't there anything they can do about that? Give him a new one?"

"No one's ever survived the Damerel rites a second time. And Harry's too old for it, anyway." Judy perched on the stool and leaned her elbows on the counter. "I hate Ryan Parish."

"Why?"

"He's being so smug about the whole thing. Called on Father

early this morning to 'discuss the situation' when what he really wanted was to make demands. He insisted the Nicolliens destroy all their familiars, and when Father refused, he wanted to restrict where they went even if they didn't bring their familiars with them. He was talking like they were all infants who needed to have their asses wiped for them. Father nearly took his head off. But that's not what really bothers me."

"That's not enough?"

Judy shook her head. "It was that he was right. Familiars have become too dangerous. I know Father still hopes they'll be able to solve the problem, but how many more people have to die, or nearly die, before he admits to failure?"

"Losing the familiars could set the Long War back by decades. How are the Nicollien teams supposed to work without their support?"

"I can't believe you're defending them. I thought you were afraid of familiars."

"I am. But I also know the Nicollien offense is completely based on familiars. And maybe now it's clear that was a stupid move. It doesn't matter, because it would be like...what's that game where you pull blocks out of a tower?"

"Jenga?"

"That one. Destroying all the familiars would be like yanking out the whole base at once. Mr. Rasmussen needs to figure out a better way to do it."

"You're so reasonable it's depressing. I just hope Harry lives. Magic's not that important."

"I never thought I'd hear you say that. I thought Rasmussens believed in fighting the Long War above all."

"There are lots of ways to fight. You and I don't have magic, and we're fighting just by running Abernathy's." Judy's smile was bitter. "That's what I tell myself every time I have to balance the books."

I went to the break room to hang up my coat and purse. "That's a valiant effort," I called out, "and definitely counts as fighting a war."

Judy didn't answer. I came back into the front of the store to find her staring at her phone. "What is it? Not—"

"He's awake. But he doesn't remember anything that happened. He tried to use magic and nearly killed himself." Judy shoved her phone into her pocket. "Give me something to do. I need a distraction."

"Labels for yesterday's auguries. Being open only four hours a day means we're falling behind on the mail-in auguries."

Judy nodded and disappeared into the stacks. I glanced through the window at the magi lining up, waiting for me to open. Well, I could let them in a little early.

"Did you hear about Harry Keller?" the first man through the door said. "They say he's dying."

"He's going to be fine. I saw him last night and he's awake and he...he's going to be fine."

"You saw him?"

I was mobbed by Nicolliens, all wanting to know about Harry. I made them shut up and repeated the highlights of what I'd seen, not mentioning what Rasmussen had said about the potential fate of the familiars. "So everything's all right," I concluded, "and you can tell your friends."

"I'm not going to wait for it to happen to me," a woman shouted. "I'll destroy Bane the minute I get home."

"I don't—" I shut my mouth. Preemptively destroying the familiars was probably a bad idea, but I wasn't going to advise anyone to put themselves in danger. "They'll figure out what's causing it."

"Not good enough," the first man said. "It could happen to anyone. And the familiar that killed Patty is still out there. It could come after you next, Ms. Davies."

"I feel safe," I said. "This building is warded securely, and I have faith in the hunting teams."

"To do what?" said a voice from the back of the crowd. The Nicolliens parted to reveal Rebecca Greenough, casually dressed in jeans so new they still had creases and a button-down plaid shirt. She looked like a model for lumberjack chic. "What do you expect your hunting teams to do?"

"Protect us against escaped familiars," I said.

"I've heard about that. Paul Pittman has already ordered all the familiars in the United Kingdom and Ireland destroyed. I wonder your Nicollien leader hasn't done the same."

"It's a drastic step. Mr. Rasmussen hasn't exhausted all the possibilities yet."

"I'm sure that's comforting to all the people who die." Greenough took a few more steps toward the shelves. The crowd moved away from her as if they could smell the poison on her. "*This* is what Abernathy's has become? This ramshackle collection? These shelves aren't even finished wood!"

"It's camouflage." Her disdainful tone of voice made me want to hit her with one of the heavier books. "And it replicates the store as it looked in Charing Cross Road. Of course, you wouldn't know this, not having Silas's diary."

"My grandfather always talked about how beautiful Abernathy's was. This clearly is the result of years of inept management. Oh, I don't blame *you*. You've only had its care for a year. It was that idiot Briggs who let it come to this, I'm sure."

I bit back a harsh reply. Arguing with her was pointless. "You've come for the augury? Do you know how it works?"

"Of course." She pulled an augury slip from her jeans pocket and handed it to me. *Should Abernathy's be restored to its proper place in London?* "Straightforward enough, don't you agree?"

"It's definitely straightforward." *And wrong-headed. I can't wait to see your face when Abernathy's turns you down.* "Excuse me." I turned my back on her, ignoring the warning itch between my shoulder blades, and entered the stillness of the oracle.

It was impossible for me to continue to feel angry while I was surrounded by such peacefulness. But I was too surprised to feel peaceful, either. The light of the oracle was blood-red, the light of a dying star, and the stillness felt oppressive, a giant thumb pressing down on my skull and driving me into the ground. "Oh, *come on!*" I shouted. "What do you mean, no augury? Listen to this. She wants to know if Abernathy's should be restored to its so-called proper place in London. There's so much wrong with that question, even I could tell her no!"

Silence spread outward as my words echoed away among the shelves. I paced between them, looking in vain for the blue light of an augury. "Do you not understand what's at stake here? You *have* to remember what it was like to move the first time. Silas said it was dangerous and you were nearly killed. You can't possibly want that again. Please, just give me an augury that will tell her you don't want this."

Still nothing. I rounded a corner and leaned face-first against one of the bookcases. "All right," I whispered. "I'm your hands. And I'll be your hands even if it's to deliver you into potential destruction. And no, I don't think that's too dramatic."

Greenough was examining the cash register when I returned. "You know, I believe this was original to the London store," she said, then eyed my empty hands. "Did you fail?"

"I don't fail," I said, which was cocky, but I was miserable and I didn't care what Greenough thought of me. "The oracle has declined to give an augury. It's not going to weigh in on your question."

"What does that mean?" For once, she sounded uncertain.

"It means it's up to the Board to make the decision. Go ahead and try to persuade them. I'll do my best to stop you."

Greenough smiled, a nasty expression. "I think your appointment was a mistake," she said, "and I'm going to do *my* best to have you removed."

"Who is this, Helena?" Jeremiah appeared from between the bookcases. His T-shirt read THERE ARE 10 KINDS OF PEOPLE WHO UNDERSTAND BINARY and there was the beginnings of a hole in the knee of his jeans.

"This is Rebecca Greenough, custodian of the Bailey Node in London." I didn't feel like elaborating any more than that.

"Hmm. Rebecca Greenough of the Bailey Node." Jeremiah approached Greenough and looked her over. "I think you may be overstepping your bounds."

"Who are *you*?"

"No one, really. One of the countless magi who fight the Long War while you sit safe in your node, passing judgment on things you don't understand."

"How dare you!"

"I dare because, unlike you, I know how well Abernathy's is run. I don't know what your beef is or why you think you can have Helena removed, but I'd like to remind you that the Board of Neutralities doesn't operate out of rank prejudice as you seem to. You have your augury, or at least the knowledge that you don't get one. I suggest you leave."

In the face of Jeremiah's calm demeanor, Greenough sputtered, unable to find words. Jeremiah treated her to his dazzling smile. "This isn't over," she spat, and turned to leave. The crowd parted for her silently. When the door shut, Jeremiah said, "I hope I didn't just make things worse."

"Not at all," I said, and hugged him.

"What was that about?" a magus said. "She can't get rid of you."

"Probably not, and I'm not worried about it. Now, who's next?"

I kept myself busy for the next several hours, too worried about Harry and Greenough to be pleased that the division of the store hours implemented by Rasmussen and Parish was being ignored while Abernathy's hours were so curtailed. By two o'clock I was exhausted and ready for a nap, but I had to go to the conference. Claude was giving the keynote address, and I looked forward to that. Plus, I might actually get to go to a party. I didn't really want to, but I knew Harry would be furious if I sat around moping just because he'd been hurt.

I bade Judy goodbye, but she had her head down over the books and just grunted at me. Shrugging into my coat, I walked through the stacks and exclaimed, "Jeremiah! I thought you left hours ago."

"I did. I came back." He had his hands shoved deep into his jeans pockets and, hunched over, looked a little like the flamingo he'd had on his shirt last week. "I wanted to talk to you."

"Oh? About what?"

"About Viv."

"Really?" I'd sounded a little too eager there, but Jeremiah didn't comment on it. "Were you going to ask her out?"

"I was thinking about it, yes."

"You don't sound very enthusiastic. Are you afraid she'll say no? Because I'm pretty sure she won't."

"I don't know if it's such a good idea, her and me. She's exciting, and funny, and I feel like an idiot whenever I'm near her—"

"Stop right there." I grabbed Jeremiah by the collar of his coat and made him look at me. "For two really intelligent people, you've both been acting stupid. Just go out for coffee. Talk to each other. See if you have anything in common beyond both of you acting like you're out of each other's league."

He smiled. "Your mysterious boyfriend is a lucky guy. I'd love to meet him someday."

I wish you could. "I'll have to introduce you. Here, give me your phone and I'll give you Viv's number. And I don't want to see you again until you've asked her out, got it?"

"Yes, ma'am." He meekly held out his phone, and I entered her number in his contacts list and handed it back. "Do you think—"

"I'm not giving you any more advice. Stop overthinking it and just call her. Coffee. Maybe a bagel. She likes muffins. That's all I'm saying."

"Have a good time tonight, Helena."

I waved goodbye to him and locked the front door, turned the CLOSED sign over, and headed back through the store to the rear door and the parking lot. Judy was still busy with the computer when I passed through the office. "You can go home now," I said.

"I'm trying to balance the checkbook. Go to your meeting and stop bothering me."

"Geez, you're cranky when the books don't add up." I waved and shut the office door behind me.

My hand was on the outer door's knob when my phone rang. *Rick Blaine.* I fumbled the phone in my excitement. "I'm so glad you called. I missed you—"

"I don't have much time. Are you somewhere safe?"

"Yes, I'm just leaving for the conference."

"Be careful going to and from your car. Portland is crawling with invaders and loose familiars."

"I thought it was just Patty Henriksen's."

"Rasmussen's keeping it quiet, but he hasn't been able to hide it from the teams. With the Nicollien teams distracted, there have been fewer fighters to destroy the other monsters, the free ones. It's only a matter of time before the news stations pick up on a surge in 'dog attacks' and fatalities. Like the ones this morning."

"Malcolm, are you in *Portland*?" A surge of irrational disappointment that he hadn't called me sooner struck me.

"I came back this morning. I've been on the streets since six, trying to clean up the mess Rasmussen made."

"He's been doing his best."

"Don't defend him. I saw a familiar savage a child today, Helena. A six-year-old child. They think she'll live. I wasn't fast enough."

"I'm sure you did your best." I winced at how inane that was.

"Not good enough," Malcolm said. "If Rasmussen had ordered the familiars destroyed the second the first attack happened, I wouldn't have had to put seven steel rounds through the head of one dragging that little girl through the streets. Quincy had to think fast to keep the illusion going. That's definitely going to be on the evening news."

"I know it's bad. Harry Keller was attacked yesterday, and he might not live."

"At least he knew what he was getting into."

I drew in a startled breath. "What's that supposed to mean?"

"He had a choice. That little girl didn't."

"So you're saying he deserved to be attacked." I remembered how Harry had looked, lying shrunken and still in his bed, and felt a flash of anger.

"I didn't say that."

"But you were thinking it."

"It's nothing I haven't said before. It was only a matter of time before the Nicolliens got what was coming to them."

I paced the tiny space between the door and the stairs. "Because all Nicolliens are fundamentally wrong-headed and part of the problem, is that why?"

"Helena—"

"Shut up. Harry Keller is my friend and I thought he was a friend of yours, too. I'm sorry you couldn't save that little girl, but her suffering doesn't make it all right for their familiar to attack Harry."

"I didn't say that," Malcolm said again.

"You didn't have to. Go back to the fight. It's what you're good at, killing things." I stabbed at my phone to end the call and dropped it into my purse. Then I leaned against the door and shook, tears of fury streaking my cheeks. How could he be so callous about another man's life?

My purse vibrated with my phone's ringing. I checked the display. Malcolm again. I didn't have anything I wanted to say to him. I wiped my eyes and ran to my car, looking around for monsters, but the parking lot was empty of anything living. If you could call invaders living.

My phone rang three more times as I drove to the hotel. I kept ignoring it, though every time it made my heart ache more. What was I supposed to do when the person whose comfort I wanted most was the one making me need comfort? *This is stupid. It's just a fight. Our first fight.* But I couldn't help feeling this was a problem that went deeper than just a fight.

I'd always thought Malcolm was fair and even-handed when it came to Nicolliens and Ambrosites, even if he did fundamentally disagree with the Nicolliens' principles. If he could be so callous about Harry's injuries, maybe that meant I was wrong. I realized I was crying again and swiped at my eyes. Crying wouldn't solve anything. It certainly wouldn't change Malcolm's mind.

I ran from my car to the hotel doors, seeing invaders in every shadow. But nothing attacked. I paused inside the door to remove my coat and caught sight of my reflection in one of the mirrors. I looked haggard, my hair falling down on one side, my eyes and nose red from crying. Quickly I went to the restroom and brushed out my hair, deciding to leave it down rather than pull it into a ponytail that would make my scalp ache. This was where powdering my nose seemed like a viable option, if it would cover its reddened tip, but I didn't have one of those powder compacts women always had in old movies. Marilyn Monroe probably was never without hers. I had to settle for splashing cool water on my face and patting it dry.

It was twenty to three when I finished in the restroom and emerged into the lobby. I didn't want to go up to the mezzanine and be stared at by other people waiting for the first session to start. Instead, I went into the bar.

Kevin was there, polishing the stone of the bar counter, and he smiled that glorious smile when he saw me. Despite the ache in my heart, I smiled back. "Is everything all right?" he said when I slid onto a bar stool. "You ran out of here so quickly I was worried. You said your friend was hurt."

"He's not doing well. But thanks for asking. Could I get a Diet Coke?"

"Sure." He put a tall glass in front of me, and I gulped it down gratefully. The carbonation burned the back of my throat.

"I needed—" I belched unexpectedly and blushed. Kevin laughed.

"Sometimes burping is what we need," he said. "Don't worry, no one else heard that."

"Just you hearing it was bad enough."

"Oh, I still think you're hot, if that's what you were thinking." He winked, and I blushed harder. "Look, I know you're worried about your friend, and I don't want to pressure you. I just think you could use some time away from all this." He gestured with the hand holding the rag. "How about you and me get something to eat later?"

For a long moment, I considered it. Kevin was cute, and nice, and I liked him, and Malcolm—well, I was angry with Malcolm, and maybe—

What am I thinking?

"That's nice of you, but I have a boyfriend," I said. "I'm sorry. Any other time—"

"No, I get it. I should have guessed someone like you couldn't be

78

single." Kevin smiled at me again. "Where is this mysterious boyfriend of yours, that he's not hovering over you so guys like me can't make a play for you?"

I smiled back. "He's been out of town. And he's not much for the conference scene, anyway."

"Not in the heating and cooling business? I guess he can't handle the action. All that excitement."

I finished my drink. "I'd better get up there. Thanks for everything."

"Hey, if you change your mind, you know where to find me."

I slid off the bar stool and headed for the exit, feeling Kevin's eyes on me. I couldn't believe I'd actually considered cheating on Malcolm. However angry I was with him, that was...it was just stupid.

I replayed our argument and stopped in the middle of the lobby, closing my eyes against the memory. I'd been a jerk, too, jumping down his throat when he probably *hadn't* meant he thought Harry had deserved to be attacked. I'd been so stupid.

I pulled out my phone and called him. It rang and rang and finally went to voice mail. I hung up without leaving a message; we'd both agreed not to leave evidence in the form of voice mails on each other's phones, not knowing how quickly we'd be able to delete them. I shouldn't have ignored him earlier. Now he was probably mad at me, at how insensitive I'd been, and he...he wouldn't break up with me over this, would he? The ache in my chest returned, and I blinked away tears. I was being stupid again. This would pass. He'd find me, and hold me until all my pain disappeared, and I would kiss him until we both forgot our own names.

Maybe.

I trudged up the stairs to the mezzanine. The last thing I wanted was to listen to another boring presentation on things that didn't matter to me, but I had to be there, if only to make sure Greenough didn't get a chance to corner a Board member or three and convince them her proposal was a good one. It was time I did a little cornering of my own.

8

The conference rooms had exciting names, but their décor was as bland as any cheap hotel. After seeing my suite, I'd have thought the Grandison would spring for something a little more upscale. But the carpeting was gray Berber with an asymmetrical pattern, the walls were a plain cream, and the chairs, while well padded, were still just the sort that stacked together to huddle in a closet when not in use. I shifted in my seat and clapped with the rest of the audience as the moderator thanked the panelists for their participation. It had been boring, a panel on changes to the rules governing faction use of the magic produced by the nodes, but it wasn't why I was here.

I stood and rapidly made my way to the front of the room. The panelists were taking their time about rising, chatting to each other, and I almost backed away to give them room. I reminded myself this wasn't about me, it was about Abernathy's, and stepped forward. "Mr. Harrison? Mr. Chukwu?"

The two men paused in their conversation and turned to face me. Both looked annoyed, though Chukwu's expression became slightly more welcoming when he registered who I was. That was reassuring. "Yes, Ms. Davies?" he said in a beautiful, liquid tenor.

"I wanted to speak to you about Rebecca Greenough's proposal to the Board. Her request that Abernathy's be moved to London." I carefully didn't say *back to London*. I didn't want them thinking in terms of where the store's rightful place might be.

"What about it?"

"I hope you'll turn it down. Moving Abernathy's is extremely dangerous, and Ms. Greenough's reasons amount to whims."

"You think you're in a position to criticize a node custodian?" Harrison said, and my heart sank, because his accent was the same perfect English as Greenough's. "Just because you are custodian of a named Neutrality?"

"I don't think I'm better than her. Abernathy's is in my care, and I do think I know what's best for it. I'd have to, don't you think?"

"Having Abernathy's located more centrally can benefit all of magery," Harrison said.

"Actually, having it slightly out of the way has benefited it. It's easy to conceal the store here. In London, in Charing Cross Road, all sorts of non-magi will visit it, and keeping the secret will be that much more difficult."

"What would moving the store entail?" said Chukwu.

That caught me off-guard. "Well...Silas Abernathy described the procedure thoroughly. It requires keeping all the books as close together as possible, and moving them as a unit. They have to go by ship, which is its own kind of complication. Magi guarded the shipment around the clock. Silas spoke of mundane officials trying to interfere with the crates, and attacks by invaders—it couldn't be warded during transit. You see how the first move was an act of desperation, guided by the oracle itself."

"And what does the oracle say now?"

"Um...well, it's declined to give instructions in this case."

"Meaning the decision is ours. As it should be," Harrison said. "We'll consider your input, Ms. Davies." He said it in a way that suggested he didn't think my input mattered at all.

Chukwu extended his hand to me. "It was a pleasure meeting

you," he said, and unlike Harrison he sounded sincere. I shook his hand. Harrison didn't offer his. I made my escape.

That was four of the nine Board members I'd spoken to, and none of them had been very welcoming. Chukwu was the only one who'd even come close to friendliness. Only my fear for the oracle kept me from falling into despair about my personal problem. I couldn't imagine any of these people being willing to change the Accords just for my benefit.

Back on the mezzanine, I checked my schedule. One more hour to go before Claude's keynote speech. I had some time to track down more board members.

The middle-aged man who'd checked me in was at the registration table. I approached him with a smile, and he straightened his tie when he noticed me. "Hi," I said. "Could you tell me where I could find Ms. Stirlaugson? It's important."

"The Board members have a private room in Annapurna, but I don't think—"

"Thanks," I said, smiling, and it flustered him enough that he couldn't finish his objection. I hurried away. Likely the Board wasn't interested in being bothered in their private retreat, but I only had so much time, and I was pretty sure I had a right to speak on the oracle's behalf.

I knocked on the door of the Annapurna room—I'd never heard of a mountain called Annapurna—and waited, trying to control my restless feet. The door opened. "This is a private room," the woman said. She had her dark hair pulled back tightly like a cheap face lift and sounded bored.

"I'm Helena Davies, custodian of Abernathy's," I said, politely but firmly. "I'd like to speak to Ms. Stirlaugson."

The woman glanced at my lanyard. She looked as if she thought I might have mugged the real Helena Davies and stuffed her in a broom closet. "Abernathy's?"

"Yes. I'd just like a few moments of the chairwoman's time."

The woman looked me in the eye, then held the door for me.

This room had all the luxury I'd expected of the rest of the conference rooms. Its high ceiling had gilded moldings, and a delicate chandelier hung over the center of the room, sparkling silver and crystal. A long conference table took up one side of the room, with comfortably overstuffed chairs on the other and a buffet table in the middle. Three people looked up when I entered. One of them was Ragsdale, the man I thought of as "my" Board member because he was the one who always showed up when there was trouble in Portland. I didn't recognize the second, an elderly Asian woman with white hair. Stirlaugson sat facing the other two, leaning back and sprawling across the sofa. I would never have expected her to be so relaxed.

"Ms. Davies," she said without sitting up. "I hope you have a good reason for interrupting us."

Interrupting what? Naptime? I controlled my impatience and said, "I wanted to talk to you and your fellow Board members about Rebecca Greenough's proposal."

"What about it?"

"I urge you to reject it. It's dangerous and unnecessary. Abernathy's is fine where it is."

Stirlaugson let out a deep, impatient sigh. "I've heard this before, Ms. Davies."

"I haven't," said the stranger. "I thought moving the store was good for business."

"I don't know your name, ma'am."

"Chao Min. Tell me why we should reject this very logical proposal." She sat with her hands folded in her lap and gazed at me curiously.

"I don't know about the Board's business. What I know is that moving Abernathy's is very risky. It only happened once before, and that was out of desperation. Please don't take this chance just because London might be more accessible."

Chao Min tilted her head to one side, her curious gaze sharpening. "Might be? It is more accessible."

"People don't have any trouble coming to Portland. And Abernathy's does most of its trade in mail-in auguries, no matter where it's located."

"That's enough, Ms. Davies. As I believe I told you, you'll have your chance to present your statement to the Board." Stirlaugson stood languidly and stretched, resuming her formal demeanor like putting on a new suit. "If you want us to take you seriously, you should stop importuning us."

Stung, I turned and fled. She was right; I'd already given her my arguments. I'd probably just hurt my cause by interrupting her naptime.

I shut the door and fumed. Abernathy's should not be at the mercy of a bunch of people who only saw it as a cash cow, as I was certain Chao Min did. I needed to talk to Judy about this. She might have an idea for organizing our arguments that would persuade the Board.

My phone rang, and I scrambled for it, hoping it was Malcolm. Disappointingly, it was Viv. "What's up?"

"Jeremiah called. We're going for drinks in about an hour. I'm so nervous!"

"Viv, why are you nervous? You're never nervous."

"I know. I just am."

"Have fun!" I immediately knew I sounded too cheerful.

"You're not blowing me off, are you? You don't sound happy."

"I had a fight with Ma—Mr. Blaine. Now he won't take my calls." I felt like crying again just thinking about it.

"Oh, sweetie. Don't worry. He's probably just busy."

"He's in Portland. He didn't even say he'd come to see me. I think I screwed up."

"Fights happen. Then there's making up. And make-up sex is *great*."

I laughed at her low, throaty purr. "I hope so. I just wish I could apologize."

"Don't let him walk over you. I'm sure, if you fought, you weren't the only one to blame."

"I wasn't. But aren't you the one who says there's always some-thing each person can apologize for?"

"I'm very wise. Sagacious, even."

I saw Diane Lakin crossing the mezzanine, headed my way. "I have to go. Thanks, Viv. And have a great time."

"I will. I hope."

"Sagacious people are optimistic, too."

I put away my phone and went to intercept Diane. "Can I ask you something?"

"Sure. I can't guarantee I'll know the answer."

"If there's a challenge to the Accords, a change someone wants to make, how do I defend against it?"

Diane nodded. "You mean the thing about moving Abernathy's."

"You've heard about it?"

She rolled her eyes dramatically. "Rebecca Greenough has made sure *everyone* has heard about it. I don't know why. It's not as if the Board cares about popular opinion."

"But what do I do?"

"They'll probably summon you to make a statement in front of them. You and Greenough both. So if you've got a little speech prepared, that will help. Otherwise...I wish I could be more encour-aging. Greenough's subtly suggesting that you're inadequate as a custodian and are clinging to Abernathy's staying here to increase your personal power."

"What?" I exclaimed, louder than I'd wanted.

Diane gripped my arm in reassurance. "I don't know that anyone's listening to her. She isn't well-liked among the custodians, except maybe by the ones who care more than they should about the unoffi-cial rankings. And I hear Lucia Pontarelli is doing her best to counter any bad impressions Greenough might spread. But you should prob-ably make an effort to make the rounds of the parties tonight, show people how nice and fun-loving you are."

"I intended to last night. A friend was attacked by his familiar and I had to see him."

Diane whistled. "That's rough. Is he all right?"

"He will be, but it's going to be a hard recovery."

"I'm sorry. I hope everything goes well."

"Thanks." I looked past Diane at the nearest conference room. "I think I've missed most of this session."

"I almost never go to the breakout sessions unless I'm presenting. They're more for the node custodians, anyway. I use the time to visit with old friends and promote my Neutrality's services."

I laughed. "Like...buy one cup of water, get the second half-off?"

"We're not quite at the point of needing to advertise, but that's what it amounts to. The Fountain of Youth isn't as guaranteed as, say, liposuction. You can never tell what part of you it will affect. I spend a lot of time explaining what to expect from it. I imagine you have a similar problem."

"I do get visitors, or mail-in customers, who think the oracle will produce a clear statement in answer to their question. Some of them get angry and refuse to pay, which is a really bad idea."

Diane's eyebrows went up. "The oracle blasts them with heavenly fire?"

"No, it refuses to give them an augury ever again. Most people don't like being cut off from the source of prophecy forever. Though some people I wouldn't mind seeing blasted with heavenly fire."

Diane laughed. "I have some of those, too. Let's go to the ballroom and get good seats for Claude's address."

The buffet had been removed, replaced with ranks of chairs like soldiers drawn up for inspection. Their blue and gold tapestry upholstery coordinated with the low-pile carpet and the gold and cream striped wallpaper. The room was cold, not quite wintry, but cool enough that I was glad I'd worn a sweater. I settled in next to Diane and said, "Is Claude a good speaker?"

"He loves to tell stories, and he knows lots of them. And how to make them relevant to us."

The room was filling up fast with custodians, their murmured conversations a tide of words sweeping unintelligibly over me. I looked around for Greenough and found her deep in conversation with a custodian I didn't know, not a Board member. The Board was taking their places on the front row, all nine of them impeccably dressed in Western-style business suits or the formal garb of their own country. It made for an impressive display of power.

Ragsdale got up and made a few announcements about the next day's events, then introduced Claude, who took the lectern to vigorous applause. "Thank you," he said. "I appreciate your welcome, though I am sure many of you are applauding the approach of day's end. The parties will be wild tonight." Scattered laughter.

"Tonight I wish to tell you a story that will be familiar to most of you. I hope you'll indulge me in a recitation of history, for the sake of a new perspective. At least I know you won't fall asleep. Someone seems to have left open a window." More people laughed, me included. "So I begin some six hundred years ago, in a town in England called Wareton. A town, and a node, that no longer exist.

"There was a man known to us only as Adam. His occupation was stonemason, and, fittingly, during the Damerel rites he chose the aegis of a stone magus. Adam labored to build the church for which Wareton became famous. He was instrumental in the construction of many of the town's buildings, and laid wards for every building he assisted with. Wareton's node was powerful, drawing the attention of many invaders, and it was due to Adam's work that the town defended itself easily against them.

"You will recall that it is the record of the traveler Jehanne du Barry that tells us what happens next. Jehanne collected the accounts of the survivors and compiled them into a single record. Many details were lost, but we know that in 1459 a stranger came to Wareton, one who performed great miracles. The magi of Wareton welcomed him as a fellow magus, albeit one with unusual abilities. The man would not reveal his aegis, claiming that he had moved beyond such things in his magical capability. He performed acts of healing beyond the ability of Wareton's bone magi, made a grove of trees grow in one night, performed illusions like no one had ever seen before—this in the days before paper magi were developed.

"What he refused to do was aid Wareton's hunters in destroying invaders. He claimed that he and his people had discovered a way to

THE BOOK OF LIES

contain the invaders, minimizing loss of life. He offered to teach this method to the magi of Wareton, asking only that they share their magic, their *sanguinis sapiens,* with him.

"The Wardens eagerly accepted his offer. Only Adam remained aloof. The stranger approached him many times, asking for his help, but Adam would say only 'My work is in the stone.' As the Wardens shared more of their magic with the stranger, Adam continued to ward Wareton.

"Jehanne's account does not say who first suspected the stranger was not as he seemed, but tradition says it was Adam himself who discovered the truth. The stranger was an invader in disguise, a thing of monstrous intelligence and power who intended to drain the magi and use their magic to allow hundreds of its smaller brethren to enter our reality. With the Wardens weakened, Adam alone stood against the monster. In an act of bravery that cost him his life, Adam triggered the binding in every ward in Wareton and caused an explosion that destroyed the invader and most of the town, including its node.

"Wareton was never resettled. Its survivors spread throughout England, with those who were Wardens telling the story of Adam to their fellows. Jehanne's story was kept in secret places until the creation of the Athenaeum, where its original now resides and where copies are available to any who choose to ask."

Claude took a drink from the glass of water on the lectern. "Now that I am finished boring you with the details, I invite you to consider —what is the lesson we should learn from this story? Beware Greeks bearing gifts? With apologies to my good friend Iakkhos." Iakkhos, sitting a few seats away from me, smiled and saluted him. "Keep your magic close and your enemies closer? But we are not magi; we have custody of magic, but not the use thereof. So what does the tale of a long-dead magus mean to us? Only this."

He leaned forward, and I was caught by the intensity of his gaze. "Adam was the first to use a ward as offense rather than defense. He saw potential where no one else did. My intent tonight is to invite you to, as the saying goes, think outside the box. As custodians, we have opportunities to serve in ways no one has yet considered. We can continue as we always have, or we can expand beyond our horizons. We—"

Someone's phone rang, not a melody or a popular song but an old-fashioned jangling bell. Stirlaugson jumped and reached inside her jacket. "Ms. Stirlaugson is excused to take this call," Claude quipped, and nervous laughter rang round the room. Stirlaugson stood and walked away, not speaking, her head bowed intently over her phone. "Now, as I was saying," Claude continued.

"Excuse me, Monsieur Gauthier, but I have to interrupt you for a moment," Stirlaugson said, returning rapidly to the lectern. "I have some news that affects everyone. You're all aware of the current crisis regarding familiars. What you may not know is that this crisis has affected our hunting teams' ability to suppress the population of invaders. The number of monsters loose in the city has reached a point where it's dangerous for someone rich in magic, such as a custodian, to venture into the streets. As of now, this hotel is in lock-down. I'm afraid we're trapped here."

9

"**B**ut I have to work!" I exclaimed, standing to face Stirlaugson. "Abernathy's can't stay closed!"

"I'm afraid we have no choice, Ms. Davies," Stirlaugson said. "There are simply too many invaders, familiar or free, for the Wardens to be able to guarantee your safety going to and from the store. We'll make an announcement and ask people worldwide to hold off on mailing in auguries, but for now, you're stuck here with us."

"How long?" a man at the back asked.

"Indefinitely," Stirlaugson said, "but in practice I believe it should be only a matter of days. If necessary, we will make arrangements for your transportation if you miss your flights."

"What about ward-stepping?" I said. "We could travel between the wards!"

"Wards have to be weakened for that to work. If we weaken the wards of this hotel, we open ourselves to even more potential for attack. Please, everyone, calm down."

The noise dimmed to a hushed murmur. "I'm sorry for this inconvenience, but I have just spoken with Mr. William Rasmussen, head of the Nicolliens in the Pacific Northwest, and he assures me they are taking every measure to end this crisis."

"Including detonating wards?" said the same man. "Is he going to destroy the city?"

"It won't come to that." Stirlaugson seemed to realize she still held her phone clenched in her hand like a baseball and put it away inside her suit coat. "I apologize for interrupting your speech, Claude. Please continue."

"I think it would be impossible to continue after that," Claude said with no rancor. "Ladies and gentlemen, I propose we retire to our rooms to ready ourselves for the evening's entertainment. We should enjoy ourselves in the face of calamity, *non?*" He smiled and bowed, then stepped down from the lectern and went to speak to Iakkhos. Sporadic clapping turned into full-out applause, in which I joined without thinking. Abernathy's closed. That never happened. Monday through Saturday, without fail.

I pulled out my phone and called Judy. Around me, everyone else was making phone calls or texting or checking the news. "Judy," I said when she picked up, "did you—"

"I know. Father told me. At least you're trapped in the lap of luxury. Father's restricted me to the house. Did you know the news has already picked up on a couple of 'dog attacks' the paper magi weren't able to cover up?"

"I don't know anything except that I'm stuck here. I was going to tell you not to bother going in to the store, but it sounds like your father has already made that point."

"I don't know that I'm in any danger. To hear him talk, the city is swarming with packs of escaped familiars, when really it's only twenty. But that doesn't include all the invaders the teams haven't had time to destroy." Judy's voice went quiet. "Did you know 'Rick Blaine' is in town?"

The ache in my heart throbbed again. "Yes."

"Nobody's giving him grief because the situation is too serious. I just wanted to warn you in case he shows up unexpectedly. I don't want you doing anything that will give you away."

"Thanks. I...don't expect to see him for a while."

"That's probably just as well."

"How's Harry?"

"Doing better. He's almost able to regenerate magic on his own."

"Tell them I'm sorry I can't come by."

"They'll understand. Harry will probably worry more about you than about himself, knowing him."

She hung up as abruptly as she always did. Diane said, "It could be a lot worse."

I was still thinking about Malcolm and absently replied, "I'm not sure how."

"The monsters could be in here with us, for one."

"Oh. Well, that's true."

"They should destroy all the familiars now rather than wait to see which will attack," Iakkhos said. "I don't know why that hasn't occurred to Rasmussen."

"I'm sure it has," I said, "but that would be a drastic step and it would make the Nicollien teams less effective. They need to find another solution." I saw Rebecca Greenough seated nearby, leaning over slightly as if listening to me. "Familiars terrify me, but I have to admit they're valuable," I added, turning away from her.

Diane stood and stretched. "That's the most exciting keynote address I've ever witnessed. I'm going to my suite to get changed, how about you?"

"I guess so. I'm not sure I'm in the mood for partying."

"Think of it as networking, and part of your job. You still need people to like you."

I made a face, and Diane laughed. "That's the spirit."

"I never thought partying could be so stressful."

We parted ways at the elevator, and when Diane was out of sight, I ran for my suite. Once inside, I bolted the door for extra security, then flopped down on one of the chairs and called Malcolm. This time it went immediately to voice mail. *He's busy, there's a lot of work to do, he's not ignoring me.* I wiped away a couple of tears and went to change into something cute but comfortable. *Why can't his work be here?* He had to know the Grandison was full of custodians, all of whom were appetizing to invaders, and he knew I was here. I zipped up my jeans and pulled a form-fitting blue V-neck sweater over my head and told myself to stop being an idiot. Wherever he was, it was where he needed to be. I wasn't the most important person in this war.

I ran a brush through my hair, dabbed on some lip gloss, and stuck my phone and key into my pockets. Stupid girl pockets. *Deep pockets ruin the line*, Viv always said when I complained, but most of the time I'd rather ruin the line of my clothes than have shallow pockets stuff tried to fall out of.

As if on cue, my phone buzzed with an incoming text. CALL ME, Viv said.

I checked the time. Thanks to Claude's truncated speech, I had plenty of time before people would expect me to show up at their parties. I called Viv's number and leaned against the wall listening to the ring. I'd almost given up when Viv said, "Hello?"

"Wow, you sound like you didn't just text me and weren't expecting this call. What's up?"

"Mom, slow down, I can't understand you."

"Oh, no. Viv, your date can't be going this badly."

"That's right."

"But you like him! And he likes you!"

"Sometimes it happens like that. Do you need me to come over?"

"Viv, Jeremiah's not stupid. He's going to know you're ditching."

"All right. Give me fifteen minutes."

"Call me later. I want to know what went wrong."

"All right. I love you." The line went dead. I closed my eyes and gently banged my head against the wall. I'd had such hopes for them, too. Well, sometimes people were just a mismatch, and Jeremiah and Viv were really different. I'd just thought...but it was obvious lately that what I thought about romance was entirely wrong.

All the same, I tried Malcolm again and once again got his voice mail. I hung up before I could leave him a long message pleading with him to love me again. I was such an idiot.

The mezzanine was empty when I reached it. The door to the vendor room was closed, but three of the other doors were open. I peeked inside Everest and saw people setting up amplifiers—magi, since the amplifiers were floating in midair. Viv would love having these guys as roadies.

I seemed to be the only person on the mezzanine who wasn't involved in party prep, so I trotted down the stairs and into the bar. Kevin wasn't on duty; it was a tall, thin girl with red hair and a mass of freckles. I ordered a beer—I wasn't in the mood to get creative—and settled in a corner to watch the rest of the customers.

My phone rang. "Thanks for rescuing me," Viv said.

"Why did I have to? Viv, I thought—"

"It was a disaster, Hel. He didn't even look like himself. He was dressed up in a button down shirt and khakis. Then he wanted to talk about music, but we don't have the same taste in bands. It was just so awkward."

"Doesn't that sound like he wanted to impress you, though?"

"I don't want to be impressed. I like him the way he is. And I tried to get him to talk about himself, but I don't know anything about software development. And to think I took out all my piercings."

"Wait—you did what?"

"Wore just the one pair of earrings. I didn't want to look too outrageous."

Light was beginning to glimmer. "So basically you changed so he wouldn't think you were weird?"

"I wouldn't put it that way."

"Viv, he likes you for who you are! He doesn't want you to tone down your appearance. I bet you wore something conservative, too."

Silence.

"Viv, give me his number."

"No! Helena, don't—"

"My love life is falling apart. I'm not going to let it happen to you. Either you give it to me or I make Judy drive over to the store to get it. And you know how she feels about driving in the dark."

Viv rattled off a number. "I'll call you back. Or he will," I said, and hung up.

Jeremiah didn't pick up right away. When he did, he answered in the tentative way you do when you don't recognize the number on the screen. "Hi, Jeremiah, it's Helena," I said. "How did your date go?"

"How did you get this number?"

"I'll make this short. You and Viv both screwed up tonight by trying to be people you aren't. You really think Viv wants you to be buttoned-down and not wear your crazy T-shirts? I promise you she doesn't."

"I appreciate what you're trying to do, but I just don't think we have anything in common."

"I think it was nice of you to try talking about music, because that's what Viv lives for. But you should have just asked her questions about what she likes and let her teach you something new. And don't be afraid to tell her about what *you* like. Now, where are you? Home?"

"Not quite."

"Change into something normal. I'm sending Viv over. And I want you to stop telling yourself she's not right for you, because I think she might be."

"I don't think that's a good idea. I'm not..." Jeremiah sighed. "You realize this is completely inappropriate for our professional relationship."

"We're friends too. That's more important."

"All right. But if it fails again, that's it, all right? No more playing yenta for you."

"What's a yenta?"

"A Jewish matchmaker. Traditionally supposed to be nosy and interfering. You've never seen *Fiddler on the Roof?*"

"It's too recent and it's a musical, so two strikes against it. I only watch musicals with Yul Brynner in them."

"You should see it anyway. Live outside your comfort zone. As you're apparently making me do."

"Just one more chance, okay?"

I hung up and called Viv. "It's all settled," I said. "Put your pierc-ings back in, put on whatever you were wearing today, and go to his house. Here's the address."

"How do you know that?"

"I looked it up yesterday in case you needed it. And it sounds like you need it."

"Helena! I can't just drive to his house!"

"Yes, you can. He's expecting you."

There was silence for a moment. "What if it still doesn't work?" Viv asked.

"Then you at least gave it your best. But I think it will." *I hope it will.*

"All right. I take it you haven't heard from Malcolm."

"He's busy. We're all trapped in this hotel because there are so many monsters running around the city."

"Why haven't we heard about that on the news? It can't be that bad."

"The hunting teams are keeping it quiet for the most part, but... remember, they look like dogs."

"Oh. That story about the little girl being mauled by a pit bull. That was them?"

"Yeah. Malcolm killed the invader, but not before it hurt her."

"He must be upset."

"To put it mildly." I sighed. "Now, go. And try to find out what Jeremiah likes that isn't software development. I'm sure he doesn't want to talk about work with you. You can talk about how pushy I am. That ought to give you common ground."

"I'm going. I'll call you later."

I put my phone away and finished my beer. That was so out of character for me, pushing Viv together with someone...but then it was out of character for Viv to be so reluctant when it came to a man. I hoped I'd done the right thing. I just wanted *someone* to be happy, even if it wasn't me.

A blast of music immediately turned down to barely audible

levels told me at least one party was starting. I strolled out of the bar, across the lobby and up the steps to the mezzanine, where colored lights from the Rainier room beckoned. The hosts had set up a table with chips and dip and a couple of coolers of drinks. The overall effect was so mom-and-dad's-rec-room I had to bite my lip to keep from laughing.

"Not this one," Diane said in my ear, startling me. "The drug use starts in about half an hour and then nobody can get any sense out of them. Come upstairs. We'll bounce from room to room."

I never would have guessed these hotel rooms, even as big as they were, could hold so many people. We moved around, accepting drinks and greeting custodians. Everyone recognized me, though after the first half hour I couldn't remember more than a handful of names because of the sheer number of people I was introduced to. The free booze had nothing to do with it. Almost nothing.

We ended up on the top floor, giggling over I forgot what. "Should I host a party?" I asked.

"It's not expected. Maybe next time." Diane drained her paper cup and threw it away in a potted tree. "Iakkhos's place is next. For someone that old, he throws an excellent party."

"Does old age mean you stop having fun, really?"

"It sure seems to. But Iakkhos is a kid at heart. He's got the biggest model train set I've ever seen. In Crete, obviously, not here."

A low, throbbing musical beat came from one of the doors ahead. Diane pushed it open and indicated I should enter. Iakkhos's suite looked just like mine, though decorated in mint green and silver. He had all the curtains shut and most of the lights off. Music with a heavy bass line pulsed through me.

"Magnifica illusion," Diane said, a little smugly. "Iakkhos's people come up with a new one every year."

"Illusion?" Of course, Diane wasn't wearing her lanyard with attached monocle. "I wish I could see it."

"What do you mean? Take off—oh, you're not wearing it."

"I thought you knew. As Abernathy's custodian, I can see through illusions."

Diane looked at me curiously. "I've never heard of anything like that. Are you sure—"

Iakkhos, his headset gleaming under the low light, came forward with his hands outstretched. "Welcome," he said. "Come, have a drink. Enjoy a taste of my homeland."

I accepted a glass of ouzo and managed not to recoil at the strong smell of anise wafting from it. This would have to be my last drink of the night. I was already feeling dizzy. "What does the illusion look like?"

"Ah, I'm sorry you can't participate," Iakkhos said. "The illusion is that of a house on a cliff overlooking the Adriatic. Smells, sights, sounds—the best magnifica illusion money can buy."

He sounded sad, as if it wounded him personally that I couldn't experience his party to the fullest. "I'm sorry to miss it. I never thought I'd *want* to see an illusion. Mostly it's benefited me to be able to see through them. Saved my life, once or twice."

"Well, enjoy yourself. Drink, eat, talk." Iakkhos smiled. "You'll just have to party the old-fashioned way."

I looked around. I knew most of the people here. Lucia was talking to Ragsdale in one corner. Claude had a beer in one hand and was chatting with the custodian of the Kiefer Node, an attractive young woman who seemed very intent on his words. "Where's Nimisha and Parvesh?"

"They were here earlier, long enough to have a drink and stare disapprovingly at the rest of my guests," Iakkhos said. "I think they'd be happier if they knew how to relax."

"They *are* out of their country for the first time. I'm sure I'd be awkward if I visited Nepal."

"I think you'd be more open to the possibility of looking foolish, which they aren't." Iakkhos smiled and went to greet someone new— oh, great, it was Rebecca Greenough. I walked quickly to the far side of the room and twitched the curtains aside to look out over the city. Iakkhos's suite looked out over the Willamette River, a long dark ribbon threaded with light where the bridges crossed it. Probably not as beautiful as the magnifica illusion, but at least it was home.

"Amazing, huh?" Lucia said. I needed people to stop sneaking up on me. "You can taste the brine in the air."

"I wouldn't know. I can't perceive it."

"That's right. I'd forgotten. Sucks to be you sometimes." She saluted me with her glass, then took a drink.

"I guess there are always compensations. Is it really that beautiful?"

"At the risk of rubbing it in, yes, it is. Paper magi have the showiest magic, I think. In a good way."

"Did you ever consider becoming a magus, Lucia?"

Lucia shook her head. "Never. But I wasn't a good candidate for Damerel, so it didn't matter."

"How do they decide? If you can be a magus, I mean?"

"It's complicated. They look at your history—how many family members survived the rites, what kind of magi they were. Like, for instance, the Campbells. Long, long line of steel magi over a dozen generations." Lucia gave me a calculating stare. I gave her my most innocent look.

"Anyway. They also look at your body, whether you've got the right combination of physical traits to endure the implantation. It's not about physical fitness, either, though being too over- or under-weight usually disqualifies you. And there's a battery of mental fitness tests to see if your sanity can handle it. Like I said, complicated."

"The thought of having something stuck into my heart just makes me shudder."

Lucia grimaced. "Me too. And it's painful—worse than the worst healing you can imagine. Which is another part of knowing if you're a good candidate. You have to want to use magic so badly you're willing to endure pain and risk death for it."

"Which I'm not."

"You've already risked your life for the oracle twice. I wouldn't be so quick to deny that."

I was saved from having to answer by someone saying, "Pontarelli. Corrupting the youth of America again?"

"I would corrupt the youth of England, but you beat me to it," Lucia said. "I thought I told you to stay away from me, Greenough."

"It's Ms. Davies I want to speak with." Greenough smiled pleasantly at me. "Or does she let you play duenna for her? I thought she was an adult, if barely that."

"What do you want, Ms. Greenough?" I asked, managing not to sound annoyed.

"To persuade you that moving Abernathy's is in everyone's best interests. I want you to speak on my behalf to the Board."

Her effrontery stunned me into more candor than I'd planned on. "I'm not going to do that."

"See sense. London is cosmopolitan and accessible by the world. Abernathy's move was always intended to be temporary. This is just setting things right."

"Ms. Greenough, you haven't been listening. Moving Abernathy's is dangerous. I don't think you understand how dangerous."

"I'll submit to you remaining custodian, even though I think your appointment was a mistake," Greenough said.

Now I was close to losing my temper. I could understand why she and Lucia were enemies. "Because I won't do what you want? Or because I'm not an Abernathy?"

"Because you've let yourself become too attached to your customers. Don't think I didn't notice how chummy you were with them when I visited this morning. You're meant to be impartial, Ms. Davies, and if you can't do that, you don't deserve to be a custodian."

"That's enough of you passing judgment," Lucia said, stepping in before I could start shouting. "I don't think Davies has anything left to say to you."

"This is none of your business, Pontarelli."

"Abernathy's is within my jurisdiction, so I'm making it my business." Lucia took two steps that put her squarely in Greenough's face. "Back off."

Greenough shoved her. "You back off."

"Lucia—" I said.

"Stay out of this, Davies."

Greenough shoved Lucia again. Lucia grabbed her wrist and spun her around, twisting her arm up behind her back. Greenough shrieked in fury and slammed her free elbow into Lucia's stomach, making her let go. Gasping, Lucia grabbed a handful of Greenough's frosted hair and pulled. Greenough stumbled backward, flailing for balance, and jabbed Lucia with her elbow again. "You're dead," she snarled.

"Not at your hands," Lucia said, somewhat breathlessly, and shoved Greenough away from her. Greenough stumbled, caught herself, and turned—right into Lucia's left hook. The sound of fist meeting flesh carried throughout the room. Greenough dropped like a stone into water, crumpling in a heap. Lucia shook out her hand, wincing. "Sorry," she said to Iakkhos.

"All part of the entertainment," he said, winking at her. "Would someone help Ms. Greenough up, and get her some water? Possibly some ice? Ah, Helena, you're not staying? Probably for the best."

"Thanks, Iakkhos, it was...memorable," I said, and hurried after Lucia. Diane followed in my wake.

In the hallway, Lucia said, "Sorry about that. Greenough pushes all my buttons."

"I didn't know you could fight like that."

"That?" Lucia made a dismissive gesture. "That was nothing. You want to see real fighting, come down to the Gunther Node when we have our annual competitions. I'm the women's judo champion six years running."

"I think I'm about partied out," Diane said. "I'll see you in the morning, okay?"

I said goodnight and continued down the hall to my suite. The dizziness had passed, but I felt a little unsteady on my feet, probably because of that last drink, which had been a mistake. I sat on one of the blue and gold chairs to take my shoes off. They were more comfortable than most of my party shoes, which Viv would probably say meant they weren't flirty enough. I flexed my bare toes and ran them through the thick pile of the carpet. Lucia had actually punched Greenough out. It had been deeply satisfying, though it wouldn't make Greenough like either of us. Not that she liked us to begin with.

There was a click, and I shot to my feet. The bedroom door swung open. I grabbed the nearest thing that could be a weapon, which was my shoe with its sharp heel. Someone stepped through the door.

It was Malcolm.

---

*H*e looked so different. The beard, obviously, but there was also the way he stood, balanced on the balls of his feet in preparation to dive or run. He wore his familiar black fatigues, filthy with road grime and dark blotches I hoped weren't blood. He looked at the shoe in my hand and said, "That isn't the best weapon."

"I know." I lowered my hand and let the shoe fall to the floor. "How did you get in here?"

"We're providing security for the conference. Evading it was easy. And I know how to bypass the lock on that door."

My heart felt like it was trying to burst out of my chest. "It's dangerous, you being here," I said, and immediately felt stupid at how ridiculous that sounded.

Malcolm took a step forward. "I don't care. I had to see you. Helena—"

"I'm sorry!" The words came flying out of me. "I didn't listen, and I said such awful things—I know you didn't mean—"

Swiftly Malcolm crossed the distance between us and took me in his arms. "I was stupid," he said, "and I let my frustration spill onto you. I didn't mean to suggest Harry deserved to be attacked. Forgive me."

"If you forgive me for being petty."

"Agreed," Malcolm said, and kissed me.

It had been so long I'd nearly forgotten how it felt to be kissed by him, how he offered me his whole heart with his kiss. He smelled terrible, but I didn't care; I clung to him and kissed him, trying to make up in one moment for months of separation.

"I missed you," Malcolm murmured. "The way you look, the way you smile...it killed me that I couldn't even keep a picture of you on my phone."

"I missed you, too," I said. His beard was soft against my face, and it felt strange and wonderful at the same time. "You don't know how many dates I had to turn down, and then make up stories about my missing boyfriend. Jeremiah Washburn thinks you're an airline pilot."

Malcolm laughed and pulled me closer. "Turning down dates, eh?"

"Don't tell me you didn't have to fend off beautiful women all around the world, Malcolm Campbell."

His amused smile went wicked. "Not as many as you probably think. But it wasn't even a struggle, because none of them were you." His hands went around my waist, his fingers working their way beneath my sweater. "You look beautiful tonight," he said, and pulled the sweater off me in one quick movement.

"You are *very* good at that," I whispered. "Maybe a little too good. Should I be worried that maybe one of those beautiful women wasn't successfully fended off?"

"I've thought about doing that every day for the last five months," he murmured in my ear. "That...and this," he added, his fingers going to my bra strap.

"Don't stop there," I said, my fingers going to his belt buckle. "I don't plan to."

VIV WAS WRONG. Make-up sex was *amazing*.

"YOU *REALLY* SHOULDN'T BE HERE," I said, my head pillowed on Malcolm's chest. "We're completely surrounded by custodians and all nine members of the Board of Neutralities."

"You don't think it makes sex more exciting?"

"Sex with you is always exciting no matter where we have it, but this makes me nervous. Or would if I weren't so relaxed." We'd made love, then showered together, then made love again, and now I felt like a puddle of warm honey.

Malcolm put his arms around me, and I sighed out contentment. "Not to brag, but I'm capable of passing through these halls without being seen even if I don't use illusions, which all these people can see through anyway. But I can't stay long. I have to return to the fight."

"Why are you here? I mean, I know why you're here, but won't they miss you?"

"We have mandatory rest periods and this is one of them. I intend to sleep beside you for a few hours, then return to my team."

I smiled in pure pleasure. "Sleep beside me. I've never heard anything so romantic. Isn't this a glorious bed?"

"I like your bed better. It's cozier." He brushed the hair away from my cheek and kissed its curve.

"This is like sleeping on a cloud. A warm, snuggly cloud."

"I think the company is what makes it so excellent."

I kissed him, slow and sweet. "I agree."

He drew me closer, and I listened to his heartbeat, a deep, measured rhythm that relaxed me further until I fell happily into sleep.

I woke some hours later when Malcolm disentangled himself from me and slid out from between the covers. "Oh," I said, disappointed.

"I didn't mean to wake you. I'm sorry." In the darkness I heard him hunting for his clothes, so I turned on the bedside lamp, making him squint.

"It's all right. I prefer not to wake to an empty bed. Will I see you again soon?"

"I can't make any promises. If the next rest period overlaps with a time when you're in meetings, probably not."

"That reminds me. I met your brother."

Malcolm paused in putting on his pants. "Ewan? What did you talk about?"

"Security things. He was angry with you."

He scowled. "I'm sure he was. That's a permanent state with Ewan. No doubt he thinks I treated Mother badly."

"He said something about that, yes."

"Well, he's a skilled steel magus, and dedicated to his job, so what he thinks of me doesn't matter so long as he keeps you safe. Which I'm sure he'll do." He finished fastening his pants and pulled his shirt on over his head.

"I didn't realize he was personally responsible for the hotel security."

"Campbell Security is, and he's head of Campbell Security while I'm gone. As far as the company is concerned, I'm still gone. They need me more on the front lines than here." Malcolm leaned over and kissed me. "Much as I wish I could stay."

"I wonder if there will ever be a time when you're not rushing off."

"Someday there will be. I swear it." He ran his fingers through his hair, then over his face. "I never did ask what you thought of my beard."

"I love the way you look no matter what. The beard is different. I like it, but I miss your dimple."

"My dimple? I have a dimple?"

I laughed. "Come on. You can't not know about the dimple. You must see it every time you smile."

"I rarely smile at myself in the mirror. Now I need to shave so I can see it."

"It's devastating. Every time I see it, I feel the urge to kiss you."

"Then I *definitely* need to shave."

I stood and put my arms around him. "It's not the only time I feel that urge."

We kissed for a while, then Malcolm said, "I really have to leave," and I let go of him. "I'll call you if I get the chance."

"Don't let me distract you. There will be plenty of time when this is over. It *will* be over soon, won't it?"

Malcolm hesitated. "One way or another," he said. "They're trying out a new binding that should keep any more familiars from breaking free, but we still have to destroy the ones that are already loose. And they have experience at fighting that an ordinary invader lacks. It's not easy."

"Good luck," I said, and he was gone.

I put on pajamas and got back into bed. The clock on the bedside table read 4:23. I could still get some sleep. A lot of sleep, if I wanted, since I didn't have to go in to work. But sleep eluded me. I couldn't stop worrying about Malcolm and the other teams, hunting monsters that could kill them if they weren't careful. Then I moved on to worrying about Harry and wishing it weren't the middle of the night so I could call Judy and find out how he was doing. And from there I went to worrying about Greenough and the possibility that I'd be moving to England—or that I *wouldn't* be moving to England, but Abernathy's would.

Finally I gave up on sleeping and turned on the television in the sitting room. There had to be something mindless on. I found an infomercial for some personal hygiene product whose use escaped me and turned the volume down low, amusing myself by providing my own dialogue. "That's right, June, this thing I think might be meant to remove excess back hair can easily be turned to fighting familiars. For the low, low price of $17.95 you, too, can own one!"

I wondered what Jeremiah had done with his familiar when Viv came over. Locked it away, obviously, but I could see him destroying it proactively. He wasn't sentimental about it, had never even named it, and thought of it as a tool rather than a creature. And I was sure he wouldn't hesitate to destroy it if he thought it was a threat.

On those disturbing thoughts, curled up in the corner of one of the soft chairs, I fell asleep and dreamed of fighting off familiars with a hand beater and one of those flails ancient Egyptian pharaohs were always depicted as having. But there were familiars fighting alongside me too, and in the dream they were named Shard and Shatter, Judy's father's familiars when she was growing up. Eventually there were so many invaders I woke, terrified that I was surrounded. It was daylight, and I'd left the drapes open, but even though I could clearly see the room was empty, I huddled in my corner for a few minutes, waiting for my heart rate to slow.

Eventually I stood, feeling as achy as if I really had spent the night in mortal combat, and checked the time. 8:35. I turned on the coffeemaker and went to get dressed, opting for casual clothes rather than my business attire. I had all day to lounge around the hotel and the idea was daunting rather than restful. I hadn't brought any books, I'd left my computer at home, and my DVD collection wasn't doing me any good back at my apartment. I had no idea how I was going to entertain myself all day.

I drank some coffee while paging through the room service menu. It looked good, but I decided I'd rather not sit in my room alone all morning. Besides, networking was important, at least according to Lucia and Diane. I grabbed my phone and my room key, stuffed the Campbell Security keychain into my pocket to make me feel more confident, and headed downstairs. As I went, I texted Judy and got back NO CHANGE. I tried to let it make me hopeful.

I hadn't been in the hotel restaurant before now. It was decorated to complement the bar, all warm colors and rich, ruddy woods. A buffet had been set up along one wall, and custodians were helping themselves to eggs and bacon and pancakes. I got a plate and accepted a fresh waffle from a woman dressed in white whose only job appeared to be making waffles on command. At least someone in this hotel was more bored than I was.

Carrying my waffle and a glass of orange juice, I surveyed the room. I didn't see anyone I knew as more than a passing acquaintance, and sitting with strangers made me uncomfortable. I found an empty table near the others and took a seat. *Nice job networking.*

Well, it wasn't as if I wore a sign saying DON'T BOTHER ME, PEASANTS.

Across the room, Claude entered. He saw me and a smile brightened his features. "Ah, Helena," he said. "May I join you?"

"Of course."

Claude filled his plate with a fluffy slice of quiche and brought an entire pot of coffee with him to the table. "I am addicted," he said with another smile. "I am never myself unless I have at least four cups in the morning. And this hotel makes excellent coffee."

"I was thinking that about the coffeemaker in my room. Delicious."

"Yes, and I would be tempted to take it home with me had I not an even better one at the Athenaeum." Claude filled his cup and took a long drink, strong and black without adulteration. He closed his eyes and sighed. "Truly it is the nectar of the gods. May I pour you a cup?"

"Please."

We ate and enjoyed our coffee in silence for a few minutes. Around us, the soft murmurs of conversation and the clinking of silverware against china made a peaceful background noise. "So you have no store to go to," Claude finally said. "What will you do this morning?"

"I don't know." I looked out the window, where a brisk wind was stirring up snowflakes. "It's the kind of day where you want to stay in and watch a movie, but I feel I should be, I don't know, making more friends."

"There will be movies shown in one of the conference rooms. And of course there is always good company to be had in the bar."

"I guess I'm not the only one at a loss, huh?"

"I had intended to visit OMSI and then Powell's, with a stop at the local Athenaeum access point. So I think, me, it will be movies today instead."

"Ms. Davies?"

One of the navy-suited Board employees stood beside our table. "Yes?"

"The Board would like to speak with you."

A chill went through me. They didn't know about Malcolm, did they? No, they wouldn't have sent a flunky if they did. "What about?"

"I'm not privy to their intentions. They did say you were to come immediately."

I exchanged glances with Claude. "There was no summons for me?" he said.

"No, sir. Just Ms. Davies."

"I'll see you later, Claude," I said, standing and putting my napkin on my plate. My hands were shaking and I shoved them into my jeans pockets to still them, wrapping my fingers around the smooth warm surface of my phone and the angular bumpiness of the keychain. Someone had seen Malcolm, regardless of his caution, and the Board was going to fire me. Or have me executed. I had no idea what the punishment for favoritism on this scale might be. *Don't be an idiot. This is probably about Greenough's proposal. Stay calm and don't overreact.*

I followed the flunky through the lobby and up the stairs to the Annapurna room. He held the door for me politely—that was a good sign, right? But no, he'd said he didn't know anything, and this was likely just him showing respect for a named Neutrality's custodian. I smiled and thanked him, then passed through the door.

Five Board members sat at the conference table. They were all dressed in business suits and looked exactly like corporate hatchet men come together to fire someone with extreme prejudice. I recognized four of them, Stirlaugson, Ragsdale, Harrison, and Chukwu, and that relieved my mind somewhat, because Ragsdale and Chukwu were at least moderately inclined to like me. Stirlaugson, on the other hand, looked like someone who'd been woken too early and then missed her morning coffee. That boded ill for me.

"Ms. Davies, have a seat," Stirlaugson said, waving her hand at the far end of the table. I sat. There was a metal pitcher and several glasses near the center of the table, too far away from me to reach them, which was unfortunate because my throat was suddenly dry and itchy. I didn't think any of them would be inclined to fetch me a drink.

"Do you know why we've called you here?" Stirlaugson said.

"No, Ms. Stirlaugson." *Don't convict yourself.*

"You're here to answer a charge of partiality."

My heart pounded faster. "Partiality?"

"Specifically, that you are inclined toward a Nicollien frame of mind."

It was so unexpected I just gaped at her. Nicollien? "I'm not partial toward Nicolliens," I said. "Why would you think that?"

"You were heard expressing the opinion that familiars should not be destroyed, and that they are valuable in fighting the Long War. We also know you have close friends among the Nicolliens. How do you answer this charge?"

"I have close friends among both factions, and I don't favor one over the other." I gripped my hands together under the table to keep their trembling from being obvious. "And I don't think it's favoritism to point out the obvious. Familiars do help in the fight, or no one would use them."

"At a time like this, no custodian should be defending familiars," said the stranger, a red-headed woman with hair cropped close to her head. She had a pen in her hand, but no paper in front of her, and she clicked the pen in and out, in and out, in a staccato non-rhythm that had me wishing I could grab it from her and snap it in half.

"Why not?"

All five of them murmured as if I'd said something wrong. The redhead looked across the table at Ragsdale. Ragsdale shrugged, the tiniest movement, and looked at me. I watched his face, hoping for a clue, but saw nothing but mild interest. None of them looked as if my fate mattered to them at all.

"You don't see it? Familiars are a direct threat to us," said Stirlaugson. "We're all trapped here thanks to them roaming free. We tolerated familiars so long as they were under control, but under these circumstances, we claim the right to ask that they be eliminated."

"Excuse me, Ms. Stirlaugson, but that's an Ambrosite point of view."

That made them sit up and stare at me. Harrison said, "You think to challenge us?"

"It's not a challenge. I'm just pointing out that that's the way Ambrosites think. And I doubt anyone would call Ms. Stirlaugson partisan. You don't have to want one side to succeed over the other to recognize wisdom in their position. I don't think the Nicolliens are right any more than the Ambrosites are, but I know what a blow it would be to their hunting teams to lose their familiars. And I think simply destroying all familiars outright is a hasty response."

"Pittman's done it, in the UK," Harrison said. "He made a wise decision."

"I don't have any idea what the situation is in the UK, and I wouldn't dare second-guess Mr. Pittman. But much as I dislike William Rasmussen, I think he understands *our* situation better than any of us, and I'm sure he'll make a wise decision too."

"You dislike Rasmussen?" Ragsdale said. He sounded surprised.

"Um, I didn't think that was a secret. He wanted—maybe still wants—me out of Abernathy's so his daughter Judy can run it. We're not friends. But if I'm truly impartial, and I am, I have to recognize his skills as a leader."

"I...was unaware of this," Ragsdale said. "Laverne, I think our reports were incomplete."

"I agree." Stirlaugson leaned forward. "And what of your friendship with a Nicollien? You rushed out of here to visit him when he was attacked."

I wondered how they knew that. "Ms. Stirlaugson, I'm not inclined to do favors for my friends, because I respect my responsibility to Abernathy's," I said. "I don't believe making connections, even close connections, to members of either faction means I'm automatically partisan." It was the closest I could come to telling them about Malcolm. I felt alone, and scared, and my words sounded thin and weak.

The room fell silent. The Board members exchanged looks that made me feel they were all secretly psychic and carrying on unheard conversations about me and my unsuitability to be custodian.

Finally, Stirlaugson said, "I am satisfied that Ms. Davies has upheld her oath to maintain Abernathy's without fear or favor. How say you?"

A murmur of assents went up around the table. I sagged a little in my seat. "Ms. Davies, as long as you're here, we might as well conduct your review," Ms. Stirlaugson said.

"My...review?"

"Every three years we review a custodian's charge, discuss concerns you might have, verify that you're performing adequately. Yours was to be this afternoon. You don't mind, do you?"

"Uh...no, I guess not."

"The rest of you can stay if you like," Ragsdale said. Harrison and the redhead stood and left, Harrison shooting me a narrow-eyed look as he did. I was pretty sure he was on Greenough's side, so I just gazed coolly back at him. I didn't need any more enemies, but I couldn't help making that one.

When the door shut, Ragsdale said, "You've had an exciting year. Murder, invaders, an attempt to destroy the oracle...what do you have to say about all that?"

"I don't know. I never have figured out why Mr. Briggs hired me, whether he knew he'd be murdered or not. But I've done my best to preserve the store, and I think those things would all have happened whether I was custodian or not."

"Possibly," murmured Stirlaugson. "The last major incident Abernathy's endured was in 1971, when Patricia Kelley thwarted some rather stupid thieves who tried to steal their own auguries. Of course it doesn't work that way, but they were quite clever in circumventing Abernathy's alarm system. That was when Campbell Security took over. Dougal Campbell and his son Alastair broke new ground—but that's not relevant. My point is that nothing this exciting has happened to Abernathy's since it moved to the United States, and perhaps we should be asking why that is."

"You think it does have something to do with me?"

"The man responsible for attacking the oracle through illusions might have thought the oracle weakened by having a custodian unfamiliar with the ways of the magical world," Chukwu said. "Not something you can be blamed for, in my opinion."

"We should have stepped in immediately and installed a new custodian," Stirlaugson said.

"But would your custodian have been able to take on the oracle's body and fight off the invading monster?" I said. "At the risk of sounding arrogant, I think most people wouldn't have thought to do it. And Abernathy's would be destroyed now."

"You don't know that."

"Neither do you." Fear made me bold.

"It's irrelevant," Ragsdale said. "What matters is Ms. Davies *did* attempt the impossible, and I'm satisfied she's earned her place as Abernathy's custodian."

"I'm not suggesting she be removed," Stirlaugson said, not very believably to my eyes.

"We ought to be asking the standard questions," Ragsdale said, "if that's all right with you, Laverne?"

Stirlaugson nodded and waved her hand dismissively. Ragsdale said, "You've had no other problems with those detectives over the stolen books?"

"None. Though I think Detective Acosta wants me to do something illegal so he can get me on some charge or other."

"Don't worry about it. We'll protect you. How's your accounting? Your books are up to date?"

"The Board accountants audited me when they did Abernathy's taxes last winter. We're ready for the coming tax season."

"Do you have any concerns you'd like to bring up with the Board at this time?"

I had so many concerns I was bursting with them, but none of them were what he had in mind. "No."

"Does anyone have something they'd like to ask Ms. Davies?"

Chukwu shook his head. Stirlaugson looked like she wanted to challenge me but couldn't think how.

Ragsdale nodded. "Then we'll approve your annual raise and bonus. Don't let this discourage you, Ms. Davies, but I don't think any of us expected you to succeed, given the challenges you faced and the fact that you came to this as an outsider. I'm personally very impressed by how well you've handled yourself." Ragsdale stood and came toward me with his hand outstretched. Stunned, I shook it.

Chukwu also offered me his hand. "I wish we were not confined here, because I wish to see Abernathy's before I return home. Perhaps there will still be time."

"I hope so. I'd love to show it to you."

"You'll present your case for Abernathy's remaining here to the Board tomorrow morning," Stirlaugson said. Reluctantly, she held out her hand, and I shook it quickly and withdrew. "We'll announce our decision at the business meeting Friday night, after the banquet."

"Thank you, Ms. Stirlaugson. I appreciate the opportunity to speak." I didn't add *I'm sure the Board will make the right decision* because it felt like sucking up to them, just nodded and made my escape.

I found the mezzanine restrooms and hid in a stall, staring at the blank wood of the door and feeling grateful for the quiet anonymity of the restroom. That had been close. And unexpected. I had absolutely no doubt Greenough was behind this attack, and it was just good luck I was well defended against it. *Imagine if they knew about Malcolm.* I wondered how many more of the Board members thought well of me, and whether that good feeling would persist in the face of a real challenge to their authority.

I let out a deep breath and left the stall. I would wash my hands, and find out where they were showing movies, and try not to think too hard about everything I had to worry me. Only a few more days, and it would all be over, one way or another, Malcolm had said. I hoped that didn't include blowing up most of Portland.

I picked up the plastic bottle of water in front of me and turned it around, reading the label. It was expensive, as everything associated with this conference seemed to be, and I couldn't help thinking it was a waste of money. They'd given us those really nice metal water bottles, but every presentation I'd attended had had these disposable bottles set out for the presenters. And now I had one of my own.

The Rainier room was more dimly lit than the other conference rooms, probably why they'd shown movies in it earlier. The sconces lighting the room were of orange glass, mottled to look like translucent marble, though I'd never seen marble that color before. It made the gray Berber carpet look brownish and gave everyone with skin lighter than Nimisha Rai's an orange tan. All the chairs were occupied, and more men and women stood against the walls. It was the fullest I'd seen any room at the conference to date.

I took a drink from my own heavy water bottle and surreptitiously looked at my fellow panelists. I'd met a couple of them at the bar the first evening, but didn't remember their names. We each had little placards with our names on them, but of course they faced the audience and were no help to me. I was near the middle of the table, with three panelists to the left of me and two to the right. I accidentally caught the eye of the man immediately to my right and had to smile in a friendly way, though my insides were knotted up with nervousness.

"First time?" he said. He spoke English with an Indian accent I liked. I nodded. "It's not so hard," he continued. "Answer the moderator's questions and speak out when someone says something you disagree with."

"That sounds like it could start a fight."

He laughed. "It can. But sometimes that's more interesting than when everyone agrees. You're the custodian of Abernathy's, right? Where do you stand on the issue?"

"I'm opposed to it."

"Well, I'm in favor, so we should have a good strong discussion." The man extended his hand to me. "Vijay Chowdhury of the Devarakonda Node."

I took it hesitantly. Chowdhury laughed and clasped my hand tightly. "Just because we disagree doesn't mean we can't be friends," he said. "I've just seen tremendous benefits—oh, it looks like we're starting."

I took another drink of water to calm my nervousness. Chowdhury seemed nice enough, but he represented the possibility of Nicollien and Ambrosite never making common cause. That made him my enemy, for the next fifty-five minutes anyway.

Chukwu took a seat at the end of the table farthest from me. "Welcome," he said. "This panel will address the issue of dividing use of the Neutralities, to restrict Ambrosites and Nicolliens from visiting at the same time. I'd like to invite our panelists to introduce themselves, starting at that end."

The woman beyond Chowdhury said, "Maggie Tennyson of the Gilbert Node in Manchester, UK."

"Vijay Chowdhury of the Devarakonda Node outside Kolkata, India," Chowdhury said.

I cleared my throat and leaned into my microphone. "Helena Davies, custodian of Abernathy's." A murmur went up through the room. I had no idea why. My presence here on the panel wasn't a secret.

The woman on my immediate left said, "Ana Ruiz, Hernandes Node in Mexico."

"Jeff Stockwell, Barrington Node outside Chicago, United States of America."

"Ishikawa Hiroshi of the Miyamoto Node near Kyoto, Japan." Ishikawa wore a glass translator like Iakkhos's, and his lips were disturbingly out of sync with his words.

"And I, Ayodele Chukwu, will serve as moderator." Chukwu leaned forward a little so he could see all the way to the far end of the table. "Let us begin with each panelist making a short statement about why he or she is here. Ms. Tennyson?"

"My node experimented with allowing the factions access only on certain days of the week," Tennyson said. She was a plump middle-aged woman who looked as if she'd be more at home baking cookies than addressing a conference, but her voice was clear and direct, though I had trouble understanding her accent. "We discovered this increased rather than decreased tensions."

"My node experienced the opposite effect," Chowdhury said. "Separating the factions has been a positive experience."

My turn. "The heads of the factions decided to restrict their followers to using Abernathy's at set times, not me. It minimized conflict, but only because they weren't in contact with each other, not because tensions decreased."

"I'd like to convince the local faction leaders to implement a division," said Ruiz, "but they're resistant to the change."

"We've had great success with separating the factions," Stockwell said. "Most magi remember the crisis that happened in Chicago some twenty years ago and don't want to repeat it."

"Like Abernathy's, use of the Miyamoto Node has been dictated by the faction heads," Ishikawa said. "I would like to see an actual resolution to the conflict rather than an artificial and temporary one."

"Let's examine the question more closely," Chukwu said. "Mr. Chowdhury, what brought you to implement this plan?"

"I heard about Ms. Davies' experiment and how successful it was—"

"I wouldn't call it successful," I said.

"You'll have your turn, Ms. Davies," Chukwu said. "Mr. Chowdhury?"

"As I said, its success led me to try it myself. We'd had magi come to blows before this, and separating the factions reduced the bloodshed to zero. The magi are more efficient in their hunting, and our resources aren't wasted on needless fighting."

"Mr. Stockwell, your comments?"

"The incident that occurred in Chicago twenty years ago, in which the Ambrosite leader incited his followers against the Nicolliens, left a mark on Midwestern magery," Stockwell said. He was a burly man with black hair on the backs of his meaty hands and a gruff voice filled with impatience. "There's never been trust between the factions, and separating them has frankly been a relief to everyone on both sides *and* the neutrals. I say it's proved its usefulness."

"Ms. Davies," Chukwu said, "you've seen the results of the policy at Abernathy's, but you disagree that it should become a permanent policy. Why is that?"

I swallowed. When had the room become so large? "Because before Mr. Rasmussen and Mr. Parish decided on this approach, Ambrosites and Nicolliens coexisted peacefully in Abernathy's. Some of them even made friends across faction lines. That's the outcome we should be hoping for, not a...an artificial peace that only exists because they all pretend the others don't exist."

"The animosity between factions is too great for that," Chowdhury said. "We've never seen that kind of relations between them in Kolkata."

"I don't want to make rules for other Neutralities. I just want to have the opportunity to make rules for myself."

"Ms. Tennyson?"

"No division we came up with made a difference," Tennyson said. "We finally addressed the problem by imposing sanctions on anyone causing trouble. Now we have peace, though it's tenuous. Requiring us to divide the Neutrality would cause the problem you're trying to solve, at least for us."

"But we need the Board's approval to convince the faction leaders," Ruiz said. "I haven't been able to enforce the policy. If the Board made this part of the Accords, I'd be able to make them change."

"If it's part of the Accords, we can't make those decisions individually," I said.

"You don't understand what it's like," Ruiz said. "The Nicolliens and the Ambrosites in my country are at war with each other. When an Ambrosite meets a Nicollien in the Hernandes Node, there is always a fight. Always. And Sanchez and Garcia—the faction leaders —hate each other so much they encourage their men and women to challenge each other. I need *something* to protect my node. This is the only solution."

"Can't you forbid them use of the node?" I said.

"Impossible. They are better armed than we, and they have magic."

"That sounds like a more serious problem than just Nicollien and Ambrosite clashing." I closed my hand around my water bottle. "Mr. Chukwu, isn't there something the Board can do about this?"

"That is not the problem at hand, Ms. Davies," Chukwu said, but gently. "Mr. Ishikawa, your thoughts?"

"Obviously I agree with Ms. Davies," Ishikawa said. "My larger concern is that the faction heads in both our Neutralities have been able to impose their rules on us. No Neutrality should be subject to that kind of demand by anyone but the Board, and then only as stated by the Accords. If the factions come to believe that they can manipulate a Neutrality without going through the standard procedure for changing policy, what else might they try to implement?"

Another murmur went up throughout the room. "An excellent point, Mr. Ishikawa," Chukwu said. "Let's pursue this. What are the, shall we say, political ramifications of making this division part of the Accords?"

I jumped on that with both hands. "It will make the Board look weak. Like it's giving in to the factions."

"Or it will look like it listens to the magi and makes wise decisions," Chowdhury said. "The Board has an opportunity here to make itself seem open-minded by acknowledging the factions' ability to police themselves."

"But—" I couldn't think of a response to that that didn't involve smacking Chowdhury. I reminded myself that he was probably a nice guy and said, "It opens the way for the factions to make other demands of the Board."

"Which they are under no obligation to fulfill."

"True, but how long will they put up with a constant stream of 'no' when they've already received one resounding 'yes'? That will increase tension, something we're here to try to prevent."

"Excellent points," said Chukwu. "Ms. Tennyson?"

"It seems to me that we really don't need to alter the Accords for this. Why not let each Neutrality police itself?"

"Because some of us don't have that power," Ruiz exclaimed.

"And I'd like to force the faction leaders in the Pacific Northwest to abandon their policy," I said.

"That's not what you said earlier," said Stockwell.

"I don't want this implemented in the Accords," I said, "and I would like each Neutrality to be able to make its own decisions. But I don't like that the faction leaders seem to think they're allowed to control my Neutrality. I was hoping the Board might have something to say about that."

"I agree with Ms. Davies," Ishikawa said. "I think it's dangerous to let the factions believe they have power over us. It's at the heart of what makes a Neutrality."

"I'm going to open up the discussion to questions from the floor," Chukwu said. "Yes? You in the second row."

"My question is for Vijay Chowdhury," said the woman. "Why does this have to be a matter of altering the Accords? Can't you just carry out the policy yourselves?"

"It's a matter of power," Chowdhury said. "So long as the policy is just my idea, there's a possibility the faction leaders may choose to disobey. The Accords, however, are binding on all of us, and they would make the policy a matter beyond faction and Neutrality. It's more secure that way."

Another woman rose in response to Chukwu's calling on her. "I'd like to address Ms. Ruiz's statement that she can't control the magi using her Neutrality. What makes you think you'll have any greater control if the Board intervenes? It seems your node is suffering from a lack of firm leadership."

"I do my best," Ruiz said. She sounded so defeated my heart went out to her. "The magi of Mexico have lost sight of the true goal of magery, which is to fight the invaders and defend those who cannot defend themselves. That is not a thing I can change. If the Board chooses not to make this part of the Accords, I will be forced to implement more drastic measures."

"Such as?"

"The running of an individual Neutrality is also beyond the scope of this panel," Chukwu said. The woman sat down, but she had a very satisfied smile on her face, as if she'd scored points in a game no one admitted to playing. I glanced at Ruiz; she was fiddling with her plastic water bottle. Had she meant that comment on drastic measures as a threat, or a simple statement of fact? I didn't like to judge, but I couldn't help comparing her to Lucia, who would never have let Rasmussen or Parish walk all over her. But she was also well-armed and had plenty of Wardens, magi or not, who were more than a match for any faction member. I felt sorry for Ruiz, and then wondered if that feeling meant she really wasn't suited to running a Neutrality. There must be some way to replace custodians who couldn't handle the job. That made me wonder further why Foster and Yamane, the Nicollien and Ambrosite Archmagi, hadn't stepped in already.

I'd missed the next question, but my name being called brought my attention back to the present. "Yes?"

"If the Board fails to ratify this change to the Accords, how will you force your faction leaders to stop the policy?"

"Well, reason sure hasn't worked," I said, and a ripple of laughter went over the crowd. "And I can't refuse to give them auguries, since that would be against the Accords. I've been thinking I'll have to talk to the individual magi, urge them to see sense. They all used to have friends among the other faction, and I can't help thinking they must miss the old days."

"Wishful thinking," Chowdhury said.

"The goal is to remind them of who the true enemy is," I said. "They were more effective when they weren't fighting each other all the time. Iakkhos Kalivas says he can remember a time before factions, when magery was unified, and he hopes that day may come again. I join him in that hope."

"The rest of us have to live in the real world. I think adding this policy to the Accords simply recognizes the way things are, the way they're going to be."

"This is for the entire panel," said a man standing at the back of the room. "How does this policy affect your own impartiality?"

"Speaking only for myself," Ishikawa said, "I believe it is more difficult to maintain impartiality when one is forced to deal only with one faction at a time. The differences between them become clearer, and one begins to empathize more greatly with one side."

"I don't think that has to be true," said Ruiz. "But, again, I can speak only for myself, and in my case I empathize with neither no matter how long my association with them."

"I agree," I said. "I think the whole thing is idiotic."

A loud murmur went up. Chowdhury turned to face me, his eyes wide and astonished. "You think the Accords are...idiotic?"

"No, I think the division between factions is," I said. "Look. You all know I came to this position as an outsider, someone who didn't grow up knowing about Nicolliens and Ambrosites and the Long War and all that. So my perspective is going to be different from yours. And what I see are a bunch of magi who all care about defending our world against invaders, who've let a difference of opinion turn into an iron wall separating them. Maybe I don't get it. Maybe the question of using familiars really is so huge people can't get past it. But I can't believe grown, intelligent men and women are so incapable of talking to each other that we're planning to make it law that they don't have to!"

Applause broke out here and there in the audience. A couple of people started shouting. "That's enough," Chukwu said. "Ms. Davies, your passion is laudable, but let us stick to the subject, shall we?"

My face reddened, and I nodded. "No, I think she's right," Tennyson said. "If the familiars are all destroyed, there's no real difference between Ambrosite and Nicollien anymore, is there? And the point of this panel will be moot."

"I wonder..." I said. "Would that really remove the animosity?"

"Probably not," said Stockwell. "The Ambrosites are acting smug about the whole thing, like they somehow came up with a way to make the bindings fail, and the Nicolliens haven't given up on finding a less permanent solution."

"Could they do that? Make the bindings fail?"

"Unlikely. That would be a prodigious feat of magic, to make it happen all across the world at once."

"Let's take another question," Chukwu said. "Ms. Chamberlain?"

I missed Ms. Chamberlain's question, because my mind had caught hold of the possibility that someone had made the binding magic fail. I didn't understand magic hardly at all, so maybe I was wrong, but I'd already witnessed a splinter group within the Nicolliens attempt to sow discord by killing Ambrosites, and this seemed like just another way to do the same thing. Not to mention how it was weakening the Nicolliens. What if a group of Ambrosites wanted revenge for the serial killings of last August?

"Ms. Davies?"

Again I startled out of my reverie. "Yes?"

"Would you like to make a final statement?"

"Oh." I cleared my throat. "I stand by what I've said today. Making the division of time between factions at a Neutrality permanent only fools us into thinking we've achieved peace. The only true peace is going to come when we allow free mingling of faction members in a neutral location. And I believe that's possible." Polite applause.

I listened to the other panelists make their final statements, then clapped along with everyone else when Chukwu thanked us for our time and dismissed us. Chowdhury said, "You made some good points, Ms. Davies."

"Thanks. So did you." *Maybe a little too good.*

"I have to say I'm convinced they shouldn't make this part of the Accords," he went on. "I'll be sure to tell them that."

"Really?"

"I'm not saying I think it's a good idea for my Neutrality, but I think you ought to have the opportunity to test your theory."

"Well...thanks."

"Are you going to Carlos's bash tonight? I hope to see you there." Chowdhury extended a friendly hand, which I shook.

"I hope so too," I said, my earlier ill feeling toward him evaporating. "I understand it's the only party tonight."

"Nobody would dare throw a party opposite Carlos. The man knows how to entertain." Chowdhury smiled and excused himself to speak to Chukwu.

"Thank you for your concern," Ruiz said in a soft voice. She had her metal water bottle in her hand and was dangling it by the plastic loop like it didn't weigh anything. "Your solution will not work for me, but I appreciate that you want to give me the opportunity to do things my way." She laughed bitterly. "Though I think my way is doomed to failure."

"There has to be *something* you can do," I said. "Can't you get more personnel or weapons from another Neutrality?"

"Neutralities operate independently, and it is a mark of weakness to petition another in such a way."

"But the Board can't want you to fail! What...what happens if the factions..."

"Take over? The Board will only send in their own people if my rule collapses entirely. Then they will either install a new custodian, or destroy the node and leave the factions to fight until one dominates."

"That sounds like anarchy. Will you be shocked if I say it's stupid?"

"Hardly," said Tennyson, coming up behind us. "But it's as the Accords state, and we are bound by the Accords. The alternative is much worse, I promise you."

"I'm sorry if I sound ignorant. I'm still learning about your world."

"Everyone understands," said Tennyson. "Ana, you really should speak to the Board about reinforcements. They can't want the Hernandes Node to fall apart. It's too important to North America."

"I have spoken with them, at my review." Ruiz sounded defeated again. "They will not intervene."

Silence fell. I didn't know what I could say to her, as ignorant as I was of the situation. "I hope dividing the node helps," I finally managed. It was banal, and we all knew it.

"So do I," Ruiz said. "But I have one more presentation to attend, and then I will go to the party and get very drunk and possibly sleep with a stranger. It cannot be more destructive than what I have engaged in so far."

Tennyson and I laughed, but it sounded weak, and I gratefully said goodbye and made my escape. Ruiz's problem made mine seem trivial—she was looking at the loss of her node, and I couldn't imagine the Board would be gentle with someone who lost them that valuable a resource in the Long War. Whereas all I had to worry about was losing my job and being convicted of sleeping with a faction member...all right, so our problems were about the same. That didn't make either of them easily solved.

Outside the Rainier room, I checked my schedule and discovered I didn't particularly want to see any of the programming for the last hour. Time to go upstairs for a short rest before changing into my party clothes. Carlos had told me there would be plenty of food at the party, so I'd eaten lightly before my panel and now the idea of a quick lie-down had some appeal.

My phone rang while I was in the elevator with a couple of burly men who eyed me as if they couldn't believe they were sharing an elevator with Abernathy's custodian. "Viv. How did it go?"

"It was wonderful," Viv sighed. "I'm so glad you interfered in our lives."

"I'm glad! Did you—" The door opened, and the two men got off. "What did you do?"

"Talked, mostly. I can't believe how much we had to talk about. I told him all about being a musician, and he told me about the fan conventions he goes to every year—he made it sound so fun I almost wanted to go myself. Then he talked about being a magus, and about having to destroy his familiar—"

"Wait—he destroyed his familiar? Did it attack him?"

"No, it didn't, but he said he didn't want to wait around for it to turn on him or someone else, and he wanted to investigate the binding, see if he could help the Wardens find a solution. I thought Nicolliens thought of their familiars as pets, but to hear him tell it he might as easily have been replacing a tire."

"Jeremiah's different."

"I know. You know, he didn't even kiss me?"

"Wow. That's different for you."

"I know. And yet I know he wants to, and he's just...waiting for the right moment. And it will be a great moment, too."

"Viv, I'm so happy for both of you."

"Don't be too happy yet. It was only one date. And not even really a date. We ordered pizza."

"Oh, let me be optimistic on your behalf. When are you seeing him again?"

The elevator door opened, and I saw Iakkhos and Diane waiting outside. I smiled and dodged past them. "Tomorrow night. We're going to the movies. He said I could choose, but I feel bad dragging him to my usual rom-com."

"Go see *Citizen Kane*. It's playing downtown."

"No, thanks, I'd rather not feel like slitting my wrists afterward. You made me watch that already, remember?"

I unlocked my door and kicked off my shoes, my feet sinking into the pile of the carpet. "Right, and you hated it. Well, don't try to second-guess him, because that turned out so well before. Just pick something you like and trust that he wants to get to know you well enough to enjoy it. Then next time it'll be your turn."

"You're so sensible. I gotta go, playing a gig tonight. Wish you could come."

"I wish I weren't trapped here. But the party tonight is supposed to be killer."

"I hope so, for your sake."

I said goodbye and tossed my phone onto one of the chairs, then went into the bedroom and fell backwards onto the bed. Malcolm was right, my bed was smaller and cozier, but this mattress was so soft I almost decided to ditch the party and snuggle up to watch movies. No, Carlos and Elisabeta would be so disappointed if I didn't show. I closed my eyes. Just fifteen minutes' rest, and then I'd get ready. Just fifteen minutes...

A knock sounded at my door. My eyes flew open. I rolled over to check the bedside clock. 8:37. That had been a lot more than fifteen minutes. Cursing, I hopped up and ran to the door. "I'm sorry, I fell—"

There was no one there. Distantly, I heard the knock again. It was coming from the bathroom, the brown marble one off the sitting room. It was more of a thump than a knock, an irregular sound like somebody trying to get out. The comparison made me nervous. Nobody else could be in my room, so...

I looked around for a weapon. The lamps were too bulky for me to hold comfortably. Ditto the chairs. I picked up my water bottle and hefted it. It was full of water and solid, better than nothing. Slowly I crept across the sitting room, twitching every time I heard the thump. My fingers curled around the lever and pressed downward. I took a deep breath, twitched at one last thump, and yanked the door open.

Something black and chitinous swarmed out from behind the toilet. I shrieked as the invader launched itself at my throat.

I swung wildly with the water bottle and felt it connect with the thing's head with a sloshing *thunk* that vibrated through my bones. It let out a squeal and fell flailing to the floor, thrashing as if in pain. I hoped it was pain. I slammed the water bottle against its head again and again, screaming inarticulate terror. It writhed, squealing, until with a pop its head caved in, and blue ichor oozed out between the cracks. With a final squeal, it went limp.

I stood over it, panting, specks of light filling my vision. I needed to find out where it had come from—and, more importantly, if there were more of them.

I ran back to the bathroom and frantically scanned the walls. It hadn't come through the shower drain; the monster was too big for that. There wasn't any water on the floor, so it hadn't come through the toilet. I looked up. The vent screen dangled over the sink, revealing a gaping black hole where the vent entered the room. Its edges glittered where the thing's rigid hide had scraped along them. In my imagination, hundreds of its fellows squeezed through, clawing at each other to be the first to get at me. The stink of its body, a sharp, nose-biting smell like paint thinner, filled the little space until it seemed a tangible presence.

I slammed the bathroom door and hauled two chairs over to prop in front of it, lodging one securely beneath the handle so it couldn't be opened. Then I went to examine the body. It was starting to sag, and more blue ichor seeped from the cracks between the plates covering its stinking body. I knelt to get a better look. A silvery harness looped around its torso, trailing a short length of chain where it had broken its leash. Not just an invader, a familiar, and it had managed to find a way through—

I stood, once again seeing spots. How had it made it through the wards on the building? Someone must have weakened them, but Stirlaugson had already said they wouldn't do that. So whoever had done it hadn't had official sanction, and probably meant the custodians harm. I couldn't think who might fall into that category.

The magi at the conference were all committed to protecting the custodians...unless I was wrong about that. The Wardens never had captured Mitch Hallstrom's masters, the ones who'd ordered him to start a war by killing Ambrosite magi. And if I was right, the problems with familiars could be caused by Ambrosites trying to prove Nicolliens dangerously wrong in their philosophy. Ambrosites who might think the deaths of a hundred and fifty custodians would be excellent proof.

Don't overreact. You know nothing about magic. This could be an accident. But where there was one rogue familiar, there could be several—

I bolted for my bedroom and slammed the door to that bathroom shut, propping more chairs against it. Then I searched the room thoroughly, using the flashlight on the keychain Ewan Campbell had given me. I stopped, looking the thing over. It was a weapon too, Ewan had said, and I almost squeezed it to test it before remembering that something this small might have limited power. Between it and my trusty water bottle, currently covered in blue ick, I might be able to make it...somewhere safe. If anywhere in the hotel counted as safe.

I sat on the bed and made myself think logically, though I was shaking from the aftereffects of terror. I knew the distance at which an invader could sense me was less than a quarter mile, probably a lot less, but I didn't know if a familiar on the street could sense me all the way up here in my suite. So I had to assume the familiar I'd killed had entered the hotel somehow and wandered around until it caught my scent, so to speak. And if one could get in, so could others. There was a good chance the hotel was crawling with them. Which meant nowhere was safe.

I bent and wiped the water bottle off on the carpet—I didn't want to get the mess all over the bedspread. I could—oh, I was so stupid.

I ran into the sitting room and looked for my phone. There, on the chair where I'd thrown it. My fingers shaking, I called Malcolm. It rang, and rang, and finally went to voicemail. This was no time to worry about not leaving evidence. "Malcolm, an invader—a familiar —got into my hotel room. I killed it, but I think there are more. You need to let the teams know the Grandison may be invaded."

I shoved my phone into my pocket and regarded the dead thing on the floor. I wondered madly if the Grandison would charge us for the carpet stain. It didn't look like anything that would come out. I shook my head, dashing irrelevancies away. I needed to figure out what to do next.

Thump. I screamed. Something struck the bathroom door, harder this time. I backed away from it, watching it shake with the impact. It sounded big, too big to fit through that tiny vent. No more time to dither. I had to get out of there.

I put on my shoes, then kicked them off. They were cute, which meant they weren't intended for fleeing from monsters. Barefoot was better than tripping and falling. I shoved the keychain and my room key—habits were hard to break—into my other pocket and ran out the door and down the hall toward the elevator.

The hall was as eerily quiet as it always was, but now I couldn't help feeling like I was in *Aliens* and the monsters were right on top of me. I passed a ventilation grate and ran faster. I didn't know where I should go. What I wanted more than anything right now was companionship. If I was going to die horribly, I wanted to do it in company. Which was an awful thing to think, but I wasn't feeling rational.

I reached Nimisha's suite and pounded on the door. "Nimisha!" I pounded again. No one came. Either Nimisha was at the party, or she was dead, and either way there was nothing I could do for her. I ran on, knocking on Iakkhos's door and then Claude's. No response. I wished I had Malcolm there, not just because I'd be safer, but because he knew how to bypass the locks and I could know for certain that my friends weren't under attack, or dead.

I rounded the corner and saw the elevator ahead. I could head for the bar, or the Kilimanjaro room where Carlos's party was. I could even try to get outside and get my car, head back to Abernathy's where I knew the wards were secure. No, that was a bad idea. Malcolm would come for me, and he needed to know where I was. I'd have to find some safe space here in the hotel.

I skidded to a halt in front of the elevator and mashed the DOWN button hard. My stockings were slippery on the carpet, and I stood flamingo-like on one foot and peeled first one, then the other off. I stuffed those into my pocket atop my phone. Maybe I could make use of them. Or not. I wasn't MacGyver or the Mythbusters or anything like that. But I hated to get rid of anything that could remotely be considered an advantage.

The elevator dinged, and the doors slid open. I checked the inside carefully, using my flashlight even though the space was well-lit. Still, I hesitated. Didn't they always say not to use an elevator in an emergency, like a fire? Though this wasn't that kind of emergency. Even so...

I looked up at the elevator ceiling, which was made of brass panels about three feet on a side. It was all too easy to imagine those panels knocked down and swarms of invaders diving through to attack and suck the magic out of my battered body.

I backed away from the elevator and began casting about for the stairs. There was a door nearby, narrower than those of the suites, and it had a bright red EXIT sign above it. I pushed it open slowly, listening for the sound of clawed feet on concrete. Nothing.

The stairwell was brightly lit, painted a very pale gray, and freezing cold. It smelled of damp concrete and nothing else, which was reassuring as what I did not need to smell was the acrid scent of a familiar's body. I checked all around for ventilation shafts and, seeing nothing, let the door close quietly behind me. The concrete chilled my bare feet, but I was willing to endure a little hardship if it got me out of this death trap safely.

I made my way down the stairs as quickly as I dared, glad I'd removed my stockings, which would definitely have made me slip on the steps. My phone began ringing after two flights, and I fumbled it out of my pocket, nearly dropping it as it slipped past the stockings. "Judy. Judy!" I'd been so freaked out it hadn't even occurred to me to call her.

"Sorry to interrupt your party—"

"No, Judy, listen. I was attacked in my room by a familiar, and there's another one trapped in my bathroom. I think the hotel is under attack."

"You *what?*"

"You need to get the hunting teams over here *now*."

"It's impossible. That place is warded more heavily than St. Paul's Cathedral, and that was built to take something half the size of a city."

"I've got blue yuck on my hands that says it's not. Quit arguing and just do it!"

Judy hung up. I chose to believe it was her typical abruptness and not a disbelief in what I'd told her. I put my phone away and continued down the stairs. My toes were growing numb and I'd lost count of how far I'd come. The slap of my bare feet against the concrete echoed faintly through the stairwell.

Below me, a door creaked open. "Hello?" I shouted, picking up the pace. "Who's there?"

Something scraped along the concrete, and I caught a whiff of paint thinner. I swore and turned to run, tripping and banging my shin against a riser. I regained my footing and took off. Behind me, the scraping grew louder, and a low moaning sound rose above it. My breath was coming too fast, I was seeing spots again, and I could hear it gaining on me.

Just as I reached the door to the next flight up, it caught me. A tendril, blood red and glistening like raw flesh, wrapped around my ankle and pulled my foot out from beneath me. I landed hard and rolled onto my back, kicking to free myself. But it was too late.

A familiar euphoria washed over me, relaxing my muscles. The familiar was bigger than the last one and its silver harness looked too small for its body, like a net bulging with fish where its muscles rippled beneath naked skin. I tilted my head to look at it from a different angle. My vision started to tunnel. It was so beautiful, and I...no, I had to fight. Slowly I withdrew the keychain from my pocket, pointed it at the monster, and squeezed.

A pulse of force erupted from the jolter, knocking the thing backward and freeing me from its grip. It lay on its back at the next landing down, twitching. I staggered to my feet and giggled, turning the jolter over in my hand. That had been *amazing*. I stepped over the thing's body—was it dead? I didn't know how to find out, and if it wasn't, I needed to get away quickly.

I giggled again and skipped down the steps like I was playing hopscotch on a slope. This euphoria was going to get me killed, but I couldn't do anything about it, so I might as well enjoy it. One step, two step, red step, no, that was the children's book. It was like being drunk, only without the furry taste in my mouth.

Now, where was I going? Why didn't they mark the floor numbers on the doors? I looked at the next door more closely. Oh. They did mark them. I just hadn't been paying attention. Ten more floors to go to the mezzanine. The buzz was starting to wear off, and I went more quickly, holding the jolter at the ready and hefting the water bottle with my other hand. Nine more floors. Eight.

Above me, distantly, I heard something moan. My old friend, coming to consciousness, or a new one on the prowl? Either way, it was bad news for me. I hurried faster.

My phone rang. I swore, juggling things in my haste to reach it. The jolter fell, I lunged after it, and my phone fell out of my stupid girl pocket and hit the concrete hard, bouncing down several steps to the next landing. The ringing stopped. I ran down the steps and picked it up, cursing again. The screen was shattered and the back had popped off. I tried turning it on and got nothing but a faint blue glow that lasted for a second and then disappeared. I shoved it deep into my pocket—once again I hated leaving anything behind—and rearranged my hold on the jolter.

Thick blue liquid the color of the oracle's glow dripped from above me to puddle, steaming, on the step below me. I looked up. Another familiar, this one built like a caterpillar with a round circle of teeth where its head should be, clung upside down to the steps above my head. I recognized it; it belonged to Brittany Spinelli. I screamed and ran, heard it fall and land on the steps with a squeal, and then it was after me, slithering along the hand rail.

I couldn't stay in the stairwell any longer. I threw open the door to the next floor and darted through it, then pulled it shut and held onto it with all my strength. The familiar hit the door with a thump, and then everything was silent. I let go of the handle, trying to calm my breathing, and backed away. Distantly, something sizzled, like bacon on a hot griddle. A blue spot appeared on the door, growing larger and brighter as the sizzling grew louder. My hands were shaking too much to hold the water bottle, and I set it down, mesmerized by the growing spot. As it grew, I brought the jolter up, holding it in both my shaking hands and aiming it at the center of the spot.

The sizzling faded away. The blue spot was now two feet across and glowed like something radioactive. I held my breath and waited.

The spot exploded outward, blasting in blue chunks in all directions as if the door were made of clay rather than metal. Brittany's familiar burst through the hole. And I blasted it with the jolter.

It knocked the monster, which screamed in pain, back into the door. I screamed with it and snatched up the bottle to bludgeon it to death, but this one was clearly dead, torn in half from the mouth down. I stood over it, breathing heavily, then screamed again, all my fear and pain finding an outlet.

"Hold on, we're coming!" Running footsteps sounded in the distance, growing louder as they neared. I realized I was still holding the water bottle in an attack position and lowered it as three people came running around the corner. One of them was Maggie Tennyson from the panel. Another was Vijay Chowdhury. "Are you all right?" he asked.

"It bit her. You need to lie down," Tennyson said.

I shook my head. "It didn't get much of a grip. I'm fine now."

Tennyson and her companions were armed, though it was a weird assortment of weapons: a curved shower curtain rod, the base of a lamp with the cord ripped out, a couple of jolters like mine. "Have you seen anyone else?" Vijay said.

"Just you and a bunch of familiars. What about you?"

"We've been working our way down from the seventh floor, looking for anyone who got stranded. Everyone's gathering in Kilimanjaro from what we hear." Tennyson waved her phone at me. "They're sending hunters—they might even be here now."

I saw the way Tennyson looked at Chowdhury and guessed why they'd been alone together on the seventh floor. None of my business. "Was anyone...killed?"

Tennyson nodded. "At least ten that we know of. I guess it could be worse. Almost everyone was at the party when they struck."

I didn't want to ask the names of the dead. Time enough to mourn them when the crisis was over. "How did it happen? How could familiars even get inside?"

"No one knows," said Chowdhury. "The stone magi are checking the wards now, trying to reinforce them to keep any more familiars out. We have to move, Ms. Davies."

"Do you have a weapon?" asked Tennyson.

"The jolter, but I've used it twice already, so I don't know how much longer it will last. And this." I hefted the bottle.

Tennyson smiled. "Not much of a weapon."

"It is if you can bash their brains out with it. If they have brains. I don't even know if they have brains!" I was feeling a little hysterical and had to close my fingers hard on the bottle to keep myself anchored to the present.

"Whatever works, right?" said Chowdhury. He turned to the other woman, who'd been silent this whole time, and said, "You still with us?"

She nodded slowly, a woman in a dream, and I saw puncture marks around her left wrist, black with reddish haloes. Chowdhury took her other arm and gently urged her toward the stairs. "We can't go that way, they keep getting in," I said.

"We tried using the elevator and had to fight off two at once, coming through the ceiling. It's a death trap," Tennyson said. "The stairs are our only option."

Both of them whistled in shock at the shattered door and Brittany's collapsed familiar. Where was Brittany? It was impossible to imagine her letting her familiar get away, and yet here it was. I wished I really were a fighter so I could punch her out. Stupid Nicolliens and their stupid familiars...no, that was no way to think. The Nicolliens would never have captured invaders in the first place if they'd known this could happen. They were just fighting the Long War as best they could.

We made our way down the stairs, moving more slowly than I had alone because the silent woman was unsteady on her feet. Tennyson took the lead with her improvised bludgeon, a brass lamp from which she'd removed shade, harp, and bulb. I followed immediately behind her. Chowdhury and the woman brought up the rear, him supporting her with one hand and holding the shower rod at the ready with the other.

"What's her name, Mr. Chowdhury?" I asked.

"We don't know," said Chowdhury. "We found her under attack, being drained by a familiar, and she can't speak. And you should probably call me Vijay, if we're going to risk near-certain death together."

"Call me Maggie," Tennyson said. "Now let's get out of this place."

1 3

---

*W*e were almost to the third floor landing when we heard the chittering. It echoed in the stairwell and seemed to come from all around us. I looked up and saw a wave of bodies, four or five of them, rippling down the stairs toward us.

"*Run!*" Vijay shouted, and we pounded down the stairs toward the third floor door. Maggie flung it open and held it for me.

"Keep moving!" she said. "They're almost on you!"

I skidded to a stop just inside the door and brought my jolter to bear on the familiar in the lead. It gave off a burst of energy weaker than before, but the creature staggered backward into the next monster in line, knocking them both to the ground. Vijay was dragging the woman, who looked like she was fighting him. He tossed the curtain rod at me and brought the jolter up to point at her face. It pulsed even more weakly than mine had, but she sagged, unconscious, in his arms. Vijay lifted her and staggered toward the door. I fled through it seconds after he did and only a few steps ahead of our enemies. Maggie dragged the door shut and held it against the thumps and scratches as the familiars tried to get through.

"Where now?" she shouted, pulling back with all her weight. At

143

least one of the familiars had opposable thumbs, because it was pulling in opposition to her.

"There's another set of stairs at the other side of the building," Vijay said. "We'll have to run for it."

"You get moving, Vijay," Maggie said. "You've got the heaviest burden. We'll hold them off to give you a head start."

"Try this," I said, snatching up the curtain rod. It was curved, not straight, and I hooked it under the latch so its far end wedged tightly into the elevator door frame. Maggie let go of the door; it bounced slightly, but didn't open. Vijay was already halfway down the hall and accelerating. "Move!" I shouted, and Maggie and I took off after him.

We outpaced him after a few strides, running all-out past blank white doors, the light sconces and floral arrangements blurring as we flew past. Behind us, the improvised barrier squealed and then made a popping noise, and the sound of the familiars scrabbling after us became louder. I risked a glance over my shoulder. Three monstrous bodies snuffled around like dogs on the scent of pheasants. One lifted its head and howled, and I stumbled and nearly fell in terror.

Maggie and I rounded a corner and found the door to the stairs. Maggie had her hand on it when I grabbed her and pulled her away, saying, "Do you smell that?"

She wrinkled her nose. "Paint thinner," she whispered. We checked the hall, but it was bare of anything that might provide cover and nothing moved. Maggie gestured with her jolter, and I took it to mean I should cover her. *This is just like* Die Hard, I thought madly, and brought up my weapon to shoot anything that might try to take her head off.

Maggie flung the door open. Something shrieked, and a dark form flew through the opening. I squeezed off a shot with the jolter, which buzzed in protest. Maggie ducked, and the familiar went sailing over her head to hit the opposite wall with a thud. Maggie darted through the doorway with her jolter out, looking everywhere for enemies. "All clear," she said as Vijay came trotting around the corner with his burden.

"We have to run," he said. "No trying to fight them. Just run."

I thought that was good advice. We ran.

We made it as far as the mezzanine door before they caught us. Vijay, helpless with the woman in his arms, backed against the door, shouting, "Open the door, let me out!"

Maggie swung at one of the monsters, a catlike creature with dirty gold fur and eyes the size of my fist. It dodged her swing and struck at her. "Helena, help him!"

I grabbed the door latch and pulled, ducking a blow by one of the other familiars with a shell like a turtle's and a million tiny cilia-like arms. "Go, go, go!"

Vijay sprinted for safety. "Maggie, we have to run!" I shouted.

"Get yourself to—ah!" The catlike thing fastened itself to her upper arm. The lamp slipped from her fingers. Maggie's eyes closed, and she screamed, the most agonized sound I'd ever heard a human being make.

I picked up the lamp and slammed it against the creature again and again, but Maggie began convulsing, and half the time I hit her by mistake. The turtle-thing's million arms tickled my leg, and a numb, pleasant sensation flooded over me.

"No," I said, "no, Maggie, come on."

Maggie went limp, her mouth slack and blackened.

"Maggie," I whispered. I tore myself away from the turtle-thing and staggered through the door, skipping in my euphoria. The mezzanine was a wreck, the carpets shredded, big chunks taken out of the corners where walls met, lamps dangling by electrical wires. I willed my body to move faster, to regain its equilibrium. The smell of paint thinner drifted past, and I gasped for clear air.

Ahead, the doors of Kilimanjaro opened, and a handful of people rushed toward me. "Keep running!" one of them shouted, and I put my head down and ran as fast as I could. Behind me I heard familiars squealing with pain, and it felt good, like justice for poor Maggie. I stumbled through the door and went to my knees, panting heavily. Hands helped me stand even though what I wanted was to lie on the ugly gray Berber carpet and pretend all of this was a nightmare.

"Helena, you've been bitten," Diane said.

"It wasn't much of a bite. I'll be fine if I can just sit down for a minute."

Someone found me one of the stacking chairs and I sat, leaning far over with my head between my knees and breathing heavily. I heard a door slam shut and what sounded like chairs being slid in front of it. When I felt I wasn't going to pass out, I sat up and said, "Is everyone here?"

"Thirteen are confirmed dead, including Ms. Tennyson," said Nimisha. Her hair was disheveled and her clothes were stained with something green and sticky. "We cannot account for twenty more custodians. Who knows how many of the hotel staff are alive."

"I called one of the hunting teams and Judy Rasmussen," I said. "They know we need help."

Nimisha and Diane exchanged glances. "We are in contact with some of the teams," Nimisha said. "They are outside. Unfortunately, so are the police and emergency medical assistance. They cannot be allowed to see the extent of the damage."

"So the teams are keeping them out? How did they manage that?"

"Not the teams," Diane said. "It's worse than that. We sent the stone magi, the ones providing the wards for the building, to strengthen them. They found—how much do you know about wards?"

"A little, from what Silas wrote. That they have to be replaced every so often, more or less often depending on how much use they see."

"So you know that wards have to have their frequencies altered to allow familiars to pass through with their masters?"

"Yes. Oh. Oh, *no*."

Diane nodded. "No one thought to re-key the wards to prohibit familiars passing through. The stone magi are trying to fix that, but they keep getting attacked. Their temporary solution, to make the wards completely impassable physically or magically, keeps new familiars from coming through, but it also makes it impossible for us to leave—or for aid to get through. We have no idea what the police make of all that."

"So we really are trapped here."

"For now. If they can't fix the problem, maybe they can shut the wards down entirely. It can't be more dangerous than what's going on now. And at least the hunting teams would be able to reach us."

"Wait. Where are all the magi from Campbell Security? Ewan Campbell was supposed to be here."

Nimisha looked particularly sour. "With the wards as strong as they are, no one thought it a problem to pull our security off to help the hunting teams in the city. We are helpless."

Her words, so final and certain, filled me with fear. I shook the feeling off. "They know we're in need. They'll figure something out." But if they couldn't get through the wards, it might not make a difference.

A thump shook one of the doors, and a mob of people rushed to reinforce the improvised barricade of chairs and tables in front of it. "Soon may not be soon enough," said Nimisha.

"And Claude and Iakkhos..." Diane said.

"What's wrong with Claude and Iakkhos?"

"Come with me," Diane said.

She led me across the room to a spot where people lay very still on the floor. Carlos knelt beside Elisabeta, holding her hand. "She will be well," he told me when I rushed to kneel at his side. "She needs her magic restored, that is all. No, my dear heart, do not speak," he told Elisabeta. "You will be well."

"Helena," Diane said, pointing, and I went to crouch beside Claude, whose normally bright eyes looked dull and feverish. "He held off three familiars while helping a dozen people to safety," she said. "Some people just don't know how not to be a hero."

Claude smiled, the faintest tug on the corners of his mouth. "I am grateful today not to be a magus," he whispered, so quietly I had to lean over to hear the words sigh out of his mouth. "If the pain of being partly drained is anything like the Damerel rites, I think I chose my path wisely."

"You're going to be fine," I said, though I wasn't at all sure this was the case. He looked shrunken the way Harry Keller had, though not to the same degree. But if Harry could recover, and Judy swore he would, I had to believe Claude and Elisabeta would pull through as well.

"Where's Iakkhos?" I asked.

Diane shook her head. "He had a heart attack when the first familiars appeared. Our resident bone magus did his best, but... Iakkhos is a hundred and two, and there's only so much magic can do about that."

Iakkhos had been isolated from the rest, with a barrier of chairs surrounding him. He looked like he was sleeping, so I didn't disturb him. "What happens if he..." I said.

"The Board will find a replacement," Diane said.

That was when I realized what had been bothering me. "Why aren't there any Board members here?"

"No one knows where they are. We sent people to Annapurna, but the room is empty."

"The *entire Board of Neutralities* is missing?"

Diane shushed me. "We're trying not to talk about it. There's nothing any of us can do."

"Can't someone at least call them?"

"Nobody here has their personal numbers. And their assistants aren't picking up."

I chewed my lip briefly in thought. "I dropped my phone."

"Do you have an idea?"

"Give me yours."

I called Judy, grateful that hers was one of five numbers I actually had memorized, along with Malcolm, Viv, my parents, and Bill's Pizzeria down the street. The phone rang, and rang, and finally she picked up. "Who is this?"

"It's Helena. I borrowed someone's phone because mine broke. What's going on?"

"Helena! There are teams at the hotel now, trying to break through the wards to get inside."

"I know. And the police are here. Why can't the hunting teams break through the wards?"

"That's a question a lot of people would like the answer to," Judy said sourly. "Somebody turned the Grandison into a death trap and filled it with familiars. I've been trying to call you for the last half hour."

"Like I said, my phone broke."

"This is what happens when you don't have a good sturdy—"

"Could we save the lecture on phone cases for later, please? I need Mr. Ragsdale's personal number. I know your father has it."

"Why Ragsdale? Isn't he in there with you?"

"We lost contact with the Board. I'm trying to reach them to see if they are in danger. Can you just give me the number?"

"Hold on." There was the sound of running footsteps, then a door opened. Judy breathlessly rattled off a number. "Are you safe?"

"As safe as anywhere is, here," I said. "I'll call you back in a bit."

I hung up and quickly dialed Ragsdale's number before I could forget it. It rang once, then Ragsdale said, "Yes?"

"Mr. Ragsdale, it's Helena Davies," I said. Beside me, Diane went limp with relief and beckoned to Nimisha to join us. "Are you all right?"

"Everything's fine here," he said. "No need to worry."

I hesitated. His voice sounded strange, maybe a little too far away. "Where are you? Everyone else is gathered in Kilimanjaro, and we—"

"We're in one of the suites. Is something wrong?"

"You haven't seen any familiars? They've invaded the hotel and are killing people."

There was a long pause. "Familiars?" he finally said. "No, we haven't seen anything like that. You're not exaggerating, are you?"

"Of course not! I've been attacked three or four times, Mr. Ragsdale. I wouldn't exaggerate that, would I?"

"You're well?" Now he sounded more like himself, and concerned for my welfare.

"No lasting damage. Are you sure you don't want us to come for you? If the familiars break through—"

"We're not afraid of familiars." A strange emphasis on *familiars*. "Did you call for the hunting teams to return?"

"We did. They're having trouble getting through the wards."

"Are they." That sounded almost sarcastic, and I was so confused I wasn't sure what to say first. "I'm sorry now that we allowed the Campbell Security forces to leave, but it seemed like a better long-term strategy to have them fight off the familiars before they got to this hotel...anyway, I apologize."

"Thanks. Um. Mr. Ragsdale, are you all right? You sound a bit strange."

"I'm perfectly fine, perfectly fine. Barricade the doors and wait for the magi to arrive."

"Mr. Ragsdale, we need the Board's presence! People are *dying* down here!"

"If the hotel is as swarmed with familiars as you say, our attempting to join you will only result in more death. I'm sorry, Ms. Davies, but we simply can't help you."

He hung up before I could say anything else. I swore loudly and handed Diane her phone. "That was weird. He didn't sound at all like himself. Not that I know him very well."

"So they're safe?"

"And not coming to join us. I don't know, it's probably sensible that they don't, but I can't help feeling we could really use their authority. What if people start to panic?"

A commotion at one of the barricaded doors drew our attention. Nimisha said, "Someone else is coming in."

It was a man dressed in Board colors, navy suit and maroon tie, and he looked exhausted. "We're unable to reach the wards to turn them off," he shouted over the noise of everyone clamoring for news. "There are too many familiars in the way."

"Then we should go with you," a woman shouted back. "We're all in this together."

"Absolutely not," the magus said. "Your lives are too important to risk."

"Helena, what do you say?" Diane said.

"Me? Why me?"

"Because with the Board absent and Claude incapacitated, you're the ranking Neutrality."

"That's true," someone nearby said. "Ms. Davies, you should take charge."

"But I—" Everyone was looking at me now. I wished I hadn't been so quick to claim I was uninjured. Then I was angry at myself. I might not be a leader, but I certainly was no coward. I swallowed, and straightened my spine. "Our lives will be forfeit if we don't help," I said. "The hunting teams are here now, and all they need is for us to let them in. I say anyone who wants to volunteer to help is welcome."

"Excuse me, Ms. Davies, but I don't think you're qualified to say that," said the magus.

"Because I'm not a fighter? That's true, but I killed three invaders on the way here, and I'm willing to kill more." Confidence was replacing my initial reluctance. "I say we find the kitchens, arm ourselves, and then protect the stone magi as they do their work. But I'm not going to sit still and wait for the familiars to overwhelm us. Who's with me?"

Hands went up here and there, twenty, thirty, thirty-five. "How do you shut down the wards?" I asked the magus, who looked as if his beloved puppy had turned around and bitten a chunk out of his hand. "I don't need the details of the magic, just how many of you magi does it take and in how many places?"

"If we weaken the wards at two key places, the whole thing will collapse," he said. "But I really can't let you do this. If Abernathy's—"

"I don't know if you noticed, but we're all in danger here," I said. "If we do nothing, Abernathy's will certainly be missing a custodian by tomorrow. And I'm not going to sit around and wait for that to happen. So it takes two of you?"

"Three at each place, and we need the familiars held off for five minutes while we work the magic." He sounded defeated.

"We can do that." I waved my arm, beckoning my volunteers. "We need to leave the defenders of this room as many weapons as we can spare. I don't suppose anyone knows where the kitchen is?"

Two people indicated that they knew the location of the kitchen.

"We go as a group until we get to the kitchen, then—what's your name?—Rufus and Maryanne will divide us to be their defenders while they remove the wards. Okay? Then let's make this quick."

We left Kilimanjaro and headed for the stairs leading to the lobby, with me in the middle of the mob, buoyed along by its motion. Kitchen, then wards—what? What the hell was I thinking? I was no fighter, no one who could lead a posse of custodians on a suicide mission to fight monsters that could kill us with a touch. What on earth had possessed me to make that speech?

I almost turned around and went back. But it was too late for that. I was nominally the head of this enthusiastic mob, and I had to lead it. Even if that was the stupidest thing I'd ever done. *Stupider than assuming the oracle's body? Or facing down invaders armed with nothing but sharpened rebar? Or going to the house of a presumed serial killer armed with nothing but your wit?* Yes, this definitely qualified.

The lobby was eerily still and hadn't taken a fraction of the damage the mezzanine had. The path to the doors was free, and the doors rattled occasionally as if someone were slamming into them with a battering ram. I almost trotted across to open them until I saw shadows moving in a funny way to both sides of them. Sticking with the team was good.

A swinging door marked STAFF ONLY led to a white corridor lined with doors, most of which opened on storage rooms filled with canned goods, linens, cleaning supplies, and (in one very cold room) frozen foods. We passed a staff break room and followed our noses to the kitchen, which still smelled good even at nearly midnight. A crumpled heap in one corner turned out to be a dead woman, her face contorted in terror. I heard a couple of people throw up, and had to breathe deeply to keep from joining them. I'd hoped the staff was safe—but that was stupid. Just because they weren't as appetizing to invaders as a custodian was didn't mean they weren't in danger from the familiars' attacks.

"Knives, carving forks, there are a lot of weapons in here," I said. My eye was drawn to a huge skillet hanging on the wall, and I

THE BOOK OF LIES

remembered Harriet killing Vitriol with her hers. I took it off the wall and hefted it. Oh yes, this felt like a weapon.

All around me people were picking over the utensils and cookware. I went to talk to Rufus. "Where now?"

"We have to get to the basement. The two loci for the magic are at opposite ends of the foundation."

"Okay. Everyone, let's split up."

"Because splitting the party always works *so well*," someone muttered, and a couple of people laughed. I didn't know what was so funny about that, but I understood what he was getting at.

"We have to split up or this won't work, even if we're safer as a group. So line up behind Rufus or Maryanne, and follow their lead. Where are your other magi?" I asked Rufus.

"Securely warded near the loci," he said. "They can't get out unless we free them."

"I thought there was no such thing as a personal stone ward."

"These aren't personal wards, they're extensions of the main wards. Our magi are like mosquitoes trapped in amber. Nothing can get them, but they can't get out."

"Got it. Free the magi, protect you from being killed, don't get killed ourselves."

I was immediately behind Rufus as we left the kitchen for the cargo elevator. My group consisted of eighteen custodians bristling with kitchen implements, and once again I was struck by the absurdity of it all. When this was over, I was going to have a breakdown, because this just wasn't me. Or maybe it was, and I didn't know myself as well as I thought. For the moment, I had to behave as if I really was this competent and daring, or it would all fall apart, and people would die, probably starting with me.

The elevator was big enough to take each of our groups all at once. I indicated that Maryanne's group should go first, as they had farther to go, and we waited tensely for them to reach the basement and send the elevator back up. Somebody shrieked, and we all jumped, weapons ready, but it was just someone brushing someone else's leg with the handle of a carving fork. Still no familiars emerged.

Finally, the elevator dinged open, and we all shuffled inside, all of us craning our necks to scan the ceiling for attackers. Unlike the passenger elevators above, the cargo elevator roof was a single piece of metal, with no joins to indicate concealed doors or passages. That didn't stop us being paranoid. Then again, all of us had seen people attacked by familiars, had heard their agonized screams, so maybe it wasn't paranoia if they really were out to get you. I was pretty sure I'd heard that somewhere before.

The elevator doors slid open, and we moved out into a wide, poorly lit hall with a low ceiling. The walls were white; the ceiling was made of those porous white square tiles that fit into a frame and could easily be knocked out of place by something that wanted to get into the ceiling—or get out of it. Fluorescent tubes flickered like they were auditioning for a part in a low-budget horror film. Once again everyone was looking at the ceiling, brandishing weapons in its direction.

I made myself watch the direction we were going, which meant I was the first to see movement in the distance.

"Watch out!" I shouted, bringing my skillet up, and then it was upon us, rushing Rufus with hands outstretched.

It howled, "Don't hurt me!"

"*Kevin?*" I said.

14

"Don't attack, he's human!" I shouted. Then I wanted to shrivel up and hide, because those weren't words you'd normally hear someone saying. But Kevin, stumbling toward me, didn't take any notice of my unusual phrasing.

"Thank God," he said. "They killed—what *are* they? Not dogs— they look like dogs, but they bleed blue—"

"Calm down, Kevin." I hugged him, felt him trembling with shock. He had blue ichor on his bartender's shirt and smeared down the side of his face.

Someone behind us screamed, and a fight broke out. I couldn't see past the bodies in the way, but I could smell the reek of familiars, and my throat closed up against it. Kevin broke away from me and stood, panting, his eyes wide. "It's another one," he said. "What the hell are they?"

"Are you all right? You haven't been injured?"

The noises stopped. "We killed it," someone shouted.

"We have to keep moving," Rufus said. "Talk on the way."

"We can't bring him with us," I said, glaring at Rufus and willing him to hear the warning in my voice: *we can't do magic with an ordinary human along.*

"He'll be killed if we don't protect him," Rufus said. "We can figure out the rest later."

"Would somebody explain *what the hell is going on?*" Kevin shouted.

"They're...wild dogs, and they...they're sick," I said as Rufus headed off along the hallway. I grabbed Kevin's arm and dragged him along with me. "That's why their blood is...different."

"You expect me to believe that?"

An unearthly howl echoed through the hallway, coming from everywhere at once. "They're on us," Rufus said. "Watch out!"

I pulled my jolter out and aimed it past Rufus' right ear. He ducked, and I squeezed. A faint buzz trembled through it, and the familiar I shot staggered but didn't fall. I shoved the jolter back into my pocket and raised the skillet, screaming defiance at the thing. Another familiar, this one white and ghostlike with fangs like a tiger, leaped on the first one's back and used it as a springboard, tearing chunks from its body and making it collapse. I stepped up and swung like a Major League batter.

Its skull met the skillet with a tremendous *clonk* and it dropped. I shouted triumphantly and swung again, crushing the head, which erupted with thick red liquid like strawberry jam. The sight combined with the paint-thinner stench made me gag. Beside me, Kevin leaned over and vomited. "Keep moving!" I said, but he was convulsing and helpless. Custodians streamed past me. I kept a firm grip on Kevin's arm. "Come on!" I said as soon as I judged he was able to walk. Wiping his mouth, Kevin followed me, and we hurried after the others.

More familiars came after us—how many could there possibly be? I thought Judy had said there were only twenty loose in the city. We'd seen far more than that. I wielded my skillet like a tennis racket, lobbing a small furry body back into two of its companions. They stopped to tear it to pieces, and I gagged again, but didn't stop running.

Beside me, Kevin was breathing hard, but at least he'd stopped asking questions. I had no idea what I'd say to explain all this. The illusions on the familiars were mostly holding, if he thought they were dogs, but the blood should have looked red...maybe the magi could remove his memories. No, I'd been told mind control was impossible, and memory removal surely counted as that. By this time we were running backwards, stumbling in our haste but afraid to turn our backs on the hallway that never stayed empty for long.

Which is why we ran into the rest of the custodians, literally ran into them and nearly knocked a couple of people down. "Why did you stop?" I gasped.

"We made it. Rufus and the magi are taking down the wards," a woman said.

"But the familiars are still—" a man I vaguely recognized began.

"*They're coming again!*" someone shouted, and I looked down the hall to see half a dozen chitinous or furry or fleshy bodies. The stench was overwhelming.

"Kevin, get back," I shouted, raising my skillet, though I was shaking so hard I had trouble holding onto it. All around me, jolters went off, taking creatures down, and then a handful of custodians ran past, shouting and wielding knives. I followed them, praying I wasn't about to die in this basement at the teeth or claws of an invader.

We fought for what felt like hours. My arms were so tired from lifting the heavy skillet, my eyes burned from the acrid smell, and I had blood on me, some of which was human. Custodians fell and couldn't be dragged to safety because we were all busy staying alive. I wiped sweat out of my eyes and spared a thought for Kevin, who'd disappeared. I hoped he wasn't dead. *That would make explaining a lot easier*, I thought, and hated myself for it.

A sudden wind blew through the hallway, carrying with it the smell of roses and sweeping away the stench. The familiars attacking us hesitated, but the wind invigorated us, and we pressed our attack harder. Distantly I heard Rufus shouting something about the wards, but the shrieking of the familiars overrode him. I slammed the edge of the skillet down on a creature's neck, nearly cutting its head off. I thought they'd be tougher than that.

Someone grabbed me by the shoulders and spun me around. "The wards are down," Rufus said. "We need to get out of here."

"They have us trapped," I said, wiping sweat away again.

"The hunters don't know we're down here. We have to get out or we'll die." Rufus glanced down the hall and pointed. Two familiars rose up off the floor and slammed into each other. "We magi can clear the way, mostly, now we don't have to conserve our magic for the wards, but you custodians need to run."

"We can't abandon the ones who fell!"

"There's nothing we can do for them now."

I swore at him, but he didn't react. "They're Wardens," he said. "They knew the risks. Now, *run!*"

He gave me a shove, and I stumbled toward a familiar that shrieked at me, but flew away into a wall before it could do more than scratch my face. Custodians began running past me. I saw Kevin in the crush and grabbed his arm. His eyes were still dilated, his face ashy. "Come on!" I shouted, pulling on him, and he stumbled along in my wake.

Once again we were at the rear of the pack, but this time there were two magi behind us, blowing familiars off their feet and tangling their wings. I tripped and went to my knees, and Kevin helped me up. My legs were shaking too much to run. Ahead, I heard voices urging us on, and then we were at the elevator. Hands pulled us in, drawing us to the center of a pile of warm bodies, and I clung to someone without knowing who it was. Kevin still had hold of my hand, and when I looked at him, he was staring into the middle distance, sightless and barely breathing.

"Something bit you," I said. "It's—"

"Nothing bit me. I'm fine."

"You don't look fine."

The elevator opened, and we all spilled out, weapons at the ready. At first I thought the little hall was empty, but then I smelled the familiar reek, and saw a couple of glistening bodies creeping around the far end. I shouted a warning. "Get back to the others!" Rufus called out, and everyone ran.

It was a total rout. Exhausted, demoralized, we all fled as best we could, not stopping to fight unless personally confronted. I held Kevin's hand tightly as we ran, ducking familiars who flew on stubby wings feathered with spikes and dodging familiars with leathery skin. We burst through the STAFF ONLY door to the lobby—

—and were nearly bowled over by a couple of men in black fatigues wielding steel knives. Kevin and I screamed and ducked. "Get upstairs!" one of the men said, but we didn't need the warning. The lobby was full of black- and white-suited figures, some of them carrying oddly-shaped guns, others with the long knives. One of them came running toward us, and I nearly fainted with relief—it was Olivia Quincy, the paper magus of Malcolm's team.

"Upstairs!" she said, putting her arm around my shoulders. "Who's this?"

"Kevin," I said, as if that explained anything. Olivia cast her eye over him, but just shrugged.

"You have to get into the big room," she shouted over the noise and screams. "We'll put an illusion on it to protect it from the cops."

"Why?"

"No time. We can't keep the police out much longer. Just trust me, okay?" She guided us toward the stairs, then left us to ascend alone. I was shaking so hard I could barely walk, and I had to lean on Kevin for support.

The doors to Kilimanjaro stood wide open, and bone magi were tending to wounded custodians. I found a chair that had formerly been part of the barricade and fell into it. Kevin crouched beside me. He looked a lot better, less shocky and more hale than I was.

"Mad dogs," he said. "You expect me to believe that?"

"I don't care what you believe," I said, and closed my eyes.

"Those were monsters."

"Yes." Judy had said it once: sometimes you had to cut your losses. And Kevin already knew more than he should.

"And you fight monsters."

"No."

"I saw you—"

159

"I fought today because I had to. Normally I leave it to the guys with the knives and guns." As if on cue, a gun went off somewhere in the lobby, and I heard the shrill, pained shriek of a familiar dying.

"I don't understand any of this, Helena. But I'm damn sure you're more than a heating and cooling system salesman."

I opened my eyes and examined him. He no longer looked like he was in shock; he was bright-eyed and his gaze was riveted on me. "I am, but I can't explain it to you." Where would I even begin? Did I need permission to tell a stranger all of magery's deepest held secrets? "I don't suppose you'll be satisfied with that?"

"Hell, no. What are wards? And magi?"

I sighed. Cutting my losses. "Magi are people who use magic against monsters like the ones we were fighting. Wards are supposed to keep those monsters out of this hotel. And the rest is too complicated to explain."

"Magic. Real magic, not card tricks."

"Yes."

"*Damn.*" He rocked back on his heels. "And what are you, if you're not a magi?"

"Magus. I run a bookstore."

"A magic bookstore?" His eagerness ratcheted up a couple of notches.

"Yes. Not like in Diagon Alley, which I can tell was going to be your next question."

"But you sell magic books?"

"Yes, sort of. Kevin, I'm really tired."

He subsided slightly. "Sorry. I just can't believe all this is happening. If I came to your bookstore, would you sell me a magic book?"

"I'm not allowed," I lied. "Only people who know the truth..." I heard what I was saying and groaned inwardly.

"But I know the truth now. Damn, Helena. This is just amazing." I heard Kevin stand, but my eyelids were too heavy to lift. He said something else, but I slipped into sleep, where everything made sense and no one wanted anything from me.

"Ms. Davies," someone said, his voice almost familiar. I dragged myself awake and blinked at him. Malcolm—no, Ewan Campbell, crouching next to me. He had a huge bruise covering one eye and most of his cheek, and his dark hair had something nasty in it. "Ms. Davies, are you all right?"

"I'm not injured, if that's what you mean." I stretched and sat upright. "Where's Kevin?"

"I don't know who that is. You haven't been drained at all?"

"They tried, a couple of times, but I don't think it was serious."

"We'll have a bone magus look at you, just in case. I'm glad you're well."

I wanted to ask about Malcolm, but thought that might give me away. Instead, I said, "Is everyone all right?"

"Everyone's accounted for." Ewan looked grim. "Twenty-five custodians were killed, as well as Parvesh Chhitri. And Iakkhos Kalivas is still very ill from his heart attack."

I closed my eyes again. "I can't believe it. So many..." My eyes flew open. "What about the cops?"

"What about them?"

"I know they were outside with you all. Why isn't this place crawling with them?"

"It is, but our paper magi pulled together one of the most incredible illusions I've ever seen. They made it look like this room is empty, left a few familiars lying around as 'dogs' to support the notion that a pack of rabid animals got inside and attacked people. The steel magi left a few familiars free for the police to kill and analyze—that illusion alone was worth all the others. We've had to allow a couple of our dead to be taken to the morgue, but for the most part our magi kept this from turning into a total disaster. I'm issuing commendations for a lot of people today. Not that I expect it will matter."

"Why not?"

"I'll be handing in my resignation in the morning. I consider myself personally responsible."

"It's hardly your fault if the Board sent you away!"

"I shouldn't have bowed to their wishes. I knew my duty and I abandoned it."

"I'm sure Malcolm won't think so."

"Begging your pardon, Ms. Davies, but I know my brother better than you do. He'd hold himself to the same standard."

I had to admit he was probably right. "How much good are you going to do the Long War if you just quit, like a...a quitter?"

"I'm not quitting. I'm resigning. There's a difference."

"I don't see it. Look, maybe you made a mistake. You're not the first. But if there's any blame to go around here, shouldn't it lie with the magi who didn't remember to change the...the frequency of the wards, or whatever you call it? I mean, I don't want to go pointing fingers, but if they'd done their job right the first time, we all would have been safe." I didn't want to bring up Rasmussen's name, but at this point, surrounded by injured custodians with the bodies of twenty-five more of them lying throughout the hotel, his refusal to destroy the familiars looked pretty stupid.

"I don't believe in putting off responsibility on someone else," Ewan said.

"If you're quitting because you think you're a liability, I won't argue with that. But if you're quitting out of guilt or something, I can't respect that. Your duty is to fight the Long War, Ewan Campbell, and sidelining yourself isn't going to help anyone."

Ewan gave me a sidelong smile and stood. "You're tenacious, I'll give you that. Thank you, Ms. Davies."

"Call me Helena."

"All right...Helena. I'll consider what you've said." He nodded and walked away, leaving me feeling achy and sad. He looked so much like Malcolm it made me long to see the real thing walk through the door, even if he couldn't hold me or kiss me in public.

I looked around the room for Kevin. There was Claude, on his feet and looking like he'd never been drained. Nimisha, sitting by herself and looking so lost my heart went out to her. No Kevin. I wondered where he'd gone. Surely no one had just let him walk away? They had to have the hotel staff somewhere, feeding them a story that would justify whatever they might have heard or seen. I hoped I wasn't going to be in trouble for telling him some of the truth.

I stood, wobbling on still shaky legs, then slowly crossed the room toward Nimisha. She looked up as I approached, but said nothing. "You're not hurt?" I said. She shook her head. "I'm sorry about Parvesh. I can't imagine how you must feel right now."

She smiled. "Parvesh and I did not get along," she said. "We were assigned this together as a sort of...penance, possibly? So I mourn him as a human being and a colleague, but not as a friend."

"Oh." I wasn't sure what to say to that. "I guess...I feel that way about the ones who died. I don't know many of the custodians personally."

"It is a blow for the Long War, to be forced to replace so many custodians at once. And Iakkhos may not survive to return to the Labyrinth. This has been a terrible night."

"I don't know what time it is, but it feels like it's gone on forever."

Nimisha nodded. "I am simply waiting for the hunters to verify that the hotel is clear of invaders, and then I intend to return to my room to sleep."

"That sounds like a good idea." I sat on the floor next to her chair and folded my arms around my knees, rested my chin on my arms. The shaking was diminishing, though I still ached from all the running and fighting, and my arms felt like overcooked macaroni. I watched the door, watched the people running in and out of it, and wished Malcolm would come. After everything I'd been through, I wanted to know he was still alive.

My eyelids sagged again, and I turned my head to pillow my cheek on my arms. I wanted to sleep *now*, and I wasn't sure I wanted to return to my suite, with the dead familiar leaking its blue blood onto the carpet. My head jerked, and I realized I'd fallen asleep, after all. Nimisha was gone, Malcolm still wasn't there, and I decided I was just going to sleep on the floor. I curled up in a tight little ball and was asleep in seconds.

Someone was shaking me, whispering my name. It was Derrick, Malcolm's teammate and an excellent bone magus. "Wake up," he repeated, and I blinked and sat up. My face felt scratchy from where it had been pressed against the carpet, and my mouth was fuzzy and dry.

"It's over," Derrick said. "We've cleared out the hotel and the wards have been restored. And properly set. The police are finishing their investigation. Are you all right? No injuries?"

"Just sore from swinging a skillet."

"What?"

"Never mind. I was bitten twice, but not for very long."

"Show me."

I rolled up my pant leg to show the pinkish crooked line where the familiar had caught me in the stairwell, then displayed my arm where the other one's cilia had brushed me. Derrick ran his hand over both sites. "You're fine," he said. "They must not have latched on long enough to drain you."

"Where's the rest of the team?"

"Mopping up. Campbell sent me to make sure you were all right." Derrick cleared his throat. "I thought you should know...we're all aware of why he's so concerned about you. In case you felt that's a secret you needed to keep."

Unexpected relief washed over me. "He told you."

"Teams that keep secrets from each other don't last long." Derrick shook his head. "I think you're both crazy for risking yourselves, but I can hardly argue with true love."

"Thanks. For everything."

"I'm supposed to escort you to your suite, just in case. We heard you were quite the fighter down in the basement. You sure you don't want to become a magus?" Derrick teased.

I shuddered. "I'm never going to complain about mail-in auguries again. I'm not cut out to be on the front lines."

"It's nice to know you can defend yourself, though, isn't it?"

"With a skillet. Not the most romantic weapon."

Derrick made me wait outside the suite while he checked it for familiars. Whatever had been in my bathroom was long gone. He put the ventilation grate back into place and used a towel to scoop up the body of the familiar I'd killed, which had mostly disintegrated. "Leave the mess," he said when I picked up another towel to mop up the blue ichor. "Most of it will sublimate into the atmosphere by morning. Their bodies don't last well once they're dead. Makes it easier to fight them, if we don't have to worry about disposal."

I made a face, but put the towel away. Derrick checked my bedroom and the other bathroom, said, "You're clear. Try to get some sleep," and left.

I showered, put on my pajamas, and got into bed, but my earlier sleepiness was gone. I had too much to think about. Twenty-five custodians to replace—why had Ragsdale behaved so oddly on the phone?—what had happened to Kevin?—would Malcolm come to me tonight? Rasmussen couldn't justify keeping the familiars anymore, not after this fiasco. I had no idea how it would affect the rest of the conference. How could anyone think about things like Abernathy's moving to London when so many people were dead?

I found the remote and turned the television on. I needed something to distract me. What I *needed* was my DVD collection, home to all my old favorites, but what I *had* was another infomercial, this one for some kind of robe you wore backwards so it was more like a blanket with sleeves. It looked comfortable and unattractive at the same time. I turned down the volume and made up my own story to go with it, something about space blanket monsters wrapping people in their folds and sucking their magic out. I might have been projecting my fears on the dumb blanket robe.

I woke from a sleep I didn't remember entering to the sound of the outer door opening. My heart pounding, I slipped out of bed and tiptoed to the bedroom door. Just as I put my hand on the lever, it depressed, and the door swung toward me. Malcolm stood there, looking as filthy and haggard as he had the previous night. I gasped, then flung myself at him, crying his name.

He held me tightly, stroking my hair, and I buried my face in his shoulder and breathed in the woody smell that was his alone. "When I got your message that the Grandison was under attack, I was utterly terrified," Malcolm murmured into my hair. "But when we arrived to find the wards impenetrable, I thought I might go mad. Knowing you were here, undefended...let me hold you, please, while I convince myself that you are safe."

"I never want to do that again. I would rather you rescue me. Does that make me weak?"

"Since I know you will fight to defend yourself if anything like this happens again, no. I swear to come to your rescue as often as you need it."

I sighed and leaned into him. "I'd like to promise I won't need it, but doesn't it seem like trouble follows me?"

"It does, a little. I'm sure it's our imagination."

I raised my head so I could look at him. "Can you stay? I'm too tired for anything but cuddling."

"I can stay a few hours, and cuddling sounds appealing." He released me only to take hold of my hand and draw me towards the bed. "Lie down, and I'll join you in a moment."

I crawled back into bed and watched him shed his fatigues and boots. "I'm starting to change my mind about the cuddling," I said, admiring the way his T-shirt fit tightly across his chest.

He smiled. "Tinsley said you fought like a demon, and that means you need rest, much as I would prefer other activities." He lay down next to me and took me in his arms. "Sleep, and we'll see what the morning brings."

I was asleep almost before he finished speaking.

15

***

*W*hen I woke, feeling tired and sore, Malcolm was gone. I stifled feelings of self-pity and shuffled to the sitting room, where I turned on the coffeemaker. A faint blue stain on the carpet was all that was left of the familiar's blood. I knelt next to it and reached out to touch it, but changed my mind when I caught the faintest whiff of paint thinner. That was never going to be a pleasant smell for me in the future. Good thing they hadn't smelled like something nice, like flowers or peanut butter.

I poured myself a cup of delicious coffee and retreated to the bed to drink it. The bittersweet aroma overrode the stink of the familiar, but that wouldn't last long. The bedside clock told me it was 9:42. I'd really slept in. I leaned back and breathed in the coffee smell again. I ought to get dressed and find out what was going on. Surely they couldn't expect the hotel staff to soldier on like nothing had happened?

I dressed in comfortable clothes, jeans and a full-sleeved tan blouse with gold embroidery around the neck, and went to Claude's suite. He didn't answer. I thought about knocking on Laverne Stirlaugson's door, but decided that was more than I could handle before breakfast. Maybe there was food still in the restaurant.

The mezzanine didn't look nearly so torn up as it had the night before. The doors to all the conference rooms were wide open, and people moved around, setting up chairs or wheeling carts full of expensive plastic water bottles. I descended the stairs to the lobby, which bore no signs of a criminal investigation other than a Christmas tree that had been knocked over, its ornaments scattered. The police had completed their work and left while I slept through it.

The restaurant was half-full of diners, all custodians, eating in ominous silence. The waffle lady wasn't there, and I had to content myself with a poppy seed muffin, a bowl of grapes, and a glass of orange juice. I found a table to myself, not difficult given the emptiness of the place, and wished more than ever that I had my phone. Being stuck in information limbo was driving me crazy.

"Good to see you're alive," Diane said, sliding into a seat opposite me. "That was some night, huh?"

"You make it sound like a party!"

"Hardly that. But you have to admit it brought us closer together, and I believe in looking for the best in the worst situations."

I wiped crumbs from my mouth. "What happens next?"

"Programming as scheduled. The police have been and gone, and the Board doesn't want this incident, as Stirlaugson is calling it, to interfere with its plans. We'll have a brief memorial service tonight before dinner."

"That seems sort of cold."

"Stirlaugson is *pissed* about the whole thing. I hear she handed Ewan Campbell his head on a platter, even though she's the one who sent him away. God forbid she take responsibility for any of this fiasco." Diane took a long drink from her coffee cup. "They've all isolated themselves anyway, the Board, I mean. I tried to talk to Chukwu earlier and he didn't have time for me. I think they're reaming out the magi who failed to adjust the wards."

"So *now* they care." I hadn't realized I felt so bitter about the Board's abandonment of us the night before. "That's nice to hear."

"They couldn't have come all the way down from the top floor without someone dying. It's not their fault they were trapped up there."

"I guess." It didn't make me happy. "What about things they still haven't decided? I don't want to make this all about me, but I need to know if I still have to defend Abernathy's against Rebecca Greenough."

"Everything's still as planned, though the schedule's shot to hell. They'll send a flunky to fetch you when it's time for you to make your statement."

"So basically I have to spend the day waiting on their pleasure."

"Basically, yeah. Sorry." She drained her coffee cup. "At least you have something productive to do. I'm going to wander the halls and reassure people, which is going to depress me after about an hour, but has to be done. Everyone's lost a friend."

"I wish I could help. I feel so at a loss—I was only beginning to know these people, and I never know what to say to someone who's grieving."

"Just be honest. Offer to listen. You might want to talk to Carlos. Elisabeta didn't make it."

A chill touched my heart. "I didn't know that. Where is he?"

"Their room. Go on, go."

I crossed the lobby to the elevators and pushed the button for the sixth floor. The man and woman at the reception desk looked at me with a total lack of interest. They seemed way too calm to have been here last night. It was reassuring to know there were people whose lives hadn't been touched by the attacks.

The sixth floor corridors were as empty as mine always were. I came to a halt in front of Carlos's door and knocked quietly, feeling obscurely that I shouldn't disturb anyone. After a short pause, the door opened, and I found myself facing a stranger. "Yes?"

"I wanted to see Carlos, if he's here." That sounded utterly stupid.

The stranger stepped back and gave me room to enter. He said something in liquid Spanish of which my mind caught nothing. Carlos said something in return, then added, "Come in, Helena."

The room contained two queen beds, with Carlos sitting on the edge of one. Elisabeta lay in the bed, looking so shrunken I might have mistaken her for a large doll if dolls were wrinkled and faded. "Carlos," I said. "I'm so sorry."

"She was in no pain, at the end," Carlos said. He took my hand and squeezed it. "She spoke to her husband, Andrei, and made her goodbyes."

"But...people recover from having their magic drained all the time. Why not her?"

"It's what happens when your magic can't restore itself," the stranger said. "It latches on to other vital parts of your body and tries to make them do the job of the magic."

I remembered what Lucas had said about Harry's magic not restoring and tears fell. "I'm sorry," I said. "It's just not fair!"

"Fair is not a thing that happens in the Long War," Carlos said, but his jaw was clenched, and tears glimmered on his cheeks. I knelt beside the bed and leaned my face against the side of the mattress. At that moment I could have cheerfully killed William Rasmussen and every familiar there was left in the city, free or harnessed. Her poor husband, waking to such awful news. And her node would need a new custodian. No wonder the Board was in seclusion. They couldn't afford to leave any Neutrality untended.

Carlos laid his hand on my head. "I would like to be alone now."

"Of course. I'm sorry. Carlos—"

He hugged me tightly. "Go. Embrace life. She would prefer you not remember her in sorrow."

The stranger—he must have been the bone magus tending Elisabeta, but I felt awkward introducing myself—opened the door for me, and I walked blindly down the hall, ending up at the elevator. I stared at the call buttons, not sure where I wanted to go: up, or down? Eventually I decided I didn't want to be alone and pushed the down arrow.

The elevator, when it arrived, held a handful of custodians, and we rode in silence to the mezzanine. Tired in spirit, aching in body, I went looking for someone I knew.

I found Claude sitting alone in Kilimanjaro, watching hotel staff set it up for that evening's dinner and business meeting. "How can they go on after witnessing what happened last night?" I said.

Claude patted the chair next to him in invitation. "They were not here last night, and know only that a pack of wild dogs entered the hotel and did a great deal of damage."

"Weren't people on the staff killed, as well?"

"Yes, but not many. With so many custodians in one place, the familiars attacked non-Wardens rarely, and the hotel's night staff is few. Did you leave before mundane law enforcement arrived?"

"I was told they were here, but I didn't see anything."

Claude made a displeased face. "I should not regret having my magic restored so promptly, but as its restoration left me in a position to speak to the police on behalf of the Board, I cannot view it with undiluted pleasure."

"Why didn't Ms. Stirlaugson speak for them?"

"The Board maintained its solitude throughout the night. We have heard nothing from them directly, only their messengers. I am concerned, me, that something else is awry, but every inquiry returns answers amounting to 'all is well.'"

"That seems really strange. I was hoping to find out if I still have to argue my case in front of them today."

"It is likely. They have been behaving as if nothing happened, which irks me, since twenty-five of my fellows have lost their lives."

"I was so sad to hear about Elisabeta Vaduva."

A look of terrible pain crossed Claude's face. "She is dead? Such a tragedy. Iakkhos will need to be told." He made no move to rise.

"Is Iakkhos okay? I heard the heart attack almost killed him."

"It did, and he is weak, but he will survive. I think it unlikely that he will see another conference."

"I'm sorry. I like him a lot."

"He and I have been friends for many years. The Labyrinth will be so different without him."

"Does he have a successor? I don't know how custodianship passes for anything except my own Neutrality."

"He does, and the successor has a successor. It is a satisfying feeling to know one's work will go on uninterrupted."

I thought about Judy, and said, "I can see that."

"Ms. Davies?" A woman in a navy suit approached us. "The Board will see you now."

"About moving Abernathy's?"

"They don't tell us the details. Will you follow me, please?"

My eyes met Claude's. "*Bonne chance*, Helena," he said. I nodded in return.

The woman led me to the elevator and pushed the button for the top floor. I'd been expecting to meet the Board in Annapurna, so that threw me a bit. Nervously I followed the woman off the elevator and down the hall, past my own room almost to the far end of the hall. The woman pulled out a key card and opened the last door on the left, then bowed me through exactly as if I were a queen. This made me even more nervous. I bobbed my head to her and entered the room. She didn't follow.

It was a suite similar to mine, though done in rose and silver rather than blue and gold. Instead of one dinette table, there were two pushed together to make a single long table surrounded by ten chairs. The sofa and armchairs had been moved to make room for the longer table, and the members of the Board sat or stood around them, like they were at an uncomfortable cocktail party where drinks hadn't been provided. They stopped their quiet conversations when I entered and focused intently on me. That didn't make me feel uncomfortable at all. Of course not. I suppressed the urge to wipe my sweaty palms on my pants and waited for one of them to speak.

"Ms. Davies. Thank you for coming," Stirlaugson said. Her suit today was pale rose that matched the décor, though I didn't believe she'd done it on purpose. "Ladies and gentlemen, let's be seated."

I let them all take chairs before I sat down, in case there was some ranking I needed to obey, but ultimately I sat where I'd guessed I should, at the bottom of the table facing Stirlaugson. Silence fell when we were all seated. I looked at the smooth, shining surface of the table and noted I could see the reflections of the Board members nearest me. One was the redhead whose name I still didn't know; the woman on the other side was Chao Min, looking as groomed and polished as the table.

"Ms. Davies," Stirlaugson said, drawing my attention, "the Board has received a proposal that Abernathy's be moved to London. You are invited to make a statement on this subject."

"Oh," I said, and caught a glimpse of the redheaded woman smiling in a superior sort of way. It irritated me enough to help me regain my composure. "Members of the Board, as Abernathy's custodian I say moving the oracle anywhere will be dangerous and unnecessary. When the store was moved the first time, it was in response to Hitler's rise to power and the premonition of the London Blitz. The move was hazardous both in terms of disrupting the oracle and in how exposed it was to attack by invaders, as it could not be warded during the move. The proposal to move it now has no compelling reason behind it, and I disagree that the supposed benefits of the move would outweigh the extreme danger the oracle would suffer."

Silence. Chukwu said, "Is that all?"

"Should there be more, Mr. Chukwu?"

"Ms. Greenough was quite eloquent on the subject," Harrison said. "She had a PowerPoint presentation."

"I don't believe that's necessary," I said, though my heart sank. Diagrams and pictures hadn't even occurred to me. "I have history on my side. Silas Abernathy was quite specific as to what moving the oracle entailed."

"Abernathy," Harrison spat. "That traitor?"

"Whatever his later actions, I don't think anyone can disagree that he saw the oracle through its greatest challenge, Mr. Harrison."

"Until last spring," Stirlaugson said. "When you prevented its destruction at the hand of a rogue magus."

The way she said the last two words sounded almost sarcastic, and it threw me. "Um...okay, yes, I guess you could say that had equal potential for destruction."

"So you believe that entitles you to make decisions for it, and not this Board?"

"Ms. Stirlaugson, I thought the point of this meeting was for me to give the Board adequate information so it could make the decision. Yes, I have an opinion, and yes, I believe it's an important one. But as far as I know, I don't have the power to make decisions about Abernathy's future. That's down to you all. I just want you to make the best one."

"And if that decision is to risk the danger, and move the store?" said Ragsdale.

"Then I'll get my passport in order and see what kind of a deal I can get on packing crates." I hoped that wasn't too flippant, but I was getting angry and was straining to keep it from coming through.

"And if the Board decides the custodianship should go to someone else?" Harrison said.

I fixed him with my steeliest gaze, though my heart quailed. "That's up to you as well. But I hope my actions have proved to all of you that I'm a worthy custodian."

Silence descended again. "Any other questions?" Stirlaugson said.

"Why is moving the oracle dangerous?" asked the redhead.

"The books have to stay close together for the oracle to...have a home, I guess would be the best analogy," I said. "If they're too far separated, the oracle dies. And in travel, it's not always possible to guarantee that kind of closeness for cargo. Particularly when you're dealing with mundane officials. Then there's the risk of invader attack—"

"We all understand that," the redhead said, a look of distaste crossing her face. "And yet it was successfully moved."

"The danger of remaining in Charing Cross Road was much greater than the risk to the oracle. Wanting to move the store because it will be more convenient isn't even in the same class."

The redhead's eyes narrowed in thought, but she nodded and said nothing more.

"Then you acknowledge there would be a benefit to moving the store," Harrison said.

"I don't know the details, but I'm told it would be a more central location for magery and would be better for holding this conference.

Those are benefits. I just disagree that they're essential enough to justify a move."

"I think the Board knows better than you whether that's true," Harrison said in a snotty kind of way. I was grateful he was a good ways up the table from me. My anger was simmering high enough I couldn't guarantee I wouldn't have smacked him.

"Like I said, I don't know the details. I'm sure the Board does understand that aspect of the situation."

"And you're prepared to uproot yourself and move to London?" Ragsdale said. His tone was neutral, almost casual, as if none of this mattered at all.

"I am, Mr. Ragsdale. I'll miss my family, but I swore to serve Abernathy's without fear or favor, and I think that's part of what it means."

"It sounds like you're clinging to the store," said a white-bearded man I didn't know who spoke with a French accent. "You ought to be thinking about what's best for it."

"Meaning what the Board decides?" I snapped, and had to pause briefly to regain my composure. "I'm sorry. I'm new to all this, you know that. But it seems to me that a Neutrality has two masters—there's the Board, who sees what's necessary for the Neutralities as a whole, and then there's the custodian, who knows her charge intimately. I'm willing to admit there are things you all understand that I don't. But I think you should be as willing to admit that I know things about Abernathy's you are never going to understand. And it's my duty as custodian to make sure you know those details so you can make the best decisions for everyone."

I leaned forward, fixing Stirlaugson with my gaze. "I've told you why moving the store is dangerous and pointless. Ms. Greenough has given you her arguments. Now it's on you to decide. You have all the power here, ladies and gentlemen. Please. Make the right decision."

The silence that fell when I finished speaking felt like heavy snowfall, muffling every sound and chilling me to the bone. Finally, Stirlaugson said, "Thank you for your time, Ms. Davies. You may go."

I pushed back my chair slowly, willing my shaking legs to support me, and said, "What about last night?"

Stirlaugson eyed me coolly. "Last night?"

This would probably kill my chances entirely, but I remembered Elisabeta's shrunken body and it filled me with rage. "Twenty-six people died last night while you hid in your suite and abandoned us. Doesn't that matter to you at all?"

"Of course it matters. But our presence would have changed nothing."

"Even so—what was so damned important you couldn't—"

"That's enough." Stirlaugson stood. "I make allowances for how overwrought your experience last night made you. The Board regrets not being present to lend its authority to the situation. But you understand *nothing* of the decisions we must make on behalf of all magery. And I will not explain myself to you. Now, leave us, and save your righteous indignation for some other event."

I clasped my trembling hands together behind me. "Thank you for hearing me out."

I managed to make it all the way through the door and down the hall to my suite before I had to stop and lean against the wall. My shaking hands needed three tries to work the key card. I staggered into the sitting room and collapsed on the nearest chair. I had no idea what the Board would make of my little speech. I might have just mortally offended them. I closed my eyes and sighed deeply. I'd done what I could, and now I just had to wait for the announcement at the business meeting after dinner. And figure out how hard it was to get a passport.

Someone knocked on my door. I staggered upright and went to open it. A young man dressed in the hotel uniform stood there, holding a small box. "Ms. Davies?" he said. I nodded. He opened the box. Inside was a new phone and a little envelope. The folded paper inside the envelope read *Judy said you broke your old phone. This should be an adequate replacement.* Malcolm never signed his notes to me; his handwriting was distinctive enough it was unnecessary. I took the phone and thanked the young man. It was identical to my old phone, and it was but the work of a moment to swap out the SIM card. I felt so competent.

The first thing I did was call Judy, who picked up so rapidly I guessed she'd been waiting for my call. "They solved the problem," she said.

"What problem?"

"The failing bindings. It was a matter of aging. Like how people today live long enough to die of cancer?"

"Judy, you're babbling."

"Sorry. It wasn't until this generation that familiars were bound for longer than twenty-five years. I don't understand the details, and I don't care, but basically the magic they used to alter a familiar to accept a harness failed after thirty or forty years of use. They're replacing all the bindings and it's never going to happen again."

"That's small comfort to the twenty-six custodians who died last night."

"I know. I'm really sorry. I shouldn't have started with that, it's just that it means the crisis is over. I hoped you'd be happy about that."

"I am. But I can't believe Mr. Rasmussen isn't just going to order them all destroyed. They're dangerous, Judy."

"You're the one who kept talking about what a boon they were to the Nicollien fighting teams!"

"I know. Now I'm not so sure they're a good idea."

"Father's been meeting with Parish a lot the last couple of days. I think—" Her voice lowered. "I think they're talking about ways to phase familiars out."

"Really? But that would be—"

"A huge change, yes. Don't tell anyone I said that, all right? I'm not totally certain that's what they're doing."

I started to tell her about the possibility of Abernathy's moving, but changed my mind almost immediately. We'd know the truth in just a few hours, and I superstitiously felt talking about it beforehand would make the decision come down against us. So instead, I said, "Did you tell Malcolm I needed a phone?"

"I might have left him a short message to that effect. Did he get you one with a nice heavy-duty case? You're way too hard on your phone for anything else."

I chose to ignore that. "Thanks, Judy. Are the travel restrictions still in place?"

"Didn't they tell you? Most of the loose familiars were involved in the attack on the Grandison, and the teams are finishing up the rest of them this morning. I was going to go in to the store, finish up a few last things before Christmas, but I hear Abernathy's will be open tomorrow from ten to two just like all week."

"That's a great Christmas present, closing up early on Christmas Eve."

"Yeah. I got you something." Her voice was gruff the way it always got when she was embarrassed.

"Good, because I got you something too." Something currently hidden in the bottom drawer of my desk back at the store. I hoped it would still have meaning after tonight.

16

There were fewer tables at dinner that night, and the sight made my eyes mist over briefly. So many custodians...I wasn't sure if I mourned more for the ones whose deaths had been concealed by the paper magi, or for the few the magi had allowed the police to see. Those bodies would go to a police morgue, or something, and maybe be autopsied, when there wasn't anything a forensic pathologist could learn about them. It just felt wrong, taking them away from us when we needed to mourn them.

The memorial service had been short but heartfelt, with pictures of the dead flanked by candles I was sure were against the fire code. The little act of defiance warmed me. It was like challenging death, daring it to overcome us. Men and women spoke about friends, Carlos read a tribute by Elisabeta's husband, and we cried and laughed, even I who didn't know any of these people as more than acquaintances. It had left me with a dull ache inside, but one that felt as if it would pass. I hoped that wasn't disrespectful of the dead.

There was no assigned seating for the banquet that night, but I couldn't bear the thought of sitting among strangers when my fate was so undecided. I saw Lucia seated across the room, talking to a man I'd met briefly after one of the presentations, and hurried toward her. "Can I sit by you?"

Lucia regarded me closely. "Sure," she said. "Did you make your pitch to the Board?"

"What pitch?" the man said. "Clive Akins, remember me?"

"I remember you, Mr. Akins. Yes, I made my pitch. The Board—"

"That's supposed to be private information, Davies," Lucia said. "Sorry, Akins, but you'll have to learn about it with the rest of us."

"*You* already seem to know about it," Akins said with a smile.

"I'm nosier than you. Sit down already, Davies."

I quickly took my seat. I'd dressed up for this occasion, reasoning if I looked good, the Board might be swayed. It was stupid reasoning, but it was all I had. I smoothed hair that was already smoothly pinned up, straightening a wayward strand, and resisted tugging my bra strap into place. I looked good in my rose silk dress and matching cashmere sweater, a nice compromise between fashionable and comfortable. Too bad Malcolm couldn't see me all dressed up.

More custodians, men and women I didn't know, joined us until all eight seats at our table were filled. Lucia, of course, knew all of them, and introduced me. It was pointless, because I was too keyed up to remember my own name, let alone those of five strangers. I smiled politely and answered questions about Abernathy's, but mostly I listened. It was sort of fascinating, the kinds of troubles Neutralities had. I watched Lucia butter a roll and speak animatedly to a woman across the table from her and wondered if she ever felt lonely. The node custodians probably talked to each other all the time, not just at the Conference, but it couldn't be the same as meeting in person.

I leaned back for the server to set the main course in front of me, herb-crusted salmon, pan-fried and oven-finished, on a bed of rice pilaf with a side of broccolini, and inhaled the delicious aroma. Sometimes I really loved living in the Pacific Northwest.

"So does anyone know what happened to the magi responsible for screwing up the wards?" Akins asked. "Lucia?"

"What, you think because they came from my Neutrality I'd have any idea about them?"

"Well, yes. That's exactly what I think."

Lucia took a large bite of salmon, I thought to give herself time to answer, though I couldn't imagine why she'd need it. "The Board called them in around five o'clock this morning, one at a time. They were gone for about half an hour each and none of them would say what they'd been asked when they returned."

"That sounds odd," I said.

"I'd already reamed them out before that, so to me it just looked like PTSD."

Lucia didn't meet my eyes. I knew her well enough to know when she wasn't being forthcoming, and knew, too, that she wasn't likely to be truthful until I got her alone. So I just said, "You're probably right. Did you fire them?"

"Of course I fired them. They were indirectly responsible for almost thirty deaths."

"That seems a little harsh," said the woman opposite Lucia.

"I expect my people to think of the worst possible scenario and plan for it. It doesn't take a genius to figure out that if familiars are breaking free, they need to be treated like regular invaders. Well, those four geniuses are going to have to find new employment, because my Neutrality doesn't need them."

"I'm with you," Akins said. "I'm surprised the Board didn't impose stricter sanctions on you. They blamed Ewan Campbell for the security failure, after all."

"They tried," Lucia said grimly. "I convinced them to get their heads out of their—"

"May I offer you dessert?" the server said. "We have a choice of three offerings tonight."

"What's the house specialty?" I said. This was something my father had taught me to ask.

The server smiled. "We are famous for our carrot cake," he said. He had a look that said he didn't expect me to go for it. Well, I already knew carrot cake wasn't as popular as in my opinion it should be.

"That's my favorite," I said. "I'll have that."

"Carrot cake?" Lucia said, making a face. "I'll have more of that key lime pie."

"This is what my father always says," I said. "Restaurants, including hotels, generally have something they're famous for. And sometimes it's not the best thing on the menu. But when it *is*, it's so far beyond everything else you wonder why anyone bothers with the other stuff. And carrot cake happens to actually be my favorite. So I'll chance it."

I sipped my dessert coffee and let its heat relax me, though probably I'd regret the caffeine in half an hour, when the business meeting was in full swing. I caught Claude's eye—he was seated at the table next to me—and smiled at him. He smiled back, but looked preoccupied, and I wished I was close enough to ask him what he was thinking. A few tables over, Nimisha and Vijay were carrying on a heated conversation I could hear from where I was, though since they weren't speaking English, it was all so much babble to me. I hoped they weren't about to start a fist fight.

The server set down my carrot cake. It came in a wide glass, not a plate, with a drizzle of caramel across it and pearly crystalline salt around the rim, like the pastry chef and the bartender had fought over the right of presentation. The tangy scent of cream cheese frosting reached my nose, and I sighed in contentment. It only had to be half as good as that smell to be the best carrot cake ever.

"Well? Is it worth it?" Lucia said. "Stop sniffing it and take a bite already." She was already forking frozen key lime pie into her mouth faster than was really healthy. There was no way she could appreciate it at that speed.

I took a bite. "Oh," I said. "*Oh.* This is amazing." Just moist enough, with the spices blended through the cake and the frosting not overwhelming it. The golden raisins were little explosions of fruitiness in my mouth. "You have no idea what you're missing."

"I hate carrots."

"Carrot cake only tastes like carrots if you're doing something wrong." I took another bite. "I may come here just for the dessert sometime."

"With a special friend?" Lucia arched an eyebrow at me. If she thought I was going to out myself in front of a table full of custodians, she was crazy. I smiled sweetly and kept eating.

I was almost finished when Laverne Stirlaugson took her place at the podium, carrying a tablet. "We hope you've enjoyed your supper," she said. "If I can have your attention, we'll begin the business portion of the evening." She didn't look like she intended to wait on us. I took one last bite, scraped up a smear of frosting and licked it off my finger, then laid down my fork and prepared myself for whatever might come.

"Once again, we mourn the loss of our friends, and salute them for their service to magery over the years," Stirlaugson said. She pulled out a pair of reading glasses and settled them on her nose. "Due to their diligence and responsibility, their successors are already in place at their Neutralities. For your information, I will read to you the list of new custodians. Hannah Warren, the Belvedere Node, Knoxville, Tennessee, United States of America; Stephen Sun, Ch'en Node, Hong Kong; Benedetto D'onofrio, Cracchiolo Node, Tuscany, Italy...."

The list went on. I tried to pay attention, but then Stirlaugson said, "Andrei Vaduva, Ionescu Node, Romania," and it startled me so much I lost track of what she was saying. Elisabeta's husband was her successor? I couldn't begin to imagine what that would feel like, surrounded every day by reminders of the wife he'd lost. I searched the room for Carlos and couldn't see him. It might be so awkward three years from now, when Andrei and Carlos met as colleagues who'd loved the same woman. I hoped for both their sakes they could find common ground.

Stirlaugson came to the end of her recitation and tapped something on the tablet in front of her. "We now have some business matters to attend to. Regardless of your feelings about the Board's decisions, we ask that you restrain yourselves from displaying extreme emotion when our conclusions are made public. First, a more cheerful matter: a node near Wichita, Kansas, United States of America has grown to the status of a Neutrality. Karen Burns will be its custodian."

A ripple of conversation passed through the room. It did feel cheerful, and even Lucia, whose normal expression was a sardonic quirk of the lips, was smiling. Stirlaugson waited a few seconds before continuing. "This is unfortunately balanced by the temporary closing of the Hernandes Node in Mexico. Internecine conflict has grown to a point that both Nicolliens and Ambrosites fail to respect the status of the Neutrality. The Board will send word when the ban is lifted. Until that time, Ana Ruiz is no longer a custodian."

The room was perfectly silent. Somebody sneezed, another person said "God bless you," and silence descended once more. I looked around for Ruiz, but couldn't see her either. At least no one was escorting her out of the room. My heart ached for her, what little I'd known of her. It made me angry that the Board wouldn't intervene...though maybe this was how they intervened. It wasn't as if I understood how they worked. I'd said it myself: they saw what was necessary for Neutralities as a whole. But it still made me mad on Ruiz's behalf.

I'd missed Stirlaugson's next statement in my distraction, but whatever it was didn't cause much stir. "Thank you for your cooperation," Stirlaugson said, and I leaned over to ask Lucia what we were cooperating about and was it something I needed to worry about.

"The Board has received an interesting proposal," Stirlaugson said, "regarding the Neutrality known as Abernathy's. Specifically, this proposal requests that we relocate the oracle to its original home in Charing Cross Road, London, England."

I sat upright immediately. Everyone was staring at me, and I flushed until my cheeks had to be as pink as my dress. I had eyes only for Stirlaugson, who was expressionless. *Please,* I thought, willing her to hear, *please see sense.*

Stirlaugson stared at me a moment longer. Then she looked away, and I felt as if I'd been released from some tremendous pressure.

"The Board has decided Abernathy's...will remain in Portland, Oregon."

All the blood drained from my face before I registered I'd won. Then I couldn't stop smiling. Lucia didn't look at me, but she squeezed my knee under the table. Whispers went around the room again, with everyone at my table quietly congratulating me, though a couple of them looked like they weren't sure congratulations were in order. I guess, if they didn't know the details, it was just as likely that I'd petitioned for the move and been turned down. Not that anyone who could see my smile would believe that. Once again I felt as if a pressure had been lifted from me. I didn't bother looking for Greenough. I didn't need to rub it in. Lucia would no doubt do that for both of us.

Once again I missed what Stirlaugson said—something about new rules for the use of *sanguinis sapiens* collected from the nodes, and irrelevant to me, but it caused a bigger ruckus than any of the other decisions so far. Stirlaugson waited patiently for the commotion to cease, then said, "If you have any questions regarding our ruling, I encourage you to take it up with a Board member." Her tone of voice indicated that nobody had better question the ruling. Silence fell, broken only by the sound of a fork tinging against china.

"Our next decision will affect all the Neutralities to one degree or another," Stirlaugson said. "Some of you have already encountered increased tensions between the factions, in some cases tensions leading to verbal or even physical conflict. A few Neutralities have chosen to implement policies dictating times at which each faction may use the Neutrality, separating the factions to eliminate contact between them and therefore reduce conflict. The Board has heard from several custodians on both sides of the subject, some in favor of it and some rejecting it, and has made a decision.

"The Board's ruling is to incorporate this division into the Accords. Beginning this coming Monday, all Neutralities will implement a policy of separation of factions."

The murmur that went up was just short of explosive. It immediately dispelled my happy glow. Make the division permanent? I wanted to stand and shout at Stirlaugson, but she was staring at me again, her eyes hard and cold and daring me to make a scene. I clasped my trembling hands in front of me and focused on the empty glass that had held my dessert. Now there was virtually no chance of Ambrosite and Nicollien making common cause. I'd almost have been willing to move to London if it meant not having to enforce that policy.

"Silence," Stirlaugson said, and such was the force of her presence that everyone shut up. "I know many of you disagree with this decision. I remind you that you are under oath to uphold the Accords, whatever your personal feelings might be. It is the judgment of *this Board*—" she widened her glare to encompass the room—"that reducing contact between the factions will allow each to focus on the true goal, which is winning the Long War. A goal, I also remind you, that every one of you shares despite being non-magi. We leave the implementation of the policy up to you. If you need help, the Board stands ready to assist you." This time she sounded sincere, but I was still pissed off enough to wish she'd fall into a deep hole somewhere.

"Now, our final matter of business is a change in Board policy," Stirlaugson said. "The Board is concerned about implementation of the Accords in the daily business of the Neutralities. In the coming months, Board members will visit each node and named Neutrality for a thorough review of your business. Don't take this as a criticism; we intend only to clarify certain aspects of the Accords as they apply to practical matters. We hope you will take this opportunity to work with us to make your Neutralities the best and most effective they can be."

Lucia whispered, "Oh, yeah, *that's* not a witch hunt at all."

I was the only one who heard her. "You really think so?"

"'Thorough review'? 'Implementation of the Accords'? They're looking for reasons to come down on us, I guarantee it." Lucia leaned a little closer to me. "You'd better be careful not to let them find you stepping outside the line at all."

"I...don't know what you mean."

Lucia snorted and sat back. "Of course not."

Stirlaugson said, "Thank you, and enjoy your evening," and sat down to unenthusiastic applause. I clapped absently, my eyes on Lucia. She either knew about Malcolm, or was a really good guesser, but I didn't think I should confirm her guess, in case she needed plausible deniability or something. I remembered being stared at by all nine members of the Board, how little they cared about me personally, even Chukwu and Ragsdale. If they found out about Malcolm, it wouldn't matter that I'd saved the oracle twice; I'd be in violation of the Accords and subject to punishment. Or maybe it would matter, and saving the oracle would be enough to simply get me fired instead of executed.

I should break it off, I thought, and pain gripped my heart so powerfully I couldn't breathe for a moment. Losing Malcolm was unthinkable. But I had a duty...a duty I was convinced I could perform regardless of the rules. I'd just have to make sure they never, ever found out. *And what happens a year from now? Two years? How long do you think you can keep this relationship secret?* I realized I had my napkin wadded in a ball in my right hand and let it fall, hopelessly wrinkled, to my lap. I couldn't think about this now.

Lucia was pushing back her chair and straightening her dress, which on her looked rumpled even though it was perfectly tidy. "I'll see you in the morning," she said. "I don't feel like socializing."

"I have to check out early, to get back to the store. Isn't it a little early for sleep, though?"

Lucia gave me her familiar smile. "I don't intend to sleep," she said. "Maxwell and Henry are waiting for me."

I gulped. "Um...Maxwell *and* Henry? I, uh, always thought it was *or*."

Lucia patted my cheek, which was flaming hot again. "Don't get conventional all of a sudden, you'll rupture something," she said, and sailed out the door.

I realized I was the only one left at the table and rose, then bent to pick up my crushed napkin and set it on my plate. When I straightened, Ragsdale was there. I squeaked, and he smiled. "Sorry, I didn't mean to startle you."

"It's okay. Thank you for choosing to keep Abernathy's here."

"I shouldn't tell you, but it was a nearly unanimous decision. You can probably guess who was the lone holdout—but don't, please, because I really can't confirm or deny your guess."

"I won't. And I don't hold it against whoever it was. There were good reasons on the other side."

"Very sensible attitude. I wanted to warn you that we'll be holding your review tomorrow, immediately after the store's closing at two."

"My review? But—oh, you mean what Ms. Stirlaugson announced." I tried to make my smile look normal and not a fear-induced rictus. "Thanks for the warning. I'll be ready. Um...can you tell me what you'll be looking for?"

"We'll let you know when we arrive. Don't worry about it. I'm sure you're doing everything right."

Guilt struck me. Here was this nice man who seemed genuinely on my side, and I was lying to him. But if I couldn't tell Lucia the truth, I certainly couldn't tell Ragsdale. "Thanks. I hope you're right."

"I wish I could go to the party, but Laverne thinks it's beneath our dignity," Ragsdale said with a smile. "I just think I'd make everyone uncomfortable."

I tried to picture Ragsdale in anything but the dark suit that made him look like a banker and failed utterly. "I'm going to have a drink and then settle in for the night."

"Well, good night, Ms. Davies, and I'll see you tomorrow afternoon."

We walked together as far as the elevator, where we said good night again, and I took the stairs down to the lobby. The bar was relatively quiet; everyone else seemed to have gone to the final party, held in the Kanchenjunga room. I was settled at the bar before I remembered—

"Hey, Helena," Kevin said. "How about another Dark 'n' Stormy? No innuendo this time."

"Oh, hi, Kevin, I—" *What the hell.* "Yeah, I'd like one."

"Is it okay for me to tell you you look fantastic tonight?" Kevin slid the drink in front of me and leaned on the bar, smiling that amazing smile. I returned it weakly.

"Thanks. For the drink, too."

He leaned closer. "So, tell me more about magic."

I took an incautiously large swig of my drink and nearly choked on the rum. "Kevin, I really shouldn't—"

"Oh, come on, I haven't told anyone about you. You can trust me."

I eyed him, so eager and so cute. "It's not about trust. I don't know much about magic."

"So tell me what you do know. Are there lots of...magi, right? Lots of magi in the world."

"I don't know how many there are. More than a few."

"What can they do? Other than kill monsters that look like dogs."

"Um..." The drink was making me feel fuzzy, on top of the wine they'd served with the salmon. "Move things with their minds, set things on fire, stuff like that."

"Do they use magic words, like Harry Potter?"

"No. They just think it and it happens."

"That's so cool! Do you have to be born a magi? Could I be one?"

"No, they're not born, they undergo a ritual that turns them into a magus. But it's very dangerous and you have to be the right sort of person."

"You don't know I'm not the right sort."

"I don't know anything about it. But no, I'm not going to ask for you."

The smile vanished. "I think I deserve a little consideration, since I nearly got killed by those things last night."

"Kevin, I didn't mean—"

"I have to help this guy." He walked away toward the same elderly gentleman I'd seen the other night, the one who'd ordered a martini. The man noticed me watching and smiled pleasantly, but didn't invite me to join him. That was a relief. Custodian or not, he had to be well over sixty and had no business picking up young women in bars. Or maybe he did. Who was I to dictate who people could be attracted to?

I sipped my drink and let my thoughts float free. Hopefully, Malcolm would come to me tonight. I could really use the company, even if there was no sex. What was the Board looking for, anyway? Maybe tomorrow they'd find out the truth, and nothing else would matter. I hoped they didn't. As stressful as keeping this secret was, it beat whatever punishment the Board might inflict on me.

"So," Kevin said, startling me, "you don't have to be born a magi—"

"Magus is singular. Magi is plural."

"Got it. You don't have to be born a magus, and there's a ritual that makes you one. Why aren't you a magus?"

I glanced around. There wasn't anyone close enough to hear our conversation, not even the custodian with his martini, but Kevin had pitched his voice low anyway, and I matched him. "For what I do, you're not allowed to be a magus."

"Selling magic books."

"Sort of. You ask a question, and I find you a book that contains the answer."

"I can't believe that's even possible. I'm not calling you a liar, it's just a really big thing to believe."

"I know what you mean. That's how I felt when I found out about it."

"You haven't done this your whole life?"

"No, just over a year."

Kevin began polishing the bar. "I don't get why you can't be a magus for that."

"It's so I won't be swayed to use the auguries for myself. I have to be impartial."

"You've never bought a book?"

"No."

"That sucks. What if you wanted to know something important? Like if you should dump your mysterious, absent boyfriend for a charming, hot bartender?"

His gorgeous smile charmed one out of me. "I'd just have to make that decision for myself."

He made a piteous face, and I laughed. "And I'm afraid you're out of luck," I added.

"I know. I'm just teasing. You want another drink? Though I'm not trying to get you drunk."

I realized my glass was almost empty. "No, I think I've reached my limit. Thanks anyway."

"No problem. Hey, Helena? Can I come by your store sometime? Just to say hi."

That can't make things worse than they already are, right? "Sure, why not?" I gave him the address and let him kiss my cheek in farewell.

In the elevator, I kicked off my shoes and rubbed one foot against my shin. If I was truly lucky, Malcolm would be waiting in my room. The thought made me nervous and excited all at once. I still didn't think forbidden sex was better when you were surrounded by people who could have you fired for it, or worse, but having him near always thrilled me. Mostly I just wanted to see him, to snuggle up in his arms and rejoice in the fact that I wasn't moving to London. I wanted to be able to talk to him as I'd done for so many nights on the phone, or curl up together and watch a movie. I wasn't a very exciting person, was I?

My suite was empty when I reached it, dangling my shoes in one hand and my little clutch in the other. Disappointed, I hung up my dress and sweater and put on my pajamas, washed my face and brushed my teeth and did all the other little bedtime rituals. It was almost ten, a little too early for bed but not early enough for a movie. Well, morning would come soon enough, and I had to work tomorrow.

I exited the bathroom and stopped, stunned. Malcolm lay in my bed, his arms casually behind his head, completely naked. He smiled at my reaction, a slow, wicked smile, and said, "I think your wardrobe is inappropriate for what I have in mind."

I climbed into bed and put my arms around him. "If that's so," I said, "maybe you should show me what I ought to be wearing."

He rolled me onto my back and began unbuttoning my pajama shirt. "Pay attention," he whispered. "There might be a test."

17

I rolled my luggage down the hall toward the elevator. I'd said goodbye to Malcolm sometime just before dawn. It had been the most glorious night, sex and cuddling and a lot of talking, and I'd probably only gotten four hours of sleep, but it had been worth it. And I could nap this afternoon, after the Board was finished with their assessment of my rigorous attention to the Accords, or whatever they had in mind.

I felt cheerful overall. I'd spent the night with the man I loved, I didn't have to uproot my life to follow the store across the Atlantic, and it was Christmas Eve day and I was getting off work early. I said "Merry Christmas" to the nice lady at the registration desk when I handed her my key cards and suppressed the urge to warn her there was a bypass to the locks. I checked the bar, but of course Kevin wasn't in yet. I was too cheerful to feel guilty about having told him things about magery. Besides, who would believe him if he said anything?

I saw Carlos coming out of the elevator and went to greet him. "You're leaving now?"

"My flight leaves in seven hours, but I intend to do my waiting at the airport. Too many memories here."

That killed my cheerfulness dead. "I'm so sorry. I liked Elisabeta a lot."

"So did everyone. Her node will be so different without her."

"I heard her husband is the new custodian. Will that..."

Carlos smiled. "Will it be a problem for me? Perhaps. But Andrei is a good man, and I hope to remember our shared affection rather than any potential awkwardness." He clapped me on the shoulder. "Farewell, Helena Davies, and I look forward to seeing you in three years."

I waved as he left the hotel, then wheeled my luggage toward the door. Someone called my name, and I looked through the door of the restaurant to see Claude, Iakkhos, Diane, and Nimisha seated at a table. "Come, join us," Claude said.

"I was going to have something at home. I have to open the store at ten."

"Your work ethic shames me," Claude said. "Sit and eat a muffin. The store is not going to disappear."

I checked the time—still early—and decided I could afford time for breakfast. The waffle lady served me a waffle heaped high with strawberries in syrup, and I sat in the chair Diane dragged away from a nearby table and poured myself a cup of coffee.

"Iakkhos, you look better," I said, taking a bite.

"I'm still weak, but I survive," Iakkhos said. "But I have to fly back to Crete. Ward-stepping is too hard on my heart."

"I'm sorry." At that moment I felt slightly guilty at being so happy the oracle was staying in Portland; a flight from London to Crete wouldn't be nearly so taxing.

Iakkhos shrugged. "It is what it is. I fly first class, at least, and have plenty of flight attendants to meet my every whim. I have the hardest time not calling them stewardesses, you know."

"You're old enough to be allowed a little slip," Diane said. "I wish this weren't the only time we all can get together. I miss these conversations."

"I will likely not see you again," Nimisha said. "Samudra chooses a different representative every time."

"That's too bad," I said, and meant it. Nimisha's prickliness had grown on me. "What will you do when you return to the Sanctuary?"

"Teach Wardens how to meditate. Guide them through the process of gaining a vision. Learn in the hopes of someday taking Samudra's place—not that anyone wishes him ill, but being the custodian of the Sanctuary is worth aspiring to."

"I understand."

"I'll have a lot to do when I get back," Diane said. "I can't believe they're making us fly out on Christmas Eve. The airport's going to be a nightmare. But I'm going to put all my responsibilities off until Monday. You're way more responsible than I am, Helena, if you're not just closing Abernathy's for the day."

"The Board is coming to review my compliance with the Accords. I don't think I should close up shop when that happens."

Diane and Claude exchanged glances. "That's...sudden," Diane said. "Did they say why so soon?"

"No, but all the Board members are in town, and I imagine it seemed like a waste of time to leave and then come back again. I don't mind. I'd rather get it over with."

"I am certain you have nothing to fear," Claude said, patting my hand. "I only wish the Board could be clearer about what it is they are looking for. As it is, it feels like they do not trust us."

That had been my feeling, as well. "Mr. Ragsdale seemed casual about it when he spoke to me last night," I said. "Maybe they're just checking on certain provisions of the Accords that people always let slip."

"Or they've got a few questions that will test our impartiality," Iakkhos said. "What's the saying—the innocent have nothing to fear from the police? I'm not sure how true that is, but it's a comforting idea."

"If you're innocent," Diane said. She looked out the window and frowned. "I'm never going to be able to look at dogs like that again."

I followed her gaze to where a tiny woman was walking a Doberman pinscher in front of the hotel restaurant. "That's right, they all looked like dogs to you. Be glad you can't see the real thing."

"You were wearing your monocle that night? I took mine off," said Diane.

"No, Helena can see through illusions. It is her gift as custodian of Abernathy's," Claude said.

"Huh," Diane said. "Are you sure about that? Nathaniel couldn't see through illusions."

I blinked. "How do you know that?"

"Because he needed the monocle last conference, and it didn't give him that headache or whatever it was you had that first night."

I looked at Claude, who seemed as baffled as I was. "Well, I'm sure I couldn't see through illusions before," I said, "so what else could it be?" But I wasn't so sure. When would I have had the chance to test that theory?

"I'm sure it's something to do with Abernathy's," Diane said. "It's just strange, that's all."

More than strange. I took a final bite of waffle and stood. "I have to be going. It was so nice to meet you all—there really should be a way to keep in touch—"

"Email," said Iakkhos. "Here, I'll text mine to you. What, you think because I'm a hundred and two I don't keep up with technology trends?"

There was a flurry of texting, then I hugged everyone, reserving a specially long one for Iakkhos, who looked at me as if he knew why. Then I waved goodbye and hauled my suitcase out of the restaurant. As I left, I saw Lucia at the front desk, flanked by Dave Henry and Martin Maxwell. I carefully didn't meet anyone's eye. Lucia and Dave and Martin were all grownups, and if they were satisfied with their unorthodox relationship, I wasn't going to criticize. It just made me feel uncomfortable.

The day was crisply cold and bright the way the sun gets before a storm. I drove east, taking the surface streets even though the freeway wouldn't be terribly congested on a Saturday morning. A Saturday Christmas Eve morning, on the other hand, might be a problem. I hummed along with the radio and ran over my plans in my head. Judy and I needed to discuss the new Ambrosite-Nicollien policy—

specifically, our two holdouts Malcolm and Jeremiah needed to know they now had to abide by the faction leaders' guidelines. I should deal with the mail-in auguries that had piled up over the last couple of days. I had Judy's gift to give her, and it wasn't something she could take home. Then the Board, ugh, but when they were gone, I was free to go to my parents' house for Christmas. This was going to be a great day.

I reached the store right around 9:30 and parked in back, hauling my luggage up the flight of stairs to my apartment. It still smelled of cinnamon and pine from the wreath I'd hung on the door. The scent followed me all the way back down the stairs and into the store, where it competed with the smell of fresh apples Abernathy's had chosen for the day. Judy wasn't in yet, so I sorted through the pile of the previous days' mail on my desk. All auguries—looked like Judy had gone through it for payments and junk mail first. I decided to get an early start on the day and picked up the first envelope.

Judy arrived at ten 'til and went straight to the break room to shed her coat and hat. "Harry's going to be all right," she called out. "They're not sure if he's still a magus, because he's not allowed to use magic while he's recovering. But he says he's just happy to be alive."

"You spoke to him?"

"Last night. They want us to come to dinner after the first of the year, when he's allowed visitors again. Lucas isn't taking any chances." She came to stand in the office doorway. "So, how was your first conference?"

"Interesting. Overwhelming. Almost disastrous. I doubt it was normal, as conferences go. I made some friends and a couple of enemies."

"Rebecca Greenough, huh? Lucia always spits when she says her name."

"She lost, though."

Judy came into the office. "Lost, how?"

"She wanted them to move Abernathy's to London."

Judy's mouth fell open. "They—why didn't you tell me?"

"There was a lot going on. And by the time I wasn't busy or

fighting off familiars trying to rip my throat out, it would have just worried you for nothing. I'm sorry."

"You're sorry." Judy scowled, but her heart wasn't in it. "So I take it we're not moving."

"It might not have been us. She also wanted them to appoint a Londoner as custodian."

"Helena, *stop keeping things from me!*"

"I'm sorry! Look, I have your present here. Will that be enough of an apology?"

Judy shrugged. "Depends on the present."

"I hope you like it."

I opened the bottom drawer of my desk and removed a sheet of paper, folded in thirds. "I was going to wrap it, but that would just have looked stupid...here."

Judy took it from me and unfolded it. She went very still. "This is an employment agreement," she said. "For Abernathy's."

"It took me a while to find the green ink. And I'm sorry it's not pretty. My handwriting sucks." I took a pen out of the top drawer and offered it to her. "You should read it. And then you sign *here* and *here*."

Judy held the paper loosely, her eyes focused on something beyond it. "You want me to be your successor."

"Well...yeah. Of course. And after what I've been through...I mean, I planned it a few weeks ago, but with all those custodians dying, I realized how important it was that the oracle pass from me to someone else as smoothly as possible. If that became necessary. And I want the someone to be you."

Judy blinked. Something sparkled on her long eyelashes. "All right," she said, and laid it flat on the desk top, leaning over it. She held out her hand for the pen, and signed swiftly in both places.

I countersigned on the line below her signature and folded the paper, put it away in the desk, and let out a deep breath. "I hope that wasn't a dumb present. I mean, you don't exactly get to take it home with you."

"It's not a dumb present. It's a *great* present." Judy swiped at her eyes. "I just got you those earrings you liked."

"That's a great present too," I said, and hugged her. Judy hugged me back. She was getting better at displaying affection.

Someone knocked on the front door, and we broke apart, laughing. "I'll go let them in, while you finish sorting through those augury requests," Judy said. "Here's hoping everyone stays home today."

There were only a few Nicolliens that morning, and I flew through their auguries in no time, leaving me free to work through the mail. The fifth one I opened made me laugh. "Look at this," I said to Judy. The augury request was simple, written in a powerful, blocky hand: *When will my sister come to visit?* Next to it was a stick figure drawing of a woman with an enormous pregnant belly. *I've got two months to go and already I feel like I'm going to pop,* Cynthia had written below it. *No augury request, just wishing you a Merry Christmas, and I'll talk to you Sunday.*

"I wish I could visit," I said. "I love this job, but it has limitations."

"I understand." Judy put the ledger away under the antique cash register. "She'll just have to come to you."

"Someday. I want to see my niece in person."

Snow began falling around 12:30, completing the picture of a perfect Christmas. Viv texted me just after that: BRINGING FOOD YOU GET THE DRINKS, so I sent Judy to the market for Cokes and settled in on the stool behind the counter, admiring our Munchkin Christmas tree and how the snow gathered in the corners of the windows.

We ate Chinese takeout at the counter, which was smooth and clear without a single chip—my Christmas present to Abernathy's. "So what exactly does the Board want?" Viv said.

I slurped up a noodle. "I have no idea. Accords compliance, probably."

"Tell me that doesn't fill you with dread," Judy said.

"It does. But I'm not admitting to anything, and if they do find out, I'll defend myself. I know what the Accords has to say about my romantic situation."

"Really? What?"

I ate another noodle. "It says 'Don't.'"

"There has to be more detail than that," Viv said.

"All I know is it says specifically that romantic relationships are against the Accords. But it doesn't say anything about close friendships, and I think those are at least as potentially problematic as romance. Mr. Briggs was killed because he wouldn't falsify an augury for a friend, but he could just as easily have agreed to do it. If I have to, I'll use that as my defense."

"Let's just hope you don't have to," Viv said. "I don't know, Hel. I've never met a man I was willing to risk everything for. I don't know if you're lucky or just insane."

"What about Jeremiah?" Judy said with a smirk.

"What about him?"

"Oh, Helena, she's *blushing*."

"All right, so I like Jeremiah. But I don't know him well yet at all."

"Did he kiss you yet?" I asked. "Oh, wow, you're blushing *harder*. Who are you, and what have you done with the real Genevieve Haley?"

"I don't know!" Viv exclaimed. "I feel like I'm thirteen again and having my first crush. He's just so *different*. It's like we could talk for hours and I'd just learn more things I want to know about him. He's not even my type!"

"I think types are overrated," Judy said. She took a drink of her Diet Coke and added, "They're just a way to narrow the field. Sometimes you find someone you never would have thought to look for, and he's the one."

"Says you," said Viv. "Are you even dating? What's *your* type?"

"I'm currently unattached. And my type is Chris Hemsworth."

"He's like five feet taller than you."

"So? Everyone's taller than me. I might as well embrace it."

"Chris Hemsworth is pretty hot," I said. "Not as hot as Malcolm."

"Says the loyal girlfriend," Viv said.

"No, I agree that Campbell's hot, even though he gets on my nerves. No offense."

"None taken."

"So we just have to find a Chris Hemsworth look-alike for Judy, and we can all settle down into relationship bliss," Viv said.

"Actually, there was someone," Judy said, a little too casually. "Someone who works for Father."

"There was? What do you mean 'was'?" Viv said, leaning over eagerly.

"She means she came to work here," I said. "You're not a custodian. You don't have to worry about the Accords."

"Employees of Neutralities are still subject to the Accords. They're maybe not as strict, but...I take my loyalties seriously. And I decided to call it off."

I felt like the biggest jerk in the universe. "Judy, I'm sorry."

"It wasn't serious. There wasn't time for it to be serious." She wasn't meeting anyone's eyes.

"Then...all those times you warned me about Malcolm...Judy, I'm *really* sorry."

Judy shook her head. "You didn't get how serious your rule breaking was at first," she said. "And then...it was obvious what you had was more than a crush. So if you're thinking I was resentful that you were doing what I wished I could do, stop. Yes, I wish I hadn't had to break it off, but he wasn't someone I cared enough about to risk my freedom or even my life for. And I never resented you."

I stabbed my chopsticks into what remained of the noodles and said, "The Accords—"

"Govern our lives," Judy said. "Don't start thinking otherwise. They don't change for people like us."

"Then who else should they change for?" Viv said. "It's not just about the unfairness. If the Accords really do need to change, how is it right that they only change if the Board thinks they should?"

"If they can be changed at a whim, they're not powerful enough to bind us," Judy said, "and they need to be powerful to keep the factions from tearing magery apart."

"That's true," I said, "but I wish I felt that the Board always has magery's best interests at heart. They're just nine people who have their own preferences and beliefs. Do you know Harrison was the only one who voted against keeping Abernathy's here? And he probably only did that because he's pals with Rebecca Greenough. So the same logic that convinced everyone else wasn't enough to override his self-interest."

"How do you know it was Harrison?"

"I don't, exactly, but Mr. Ragsdale implied it strongly." I let out a sigh. "It doesn't matter. Either they find out about me and Malcolm this afternoon, or they don't, and there's nothing I can do except keep my secrets as best I can and pray they aren't omniscient."

Viv left after giving us both presents, me a turquoise sweater with a three-quarter-length sleeve, perfectly matching my favorite bracelet —"It's not your color, but I'm never going to convince you of that," she said—and Judy a vintage choker she put on immediately. A few more magi came in, not many, and by 1:30 I told Judy she should go home. She didn't argue.

Snow fell more heavily now, turning the world gray, and I sat on the stool and watched the flakes fall. I couldn't remember the last time it had snowed this heavily in December, and I dreaded the moment I'd have to get out on the roads to go to my parents' house. But it was hard to feel unhappy when the world was so beautiful. I checked the time. 1:45. Maybe I could close up early.

The door swung open, setting the merry bells jingling. "This is a hard place to find," Kevin said, brushing snow off his hat and coat.

"What are you doing here? I was about to close up."

"Then I'm glad I made it. I wanted to see where you work." Kevin took a few steps toward the nearest bookshelf. "I pictured something a little more magical."

"The magic is all hidden. If it looked magical, everyone would notice it."

"That makes sense. These books aren't in any kind of order. Don't you have anything by Stephen King?"

"I don't know. It doesn't work like that."

"Okay, so how does it work?"

"Kevin—"

"Come on, Helena, I just want to know more. That's not against the rules, is it?"

What was probably against the rules was telling a complete stranger the details of how Abernathy's worked. At least when I'd revealed its secrets to my sister Cynthia, I'd known and (mostly) trusted her. *Well, at the risk of being classist, what are the odds a bartender can afford an augury?* As if I had any idea how much bartenders made. I might be making a huge mistake.

"People write down questions," I said. "The store won't answer every question, like nothing beginning with 'who?'"

"Why not?"

"I don't know. And it won't help you commit a crime. But everything else, they give to me, and I go in there and find the book the store chooses to answer the question."

"So is it, like, a riddle? Or does the title answer the question?"

"Neither. You're supposed to study the book, and it reveals the answer."

"Are they expensive?"

"They can be. Usually they're around a thousand dollars."

Kevin whistled. "That's a lot. But I guess if you're predicting the future, it's worth it."

"That's how people feel about it, yes."

"So do an...an augury for me."

"I can't do that."

Kevin took a few steps closer to me. "Why not? I can pay, if that's what you're asking."

"I...don't think I'm supposed to do it for someone who's not a magus." That wasn't true. I just felt uneasy, like I'd already told him too much.

"Just once. Then I'll leave. I won't even come back, if that's what you want. Though I'd like to see you again."

"I told you, I have a boyfriend."

"Not like that. You're interesting and you're part of an interesting world."

"I just don't think I should."

"I won't tell anyone. *You* won't tell anyone."

"That wouldn't make it right."

"Are you afraid the Board will find out? You think Stirlaugson will punish you? She doesn't have to know."

"That's not—" I stopped. "Where did you hear those names?"

Kevin smiled at me, cocking his head to one side. "Now, what you should be asking yourself, Helena," he said, "is, did I slip up, or did I say those words on purpose?"

He took another step toward me. I stepped backward and bumped into the counter. My face and hands felt numb with fear. "Don't come any closer," I said, fumbling for my phone.

"I'll break your phone if you touch it," Kevin said, smiling more broadly. Black streaks like ink in water swirled across his teeth, and when he blinked, his eyes were solid black. "I think you and I should talk, just the two of us. After all, I went to a lot of trouble to reach you."

I swallowed, and said, "What are you?"

18

$\mathcal{K}$evin's mouth stretched wider, too wide for a human body. More black streaks swirled across his lips and gums. "You *are* clever," he said. "'What' is the right question. I'm wearing poor Kevin like an ill-fitting suit, for one. For the rest—you tell me what I am."

I cast my mind back three days, to Claude's abbreviated keynote address. "You're an invader," I whispered. "You're one of the intelligent ones, the ones they tried to communicate with centuries ago."

The Kevin-thing applauded. "Obviously we don't call ourselves invaders, but we'll go with your terminology for now. Now, why do you think I'm here?"

"You want to destroy the oracle."

It shook its head. "I could have done that when I first entered, if that's all I wanted. This body is a good shield against Abernathy's wards, lets me enter the store when I'd bounce right off them in my natural form. If I were to crawl out of my Kevin suit here, it would trigger the wards explosively, taking you and me and, unfortunately, the oracle with it. No, it's not the oracle's death I want. It's you."

I slid sideways along the counter, trying to get away from the Kevin-thing. "Me? Why me?"

"For that, I have to tell you a story. Do you mind?"

I shook my head. Maybe if I could get behind the counter, I could pull my phone out without it noticing, and...do what? I couldn't call someone without having to look at the screen. For the first time I missed the phone I'd had in middle school, with its raised buttons and complete lack of internet access.

It saw me moving but did nothing to stop me. In fact, it smiled again, as if I were some kind of precocious pet. "This story begins several hundred years ago, when my people first entered your world. It's a beautiful world, don't you think? So rich in all kinds of life. Now, I don't know what the Wardens have told you about us, but I guarantee you it's wrong in at least one respect—we don't want to drain your world of all its magic. That would make you useless to us. We just want to be able to share it. A few people, here and there, nothing really."

"Not to those people," I said, and put myself behind the counter.

"I like you, Helena. You're spunky. Do people still use that word? I haven't been in your world for many years, so I don't know what the right terminology is. Kevin doesn't seem to know it, so maybe it's outdated."

"You know his thoughts? Is he...alive in there?"

The Kevin-thing looked sorrowful. "I'm afraid not. There's really only room for one person in these meat sacks you call bodies, and Kevin had to make way for me. But I get some of his memories—do you have *any* idea how much mental space he had devoted to mixed drinks? It's really fascinating. Too bad the body starts to degrade over time. I enjoyed being a bartender for a while."

"When did you kill him? This morning?" The idea that I'd been talking to this...thing...the whole time I'd thought it was Kevin—it had *kissed* me—

"No, it was Wednesday morning. Well before the wards sealed everyone in. Did you like my impression of a terrified young man, faced with horrible monsters?" A snarl crossed its face. "I should make you pay for what you did to my poor idiot cousins who never did a thing to hurt you."

"What?" I shouted. "They would have killed me!"

It made a dismissive gesture, and I saw Kevin's nail beds were black and oozing. "Technicalities. They're hungry, they need magic to survive just like you do—would you deny them their natures?"

"What do you mean, cousins? Aren't you all the same?"

"The...invaders...you Wardens fight are as close to being like me as a chimpanzee is to being like you. Which isn't to say I feel loyalty toward them the way I do toward my own kind, but you'd fight to defend a chimpanzee that was about to be destroyed, wouldn't you?"

"I don't know. If it were hurting someone, probably not."

"It's irrelevant. The point is the story. Should I go on?"

I nodded. My mouth was dry, my palms were itchy and sweaty, but the urge to know was more powerful.

"As I said, we're not interested in draining your world, all you humans, of your magic. But the Wardens, most of them, don't want to compromise. They'd rather see your world die than coexist with us."

"Because you kill people to survive." Then something struck me. "What do you mean, most of them?"

"*Very* clever." Its hands clapped again, slowly. "You've met a few of our allies. Thwarted a few of our allies. I'm sorry to say we did try to destroy the oracle once, with that origami illusion, but I promise you it was only a test—we wanted to see what kind of woman the new custodian was."

"But—we had proof Matt McKanley had a grudge against the oracle. He wasn't one of your allies."

"He was, actually. It's true he wanted revenge on the oracle, but we gave him the idea. It was unfortunate he had to die, but we couldn't allow him to reveal the truth. You surprised us. We realized you were someone to watch, though we didn't expect it would be you who discovered Mitch Hallstrom and stopped him harvesting *sanguinis sapiens* for his fellows."

"Hallstrom was one of you?" I remembered how he'd laid his hand across my belly and wanted to throw up.

The Kevin-thing looked aghast. "Oh, no, we didn't wear Hallstrom," it said. "He was one of our human allies. We don't like wasting your kind. And Hallstrom was rather stupid, and it's unpleasant to take on a stupid human. All the memories are so dull. My point is, there are Wardens who've seen the light, so to speak, and we and they work together to bring this Long War to an end."

"Then what do you want from me?"

"What I said. I want an augury."

I shook my head vigorously. "No. No way in hell am I doing an augury for you."

"Why not? Don't the Accords state you have to accept an augury request from anyone who can pay?"

"The Accords don't include you. They're meant for fighting things like you."

"Ah, Helena. Sweet Helena. What makes you think you haven't already given auguries for things like me?"

It was like a brick to the face. "I," I began, but couldn't find words to finish. I'd had no clue Kevin wasn't human anymore until the thing revealed itself. So much for my perceptiveness. "Well, I know now, and I'm refusing."

It stepped closer. I could smell its breath, hot and stinking of rotten flesh. "What if it's an augury that benefits both of us?"

"How?"

"A simple question. 'Who will win the Long War?'"

"It won't answer questions beginning with 'who,'" I said, feeling bolstered by this little slip.

"Interesting. What about, 'What action will bring the Wardens success in the coming year?'"

I swallowed and tried to close my nose against the stink. "That still benefits you. It will tell you what to do to stop that action. I'm not going to betray my friends by helping you."

"It's not a betrayal. Helena, I wish I could convince you of my sincerity. I don't want to hurt you. I just want you to work for the winning side. Because I promise you, *we are winning.* Your Wardens fight a losing battle against the small creatures you call invaders— there are millions of them, Helena, millions upon millions, all of them slavering to access your world even for a few minutes. We don't have to attack you. We just have to wait."

"So what you want," I said, "is for us to capitulate. You'll take a few humans here and there, and the rest of us will be...what? Cattle?"

"Hardly that. We consider human intellect a valuable resource. We've even been known to have friends among your kind."

I came out from around the counter. It felt like shelter, but really it was a trap. Could I make it to the front door? No, I'd have to run past the Kevin-thing, and it would catch me and probably kill me. The back door was farther away, but I knew the path through the bookcases, and I had a small chance going that way. The Kevin-thing smiled at me as I emerged. Probably it thought I'd given up. Well, that wasn't going to happen.

"Who decides who lives and who dies?" I asked. "Is there a lottery? Or do you take only criminals?"

The black eyes glistened. "That's an interesting idea. I'm not sure anyone's ever thought of that. Would that be acceptable to you? Let us rid you of your criminal element, and everyone else lives free and happy?"

I shifted my stance, ready to run. "I've seen people killed by your kind," I said. "It's not a death I'd wish—"

The door opened. The Kevin-thing half-turned in response. I almost ran. It was the perfect opportunity. But I couldn't leave whoever this newcomer was alone with the monstrous creature.

Instead, I shoved the Kevin-thing, hooking his ankle with my foot to make him lose his balance. Half-turned as he was, he went down hard. "Help me, he's a—a robber!" I shouted, then felt like an idiot, because what I needed was to get it out of the store before it decided to leave Kevin's body and make the whole place explode.

The Kevin-thing shoved me away and began to rise. "*Help!*" I screamed, tackling it again.

I was suddenly surrounded by the members of the Board of Neutralities. Hands dragged me away from the thing. "A robber?" Stirlaugson said. "That seems oddly—"

The Kevin-thing's mouth opened widely, and black tendrils

emerged from it. *"Get it outside!"* I shrieked. "Don't ask questions, just do it!"

Four of the Board members grabbed the thing and hustled it through the door, throwing it to the pavement. "Inside, inside," I gasped, and shut the door and threw home the dead bolt. I leaned against the door, too spent to worry about whether the Kevin-thing had the means to break through it.

I heard gasps, and swearing, and looked up in time to see something black and angular emerge from the Kevin-thing's mouth. It had waving tentacles where its mouth should be, and the back of its head came to a wicked point. Eight multi-jointed legs that ended in spikes pulled free of what was left of Kevin's head. Black vapor pooled beneath it, rising up from its chitinous skin and melting the snowflakes that touched it. It had a dozen eyes like beads of blood, lidless and filled with a terrible intelligent menace, that it turned on me. It couldn't have smiled, not with that mouth, but I could swear it was laughing as it looked at me. *"You'll have one more chance, custodian,"* it said in a voice that hit every one of my primal panic buttons. *"One more, when all hope is lost. Remember."*

It turned and took a few steps toward the market, but before it could go farther, it shimmered like it was passing through an oil slick. It hurt to look at it, but I squinted and saw it flatten out into a two-dimensional caricature of itself, then fold like the most complicated origami I could imagine. Then it was gone, and snowflakes began to drift into the space where it had been. Kevin's body, which looked like an empty, distorted suit now, lay on the pavement in front of my door.

"Thanks," I said to the air, not sure how I was going to explain this to the Board.

There was silence. I turned around to find them all looking at me with...was it pity, or shame? Either way, it made no sense. "We should probably get Kevin's body before someone notices it," I said.

"Tim, Erich, see to it," Stirlaugson said, and Ragsdale and Harrison opened the door and hoisted Kevin's body back inside. I hovered nearby, just in case the invader was still there and hiding well, but nothing happened. Ragsdale turned the dead bolt again and, as an afterthought, turned the sign to say CLOSED.

We all stood there in silence, me feeling exhausted and terrified and confused. Why weren't they asking questions? *I'd* ask questions if I were them.

Finally, Stirlaugson said, "The Board wishes to apologize to you, Ms. Davies. We had no idea they would act so quickly or decisively."

That confused me more. "What are you talking about? Are you saying you *expected* this?"

Stirlaugson sighed and sat on the metal chair just inside the door, wobbling a bit. "We didn't intend to tell you anything," she said. "The point of this visit was to determine if you'd already been corrupted. If not, you need never know the danger; if so, we were prepared to...deal with you."

"I don't understand. Corrupted how? You mean, how that thing wanted me to work for it?"

"Exactly."

"And you knew it would try something like that. You know about the Wardens who work with the invaders. Why haven't you told anyone?"

Stirlaugson looked at Ragsdale, who was wiping his hands on a handkerchief that looked just like the ones Malcolm carried. "The night the familiars attacked the hotel," he said, "the Board was... visited...by an invader who wore human form. It told us of the invaders' alliance with a handful—maybe more than a handful—of Wardens, how they'd been working with them for centuries. It laid out their plan for conquering the world and invited us to join them. I apologize for how distant I sounded when we spoke, but it threatened to...discorporate...as that one would have, destroying the hotel and killing everyone in it, if I gave its presence away."

"That's why you couldn't come down. Not the familiars, but one of them. How did you escape it?"

Ragsdale smiled. "We're more physically competent than we appear. We subdued it long enough to get it out of the hotel before it could injure anyone. Then we set about doing damage control."

"They let the familiars into the hotel! No—were they behind the bindings failing in the first place?"

"They were not. That was a simple flaw in the Nicollien binding. They just took advantage of it."

"What do you mean by 'damage control'?"

"We have no way of knowing which Wardens are in league with the invaders," Stirlaugson said. "We began by interrogating the magi who created the flawed wards, to see if they had done it on purpose. During the interrogation, we rendered them unconscious and conducted a thorough physical. We hoped to find some alteration in their bodies that would indicate they had accepted the invaders' promises. It was something our visitor had implied might exist."

"You didn't find anything."

"We found *something*," said the red-headed Board member, "but it occurs naturally in perhaps one out of three humans. Hardly conclusive."

"But something to go on," said Harrison. He seemed not at all antagonistic toward me now.

"Wait," I said, "you're not magi. How could you conduct that kind of physical? Because I'm sure it was more complicated than checking their pupil dilation."

"We enlisted Lucia Pontarelli's aid. She's loyal to us, and has proved that loyalty time and again." Harrison wouldn't meet my eyes.

"But—I have faith in Lucia, but how could you be sure she wasn't a traitor? You can't trust anyone!"

"At some point we simply have to act on faith," Stirlaugson said. "We are cleaning house, Ms. Davies, beginning with the Neutralities, and we hope to do so quickly, before knowledge of this...this shadow cabal spreads."

"You have to tell people."

"And do what? Incite riots as Nicollien and Ambrosite go to war, this time over a real threat? If you have a better solution, we're listening."

I shook my head. "I understand. Nobody will be able to trust anybody else. The factions will be even more divided than they already are. You want to figure out who's really on our side and get as many allies as you can before the war begins, so you'll have people you can trust."

"Which is why we're going to ask you not to tell anyone about this," Stirlaugson said.

"What...no one? You can't expect me to keep this a secret from Judy!"

"Judy Rasmussen's loyalties are already strained. She might be innocent, but she might also feel obligated to tell her father. And we are by no means sure that William Rasmussen is not a member of the shadow cabal."

"I trust Judy with my life."

"We appreciate that. Nevertheless, you will not tell her. We will let you know when you're allowed to speak."

"But—"

"Consider yourself bound by the Accords, Ms. Davies." Stirlaugson stood and brushed off her skirt. "We intend to find a way to identify traitors, and when that happens, secrecy will no longer matter. Until then, hold your tongue."

I nodded, feeling mulish. I couldn't tell Judy. I couldn't warn Malcolm that his allies might be traitors...oh, no, *Malcolm* couldn't be one of them, could he? I thought of how he'd looked every time I'd seen him fighting invaders. No. It was impossible. But I'd promised not to tell, and I had to stay quiet. This really was a violation of the Accords that would see me executed.

The nine members of the Board closed in around me. It felt menacing, and I readied myself to fight free of them. But they just offered their hands for me to shake, one at a time. Ragsdale looked at me with compassion, when it was his turn, and Chukwu nodded to me as to an equal. Stirlaugson was last, and she held onto my hand when I would have let go and said, "We know what we're asking of you. We honor you for keeping the secret."

"Thank you."

"We'll leave by the back way." Stirlaugson pulled out her phone and turned away to hold a short conversation with whoever was on the other end. "Some of you, bring the body. We'll dispose of it. He can't ever be found, not looking like that."

Kevin did look like an empty skin, deflated and torn, and I swallowed around another lump in my throat, remembering the cheerful, flirtatious guy I'd met that first night. I didn't want to know if he'd died in pain.

I showed them the back way out, then locked the door behind them and trod slowly upstairs to my apartment. I kicked off my shoes and sat on my couch with the lights turned off. It was still afternoon, but the heavy snowfall turned the light gray and made everything look dismal and dull. I curled into a ball and shook uncontrollably. This was too great a disaster for tears. I'd come face to face with death, but that wasn't what terrified me. It was the knowledge that likely somebody I knew was a traitor to the Wardens' cause. Someone I knew thought that invader, with its smooth speech and gentle logic, was right, and a few humans could and should be sacrificed for the sake of the rest of humanity.

I shook, tearless, until my body calmed enough that I could stand and walk to the window. I looked down at the spot where Kevin's body had lain, where the invader had disappeared like folded paper, and tried to breathe normally. The Board would figure something out. They were ruthless and committed to the truth.

Unless one of them is a traitor, too.

Why would the invaders make a move now, if they'd had centuries to infiltrate magery? The Kevin-thing had implied it had something to do with me—that they'd wanted to test me, see if I could hold strong and keep the oracle alive. That didn't make it my fault, but it made me utterly determined to fight them. "I won't let you win," I whispered, and my words echoed in the stillness of my apartment. "I won't let you win."

19

*W*hen I was younger, our family living room had always looked like a disaster area at ten o'clock Christmas morning—wrapping strewn everywhere, toys stacked up in our separate corners like a three-way game of Jenga. Now it looked more sedate, though the piles were still there, smaller piles now that Tickle Me Elmo wasn't a likely gift. "Maybe we can get Cynthia and Ethan out here next year," I said, dangling my new watch by its strap and watching the Christmas lights on the tree reflect in its face. "It would be fun to have a baby around."

"She won't be even a year old yet," Mom said. "Not old enough to really have fun with Christmas. Give it a year or so."

"I can't believe I'm going to be a grandpa this time next year," Dad groaned. He was lying on the couch with his eyes closed and the Sunday newspaper tented over his chest. "I'm too young for this."

"Cynthia's twenty-six. That's not too young."

"I didn't say *she* was too young, I said *I* was too young. I'm barely thirty."

"Mentally, you're six," Jake said. Dad threw a ball of crumpled wrapping paper at him, but it fell short by a foot.

"I have to check the turkey," Mom said. "And the potatoes."

"She's barbecuing it," Jake whispered when she'd left. "Barbecuing Christmas turkey. That's got to be a crime."

"Come on. If Mom's doing it, it will be great," I said, though secretly I had reservations. I'd never gotten the deep-frying craze, and barbecuing seemed like just one more wacky experiment that had huge potential for disaster.

Jake shrugged and pushed himself upright. "I'm going to put my loot away and sleep until dinner. Lunch. Whatever it is when you have Christmas dinner at noon."

I strapped the watch to my wrist. No more fumbling for my phone to check the time. It was a vintage piece my parents had found for me, and I loved it. "Dad, don't sleep on the couch. You know Mom hates it when you do that."

"If I sleep, she can't find things for me to do," Dad said, but he sat up and folded the paper. "You still liking that job of yours?"

"I love it. I'm so glad you still read the actual newspaper, or I never would have found it."

"I just can't believe it put you in danger. When we learned you'd been in that hotel where the wild dogs attacked...that's the weirdest thing I've ever heard of."

"It was scary. I'm just glad so few people were hurt." The lie hurt, like denying my colleagues' suffering, but what else could I say?

"You must have been terrified. You've always been afraid of big dogs," Mom said, coming into the room with an apron in her hand. "Ever since you were three and that dog came after you."

"I don't remember that."

"We were having a picnic in the park. Some woman was walking her dog—I can't remember what kind it was, but it was easily as tall as you were and probably outweighed you—and it got loose. Came running right up to us, snarling and barking."

"I don't think it came after you specifically, but you probably didn't care about the distinction. You shrieked like it was going to kill you," Dad said. "The woman got hold of it, very apologetic, and it didn't hurt anyone, so we just let it go. But for weeks afterward, you had to sleep with the light on. Kept screaming about monsters coming after you."

I sat with my hand on my watch band. "Monsters?"

"Yes, and you drew the most awful pictures and kept asking when they were coming back." Mom laughed. "It's funny now, but at the time we came close to taking you to a specialist."

"I don't remember," I repeated.

"Well, you *were* only three. I don't know how many memories any of us have from that age," Dad said. "And it passed. We were worried you'd develop a fear of dogs, but mostly you were just wary of the big ones, like any small child might be."

"Yeah, dogs don't frighten me." Monsters? That was far, far too long ago to be explained by my being Abernathy's custodian. But if Mr. Briggs hadn't seen through illusions.... "I must've just had an overactive imagination."

"Probably. Though you've always been our level-headed child." Mom patted my level head and smiled. "Why don't you come set the table?"

"Why do I always have to set the table? Jake should learn how so he can impress his girlfriends."

"Because it gives me a chance to talk to you." She put on the apron and made a little "come here" gesture with her right hand.

I grumbled, but got out the silver and china and laid places around the table. "Speaking of girlfriends," Mom said, "are you seeing anyone?"

"Not a girlfriend, Mom."

"It was by way of being a segue, smart girl. Well?"

"I..." My parents had no contact with the magical world and were unlikely to tell anyone who mattered about my relationship. "Actually...yeah, I am."

"Really?" Mom's voice ratcheted up into Maternal Busybody mode. "Who is he? Why haven't we met him? How long?"

"Mom, calm down. We've been dating for a few months, but he

travels a lot, so we haven't seen much of each other. And I was going to bring him over when I felt it was serious." Two-thirds of that was a lie, and I hated myself for it, but I couldn't tell my parents the truth about Malcolm. As for not bringing him over...I never felt awkward about how much older Malcolm was than me, except when I thought about my parents meeting him. It wasn't as if I were dating someone their age, which would be truly awkward, but...it was irrational, and I should get over myself. "Maybe we could come for dinner some night?"

"Of course. I'm glad you're dating. You're too young not to be having fun."

Oh, we have lots *more than fun, Mom.* Another thing you didn't talk to your mother about, even if a healthy sex life was a good thing. "I think you'll like him. His name is Malcolm and he loves old movies. It's sort of how we got together."

"So, dinner and movie night. Just let me know when you want to come over, and I'll make something special."

I set out the final napkin, folded the way I'd learned in home ec, and said, "I'm going to get my things packed up. I should probably leave after dinner."

"I'm glad you came." Mom slipped out to check the turkey again, and I gathered my little pile of gifts and trotted downstairs to my old room. The purple carpet, as ugly as it was, filled me with nostalgia, and I sat on my old bed and breathed in the lavender smell of the potpourri my mom scented the sheets with. Coming home, even if only for a visit, always left me with the strangest mix of feelings: irrational regret, quiet happiness, and an urge to leave and return to my actual home as quickly as possible.

I packed my suitcase—I was starting to get sick of the sight of it, after five days—and made the bed, something I normally would not have done. I saw no point in making a bed you were just going to mess up again. But I was a guest now, not a resident, and I wanted to leave this room, now a guest room, as nice as possible. Even if Mom would probably change the sheets after I left.

My eye fell on one of my old stuffed animals wedged into the upper shelves of the ceiling-high bookcase. Snoopy wasn't as white as he'd once been, thanks to age, and his bright black eyes regarded me with indifference. I remembered the Kevin-thing's eyes, not the blood-red ones of its actual body, but the black, malicious beads that had stared out at me from Kevin's body, and turned Snoopy to face the other wall.

So. I'd had nightmares about monsters. I really didn't remember that at all. Could there be something magical about me that didn't have anything to do with Abernathy's? It wasn't being attractive to invaders, or I'd have seen a lot more attacks growing up. Or been killed by one. No, in that respect I was a typical custodian. But if Diane was right, being Abernathy's custodian didn't have anything to do with my ability to see through illusions.

I sat on the bed and turned my watch around and around on my wrist. No one had ever mentioned anything like this before. You either had an aegis, which made you capable of working magic, or you didn't, and you were as nonmagical as a brick. Possibly more so, if a brick could be imbued with a ward. No, that wasn't totally true; I remembered Lucia saying once that some humans had unnaturally enhanced senses, what we'd call second sight. So was I one of them? I certainly didn't feel special. And seeing through illusions hadn't been useful until I was part of the magical world, so it wasn't as if I had some kind of superpower.

I sighed and dragged my suitcase off the chair. I could ask Lucia about it tomorrow, or Malcolm tonight, if he came over. I hadn't called him this morning, reasoning that he would want to spend time with his family, but I had a gift for him, and I sort of hoped he had a gift for me. Not that mine was all that exciting, because what do you get for your wealthy, successful boyfriend that he doesn't already have? Still, I'd done my best, and the truth was I just wanted to spend time with him. Even if I couldn't tell him what was troubling me.

I'd been grateful to reach my parents' house the night before, with its familiar comfort and the rituals of Christmas. I'd spent the entire drive scanning the streets, dark with snow, for the angular form of the invader. It knew who I was, knew my name, and I was certain if it wanted me dead, I'd be dead. I twitched every time the lights changed, terrified that something would rush at me while I was trapped between cars. But nothing had.

It took most of Christmas Eve dinner (assorted cold cuts and cheeses on sandwich rolls, with cheeseball, crackers, and pickles, because even my mom got tired of cooking sometimes) for me to relax. The traditional viewing of A Christmas Story (not It's a Wonderful Life, which my father insisted was not a Christmas movie) failed to keep my attention. I kept remembering what Stirlaugson and Ragsdale had told me, about the crisis magery faced, and the thought that I was privy to the secret made me want to run shouting it in the street. But I would keep my mouth shut, even though I wanted more than anything to share the burden with Malcolm and Judy and even Viv, for whom it wasn't so personal.

But I'd slept well, visions of Christmases past dancing in my head, and woke to a sparkling Christmas morning, and now everything was slightly at a remove, as if my heart and mind had come to an agreement that I'd go crazy if I couldn't put it a little bit behind me. I couldn't help the Board except by running Abernathy's, and I couldn't help anyone by fretting. Even if I was going to wonder, every time someone walked through the door, if it was an invader I was helping.

I bumped upstairs with my suitcase and rolled it over to the front door. "Don't take this as a sign that I'm impatient to leave," I called out. Mom laughed from the kitchen. Dad was snoring on the couch with the paper lying on the floor next to him. I could see Jake through the front window, shoveling snow. "Was that his idea, or yours?" I asked.

Mom came to join me at the window. "His idea. He's become surprisingly responsible ever since he started applying to colleges. Meeting all those deadlines for applications, scholarships, financial aid...he's done all the work."

"Impressive." Weird. My little brother, getting ready to become an adult. "Where does he want to go?"

"University of Oregon. He says it's for the science program, but I know he just wants to stay close enough to home that he can get a real meal occasionally."

"I thought he wanted to play football."

"He's practical enough to know he's not good enough to play at a college level. He'll always love football, but he wants to make a living."

"Wow. Responsible *and* practical."

"Just like you," Mom said, patting my cheek.

THE BARBECUED TURKEY WAS INCREDIBLE, moist and rich with juices. I ate more than I should have and was happy to crash in a turkey coma for an hour or two after the meal. Then I said my goodbyes and headed home. *Home.* I had a place of my own, a job I loved, a wonderful family, and the best boyfriend in the world. Sure, there were monsters infiltrating the organization meant to stop them, and I probably shouldn't trust anyone except Viv, but for now, I was happy.

I unpacked my suitcase and stowed it in the closet, hoping I wouldn't need it again for a long, long time. Then I went into my living room and surveyed the Christmas decorations. They could stay up another day. This way Christmas didn't have to end yet.

I pulled out my phone and checked my texts. Nothing from Malcolm. I hesitated, then dialed his number. It went to voice mail so quickly I felt hollow inside. He was just busy with his family, that was all. He'd call soon.

I lay on my couch with my phone resting on my stomach and watched the light grow dim as the sun set. The rosy glimmerings of the tiny lights around my windows turned the living room warm. I kicked my shoes off and stretched my toes. Even without Malcolm there, it was a beautiful evening.

My phone rang. I snatched it up. "I'm sorry I'm calling so late," Malcolm said. "May I come up?"

"Are you downstairs? Yes, come up." I ran down the hall and

threw open the door to see Malcolm ascending the stairs. "Is it really snowing again?"

"Not much." He brushed off the shoulders of his overcoat, transferring the wrapped package he held from one hand to the other. I tried not to stare at it. "I would have come sooner, but my mother's plans for the day went on longer than I'd anticipated."

"I don't mind. I was with my family most of the day, too. Come in."

Malcolm shed his overcoat onto one of my living room chairs and set the package, something oblong wrapped in gold-figured paper, on its seat. He turned and took me in his arms, kissing me with an intensity that surprised and pleased me. "I thought of you all day," he said. "Merry Christmas."

"Merry Christmas."

We stood, kissing, for several minutes until I pulled away and said, "I have something for you."

"As do I. Though I'm not sure how you'll feel about it. It seemed perfect when I bought it two months ago, and now..."

"Malcolm Campbell, are you *embarrassed?*"

He smiled at me, his eyes twinkling. "Normally I would have bought you jewelry, but you couldn't wear anything I got you publicly, not to mention you're not a typical woman."

"I'm not sure if I should be insulted by that."

Malcolm grabbed my hand and pulled me back into his embrace. "Wonderful. Extraordinary. Beautiful. But never typical," he said, punctuating his words with kisses. I laughed with joy.

"Well, mine isn't much. I ran into the same problem you did—what to give you that wouldn't give us away." I ran to my bedroom and came back with a flat box and a little square box, both of them wrapped in bright paper with snowmen on it.

"You first," Malcolm said. "I've worried about this all day."

"Malcolm, I will love whatever you give me." I tore the wrapping off and opened the box, which was hinged along its long side. I gasped, then laughed. "It's the Maltese Falcon."

"You like it?"

"I love it. It will go perfectly next to the radio cabinet." I ran a finger along its smooth matte-black surface, then was struck by a horrible thought. "This...isn't the *original*, is it?"

He laughed. "I didn't think you'd want four million dollars' worth of movie prop in your living room. This is a replica I found in Hollywood, in a little store that specializes in movie memorabilia. And your reaction is exactly what I'd hoped for."

"The fact that you didn't lead with 'I can't afford four million dollars' worth of movie prop' makes me wonder about your net worth."

"Mmm. Do you love me more now you know just how filthy rich I am?"

I set the box aside so I could put my arms around him. "I love you more because you love *me* enough to pick the perfect gift." I kissed him quickly, then disentangled myself to hand him the larger of my boxes. "It's *really* not much. Actually, it's a tie. I know it's a cliché, but I thought...it's something you could wear that no one would know came from me..."

"It's beautiful. You have excellent taste."

"I had some help from the man in the store, who was under the impression I was shopping for my father. Is that creepy at all?"

Malcolm burst out laughing. "I'm not *that* much older than you, love."

"I certainly wasn't thinking about my father when I picked it out. Anyway, that's the one gift. It's in case the second one isn't as meaningful as I hope."

Malcolm raised his eyebrows. "Now I'm curious." He accepted the little box and opened it. "A key," he said, his tone of voice inquiring.

"Yeah. Um. Specifically, the key to this apartment." His face had gone utterly expressionless, and I stammered, "See, I know the only reason you don't just walk in here whenever you feel like it is politeness, because you're a steel magus and that lock is meaningless to you, and I wanted you to know, you know, that you're welcome here. Even though we can't be together openly. My home is yours, whenever you need it."

Malcolm slowly closed the box and set it down. "That," he said quietly, "may be the best gift I've ever received."

"I hoped you wouldn't think it was stupid."

"Not stupid. Not at all." He smiled at me, and my heart did a little flip-flop. "Helena," he said, laying his hand along my cheek, "I love you, and when I'm with you, wherever we are, it feels like home."

I put my arms around his neck. "That's exactly how I feel," I said, and pulled him close for a kiss.

ACKNOWLEDGMENTS

My thanks to Bryan and Jana Brown, for providing the menu for the Grandison Hotel, and to Jacob Proffitt for reading this book in draft and giving great feedback.

ABOUT THE AUTHOR

Melissa McShane is the author of more than twenty-five fantasy novels, including the novels of Tremontane, the first of which is *Servant of the Crown;* The Extraordinaries series, beginning with *Burning Bright;* and *The Book of Secrets,* first book in The Last Oracle series. She lives in the shelter of the mountains out West with her husband, four children and a niece, and three very needy cats. She wrote reviews and critical essays for many years before turning to fiction, which is much more fun than anyone ought to be allowed to have.

You can visit her at her website **www.melissamcshanewrites.com** for more information on other books and upcoming releases.

For news on upcoming releases, bonus material, and other fun stuff, sign up for Melissa's newsletter at http://eepurl.com/brannP

ALSO BY MELISSA MCSHANE

Printed in Great Britain
by Amazon

23966817R00136